SCOTT WESTERFELD
MIRROR'S EDGE

SCHOLASTIC

Published in the UK by Scholastic Children's Books, 2021
Euston House, 24 Eversholt Street, London, NW1 1DB, UK
A division of Scholastic Limited.

Scholastic Ltd Ireland offices at:
Unit 89E, Lagan Road, Dublin Industrial Estate, Glasnevin, Dublin 11.

London – New York – Toronto – Sydney – Auckland
Mexico City – New Delhi – Hong Kong

SCHOLASTIC and associated logos are trademarks and/or
registered trademarks of Scholastic Inc.

First published in the US by Scholastic Inc., 2021

ISBN 978 0702 31044 7

A CIP catalogue record for this book is available from the British Library.

Printed by CPI Group (UK) Ltd, Croydon, CR0 4YY
Papers used by Scholastic Children's Books are made
from wood grown in sustainable forests.

1 3 5 7 9 10 8 6 4 2

www.scholastic.co.uk

To everyone who's afraid to go home

PART I

DESCENT

I am not going to die,
I'm going home like a shooting star.

—Sojourner Truth

ASCENT

The black airship looms above our heads, blotting out the stars.

Woven from filaments a thousand times thinner than human hair, the hundred-meter craft weighs almost nothing. Inside is hard vacuum—a profound emptiness with more lift than hydrogen. We dangle from the undercarriage, seven commandoes, watching the earth fall away below us.

We're thirty thousand meters up. Halfway to the drop height.

Tonight I'm going home.

The city of Shreve, where my father rules with force and lies, isn't going to welcome us. So we're floating to the top of the stratosphere, then falling like an unexpected rain.

At this altitude, the weather is a rippled sheet of clouds spread out beneath my feet. The outline of the continent peeks through, framing the great wheel of a tropical storm in the Gulf. The tendrils of the Mississippi floodplain reflect the sky. The midwest glows softly, covered with a pale expanse of white weed, an engineered species that chokes out all other life.

But the most headspinning sight is a bright sun hanging in a black sky. We've almost reached the fringe of space, the atmosphere a fragile band of blue hugging the curved horizon.

From his position beside me, Col reaches out to grasp my shoulder. Our pressure suits are too stealthy for radios, but his voice is carried by touch.

"Minus forty degrees!"

Through the thick visor of his helmet, Col's awestruck expression sends a tremor through me. The planes of his face are askew, his lips thinner, his eyes blue instead of brown. Part of my brain reacts uncertainly.

Do I know you?

The camo-surge was three weeks ago, a full-body operation to hide our identities from the surveillance dust of Shreve. My father's city will be watching us every second. There was no choice but to remake ourselves.

Col has a new voice, new fingerprints, a layer of synthetic skin that sheds fake DNA.

I have all these things too. My face is not my own.

Maybe it never was.

It takes me a moment to see Col in there—the boundless smile, the way his hands move when he talks.

The way he thinks.

"Celsius or Fahrenheit?" I ask.

"Both! Minus forty's where the scales cross." Col's new eyes narrow. "I told you that already, didn't I?"

"You enjoyed telling me again," I say. Fahrenheit is some oddball Rusty scale I'd never heard of before yesterday.

"Very funny," he says.

I smile back at Col, trying to ignore the feeling that I'm watching a stranger impersonating him.

"Either way," he says, "minus forty is *cold*. If you took that suit off, you'd have frostbite in three minutes."

"Wouldn't I suffocate first?" There's not much oxygen up here at the edge of darkness—hardly any atmosphere at all.

"Probably." Col sounds disappointed, like he had his heart set on freezing to death.

But it's toasty warm inside our suits, and we're breathing almost pure oxygen to prevent decompression sickness on the way up. If any of us die tonight, it won't be from cold or suffocation—it'll be from hitting the ground too fast.

Have I mentioned we aren't wearing parachutes?

Chutes would slow our descent too much, making us easy for ground defenses to spot. We have to flit into Shreve invisibly fast, taking the risk of crashing into a tree at forty meters per second.

The risk is worth it, because my friend Boss X is in a cage down there.

I've come to set him free, to shore up the alliance between the rebels and the free cities. To repay everything he's done for me and Col—rescuing us from Shreve, allying with us against my father.

3

But mostly I need to save X because I killed his love.

Who was also my brother, Seanan, it turns out.

X told me all this in the minutes before he was captured, my whole life thrown into chaos with a few words. Everything I thought I knew was wrong or backward.

Wearing this strange face, this new skin, I'm here to set myself right again.

HAPPY
BIRTHDAY

The night before the jump, my sister tries to talk me out of it.

"Don't go back to him, Frey."

I shake my head. "This isn't about our father. We'll rescue X and get out."

"The last time you went to Shreve, he caught you."

"No one caught me." My voice stays level. "I gave myself up to save Col."

Rafi sighs at this—she still doesn't think much of my boyfriend—and keeps leading me into darkness.

We're in an ancient Rusty coal mine, the home base of her rebel crew. It's a warren of passages gouged into the earth, lit with torches and the pale green luster of glowworms.

She's taking me down a tunnel, deeper into her mountain than I've been before. Our shadows jitter on the uneven floor. She speaks softly, but her words echo hard as stone.

"Walking into the dust *is* giving yourself up, little sister."

Surveillance dust. The air in Shreve is full of machines, always watching and listening. Every breath you take contains hundreds of microscopic cameras, microphones, transmitters.

"The dust won't recognize me," I say. "My new face went into the Shreve database last night."

Rafi turns to stare at me, the same way she has since I got the camo-surge. Like I'm a stranger—or a traitor.

Like I've broken her heart.

Since we were born, my twin sister and I have shared everything. Not just the same looks, also mannerisms, clothes, speech patterns. My father didn't want his enemies to use his heir against him. So he made sure Rafi was born with a twin.

A body double, a protector, a spare.

But for the first time in my life, I look nothing like my sister—my flatter nose, my wrong-colored eyes. I'm a centimeter taller and walk differently.

I'm not hers anymore.

"This is temporary, Rafi," I say.

"Not really," she says. "It's changed you, changed *us*."

I try to argue with her, but no words come. When I look in the mirror now, there's someone new in front of me. It's bland Shreve surge, pretty in a boring way, but it's a face that no one else in the world has—mine alone.

She's right. Seeing myself this way is changing me.

"After the mission, we'll be twins again," I say.

"We're twins now," she says, and walks away into the darkness.

I follow.

It isn't fair—Rafi changed herself first.

A few months ago, she stole my name and used it to take over a rebel crew. As Boss Frey, she dressed in leather, furs, and shiny stones dug from the abandoned shafts around us. She became an exaggerated version of me, the deadly sister.

Of course, she also raised a rebel army against our father. The mission to rescue Boss X is based here in her lair, and we're borrowing her best commando, Riggs.

Even if she thinks our plan is logic-missing, Rafi can't say no to helping me.

As we descend, the darkness grows—I'd be blind without my infrared implants. Rafi is making her way by feel, her fingers brushing the rippled stone.

"Where are we going?" I ask.

"I'm giving you an early gift."

I'd almost forgotten. We turn seventeen in a week, our first birthday since we left Shreve.

Growing up, Rafi was the only one who ever gave me presents. My father didn't want to make a connection with his disposable daughter. My tutors knew better than to bond with me, and no one else had any idea I existed.

A twinge of guilt goes through me. "Rafi, I didn't get you anything."

She turns and takes my hand, squeezes it. "You'll find me something good in Shreve, I'm sure."

Her smile glimmers in the dark, and then we're walking again, the gentle slope carrying us down. The air grows cooler, wetter. The silence looms, huge and imperturbable, like the mountain around us.

In this nothingness, Rafi asks, "Do you trust this spy of yours?"

It takes me a split second to process—she isn't supposed to know about our spy in Shreve, the deep secret that makes this whole mission possible.

"What spy?" I ask. Too late.

"The one you just admitted to having." Rafi's smile lingers in her words. "I wasn't sure."

A sigh slips from me. For sixteen years, I deceived the whole world, but I can't fool my own sister.

It's a logical enough guess. Hacking the Shreve database from the outside would be almost impossible.

"Do you even know their name?" Rafi asks.

"Not even Zura knows, and she's the only one talking to them." Their messages are deep-coded and anonymous. All we can be certain of is that the spy is high up enough in the Shreve government to create new citizens.

"Why trust an enigma with your life, Frey?"

At this point, my sister might as well know the rest. "Because Col and I *already* owe them our lives. When Boss X's crew and the Victorians rescued us from Shreve, the spy helped."

Rafi frowns. "Back when I was with the Vics? No one told me."

"Me either, till we started planning this mission—and it has to *stay* secret. A rumor spreading through your crew while we're in Shreve could get us all killed."

Rafi stops walking, reaching back for me again. "I would never endanger you, little sister."

Here in the darkness, where she can't see my strange new face, her voice is tender. Like when we were littlies, sharing a bedroom every night.

"I'm just worried about you," she says. "This spy may hate Dad, but that doesn't mean they're on your side."

"There's no other way to get into Shreve. And I can't leave X there. He's our only link to . . ."

Rafi stays silent, daring me to finish the sentence.

Our brother, the one I killed.

"They loved each other," I say. "Isn't that enough reason to save X?"

"Seanan's dead," Rafi says. "I don't want to lose you too, just because you feel guilty."

I turn away from her, but there's nothing to look at, even in my infrared. The stone walls are cold and black, carved centuries ago by long-dead Rusty digging machines. My sister lives in darkness, surrounded by the wounds of the past.

I don't know how I feel about killing my own brother, but *guilt* is too simple a word.

We never even met Seanan. He was kidnapped before Rafi and I were born, raised by rebels to hate his own family. He came home in disguise when we were fifteen, planning to assassinate our father. But he picked the wrong day. Father was stuck on the other side of town, so Rafi stepped in for her first public speech.

Nothing went as planned.

Except me doing what I was born to do—protect my big sister.

It's logic-missing, feeling guilty for killing someone who was shooting at me and Rafi. But I don't know how else to feel.

I used to have rows of buttons on my arm that would give me any emotion I wanted. At the touch of a fingertip, Grief or Anguish would flow through my veins, strong enough to settle this tangle inside me. But I lost my feels in battle, and now all I can summon for my brother is a tightly wound cord of confusion.

I'm certain of exactly one thing—Boss X is my friend and ally, and I can't let him rot in a cell.

"Are you jealous of X?" I ask softly. "Because he knew Seanan and we didn't?"

Rafi gives me an angry shake of her head. "Seanan mattered when there was a chance he was alive. Now he's just a ghost of someone we never knew. All I have left is *you.*"

That last word hangs heavy in the darkness. Like she needs me to say that she's all that matters to me too.

But that isn't true. Not anymore.

"X is crew to me," I say. "He's family. Don't you feel that way about your rebels?"

"Of course." Rafi drops my hand, turns, and starts walking again. "If Dad had one of mine in prison, I'd wreck the earth to save them.

But I wouldn't risk *you*, Frey. What you and I have comes before crew, before allies, before friends."

She says that last word sharply. I've met Rafi's friends back in Shreve. Named after gods and goddesses, like Demeter and Sirius, they were wealthy and beautiful, their faces sculpted by the best cosmetic surgery money could buy. But they didn't love my sister.

None of them even knew her biggest secret—me.

I grew up thinking that I was the isolated one, hidden away, trained to kill. But Rafi was our father's protégé, taught from birth to charm, deceive, and manipulate everyone she met.

When I left home, I found allies and crew, and fell in love with Col.

When Rafi left home, she raised an army. They worship her, but that isn't the same as love.

I didn't always understand the difference, because I was raised to love *and* worship my sister—my only friend, my purpose in life. Rafi's love saved me from becoming the killing machine our father tried to make me, but I was still just a copy of her.

Now I have Col, who'd only laugh if anyone tried to worship him. Who looks at me the exact same way, even if my face is new and strange. Who fights for me.

If X and Seanan had what Col and I do, then I owe this mission to my brother.

"We're almost there," Rafi says. "Cover your eyes."

I obey, and a wash of light fills the room.

The tunnel has widened into some kind of maintenance area. Along the walls are stacks of rusted tools, and the old trolleys that once carried coal to the surface. The space is lit harshly by a tiny lamp Rafi's taken from a hook.

"Welcome to my armory," she says.

I blink. "Where are the weapons?"

She walks across the room, the shadows swaying around her. She yanks a tarp from one of the trolleys, spilling dirt across the floor.

I follow and look inside.

It's a rebel crew's dream—pulse bombs, mini attack drones, plasma rifles that could knock down a hovercar. Or a skyscraper.

"Where'd all this come from?"

"I've been collecting them."

"You used to collect *shoes*, Rafi. These are war machines!"

She smiles. "The Rusties left weapons caches everywhere. Dad taught me where to look."

"But why do you need them? The free cities are going to handle Father. Since he tried to take over Paz, the whole world is against him!"

"That's what scares them," Rafi says. "Dad's in a corner. Do you think he's above setting everything on fire? A little mutually assured destruction?"

I take a step back from her.

Mutually assured destruction was a Rusty term in the age of atomic warfare. It was a grim, simple concept—it's better to kill everyone in the world than to die alone.

"You think he has nukes?" I ask.

"He'll be ready with something," she says. "Or, at least, the other cities will be too afraid to find out."

12

I shake my head, wanting to explain that Diego has already promised to end our father.

But Rafi doesn't know about the free cities' plans for me.

They don't trust her to rule once he's gone. And if I tell her they plan to put *me* in charge of Shreve, it will only confuse things between us. I don't want my sister thinking that I'm plotting against her.

There's too much between us already.

So I change the subject. "Thanks for the thought, Rafi. But I can't take these weapons into Shreve. The dust would spot them in a second."

"Not this one." She reaches in and pulls a velvet bag from the depths of the trolley. "Hold out your right hand."

I do. Rafi takes three rings from the bag and slips them onto my fingers. They're a pale color that almost matches my new skin.

"What are they?"

"Smart plastic," she says. "Make a fist with your thumb on the inside."

"That's not how you make a fist."

"Exactly. So you won't do it by accident."

I follow her instructions, and the plastic comes to life, squirming in my hand. A tendril pushes out of my fist, displacing my thumb to form . . .

A knife.

When I squeeze, it grows into a rapier, the blade thinning.

We commandoes have lots of makeshift weapons hidden in our gear, but nothing as elegant as this.

The Rusties were always at their cleverest when inventing ways to kill people.

"It's called a variable blade," Rafi says, beaming. "I know you'll hate not having a pulse knife. Happy birthday, little sister."

"Thanks." When I open my hand, the plastic slithers around my fingers again, re-forming the innocent-looking rings. "I don't have anything for you."

She shrugs. It was always this way. I've never had money to buy presents, and Rafi possessed everything she wanted.

"Just come back to me," she says. "That's my present."

"Don't worry, Rafi. They won't catch me."

She gathers me into a hug.

"Not only that, little sister. I mean *come back to me*."

And there, in the warmth of her arms, I realize that she means changing my face back to hers.

DROP

We reach the drop height just as the sun sets, turning the thin arc of atmosphere from blue to blinding white.

Below us, it's night already, the lights of Shreve visible in the distance. We aren't dropping from directly overhead. We're falling at an angle, letting our wingsuits and the winds of the jet stream carry us across the border.

The airship has expanded as we've risen, two hundred meters across now. But we're invisible from the ground. The ionosphere around us reflects most radar waves, and everything we're carrying is made of ceramics and plastic. No metal to ping Shreve's air defenses.

The free cities have provided us with their best tech—hidden weapons, this airship, even cloud-seeding stealth craft to increase the chance of dust-clearing rain while we're in Shreve. The cities may not care about Boss X, but anything that hurts my father strengthens the alliance against him.

Zura, one of Col's soldiers and the official commander of this mission, flashes her wrist lights to get our attention. She holds up two fingers.

Two minutes till we drop.

A trickle of dread starts in my stomach. By reflex, I reach for my feels, but of course they've been gone for weeks. Up here in the void, I'm stuck with my own emotions.

It's headspinning, the idea of falling for twenty solid minutes. There's some animal part of me that doesn't believe I'm really this far above the earth. There's no sense of scale up here—nothing visible below but the city and a few winding rivers glinting in the moonlight.

Col waves a hand. I smile at him, trying to look brave.

He unsnaps the shoulder pocket of his pressure suit and pulls something out . . . a flower.

He hands it to me, mouthing two words.

Happy birthday.

I hold it close, staring through my helmet visor. It's a single shaft of the goldenrod that grows around my sister's mountain hideout. Its yellow petals glitter with ice against the setting sun.

The altitude has frozen it solid.

I want to tell Col that I've never seen anything so beautiful. That it's the first birthday present anyone besides my sister has ever given me.

Col gestures with his gloved fingers, a flicking motion.

When I bat the flower, it shatters into a galaxy of tiny golden stars. The sparkles spread out, floating uncertainly around us for a moment before they start to fall.

I take Col's hand, laughing. "How long have you been planning this?"

"All week," he says. "I *knew* it would shatter—like using liquid nitrogen! It's minus a hundred and forty up here!"

"That's . . . cold."

He cracks up at this. His surge-altered laugh sounds wrong, but I'm pleased that Col loved his gift as much as I did.

"Hard to believe it's a warm spring evening down there," he says.

I look down at my father's city. The floodlights around the border look white and cold.

"Fall safe," I say.

"You too, Islyn."

A pulse of strangeness—*Islyn* is my Shreve name.

In twenty minutes, I have to become someone else. Every word, every gesture, every second.

"You too, Arav," I reply in kind, then realize something. "Wait. I haven't missed *your* birthday, have I?"

"Don't worry, Frey," he says. "I'll remind you."

The sound of my own name settles me. But I can't help wondering, how do people find out each other's birthdays?

Do you just ask?

What am I supposed to get the boy I love?

Another flash of light comes from Zura. Col lets go of my hand to check the straps of his wingsuit harness.

Zura counts down on her fingers.

Three, two, one . . .

On zero, the nanofilaments of the airship above us disassemble all at once. The huge black shape disintegrates, imploding into swirls of smoke, a dark ghost vanishing.

The grip of my harness goes slack—but this high up, there's not enough atmosphere for the rush of wind. My stomach knows I'm in free fall, but my fellow commandoes seem to be hovering in the stillness around me.

I breathe slow and deep, letting my training kick in. My arms and legs spread out, stretching out the membrane of the wingsuit, like I've done a hundred times in practice.

But this isn't anything like the simulations.

Something huge has filled my body—a primal, terrifying knowledge that nothing is holding me up.

I feel weightless, motionless. As if time is frozen in these moments before returning to my father's city.

Sixty kilometers left to fall.

TERMINAL VELOCITY

A month before the drop, Zura tells us all the ways we can die.

"Hitting the ground at ten meters per second will usually kill you," she says. "Terminal velocity for a human body is five times that speed."

"Terminal," I repeat. "Is that when you *definitely* die?"

Zura shakes her head. She waves a hand, and a little person appears in the airscreen over the conference table. Belly down, arms out—the skydiving position. Its clothes flutter as if wind is rushing past.

"Terminal velocity is the top speed a human can fall. At fifty meters a second, air resistance equals gravity—you stop accelerating. But it's fast enough to liquefy your insides if you hit the ground."

"*Liquefy?*" Col says. "Are you trying to scare us out of this mission, Zura?"

"You, sir? Never."

Col shrugs. "Cats can survive falls at terminal velocity."

"Well, maybe you have nine lives." Zura's smile flashes in the light from the airscreen. "I've stopped counting."

We're in the Spider Room, deep in Rafi's mountain. It's us three, plus Yandre and X's old friend, Boss Charles. The rescue mission is still in the planning stage, known to only a handful of people.

I haven't even told my sister yet.

Zura gestures again, and the little person on the airscreen sprouts membranes between legs and arms, like a flying squirrel.

"With wingsuits, we'll fall much slower—ten meters a second. That's still deadly fast, though, and we'll be moving *forward* three times that speed."

Pulsing arrows appear around the little person, showing airflow across the wings. Terrain rushes past below.

"So we die if we hit anything," Yandre says. "Even a bird."

"But at least we won't be liquefied," Col mutters.

"More like *splattered*." Zura waves the image aside. "But it's the only way to get into Shreve without being seen."

Boss Charles speaks up. "What happened to walking?"

"The dust would spot us." Zura waves a hand, and familiar images of surveillance dust appear. "The air in the city of Shreve is full of nano-scale cams, microphones, and transmitters. Every word, every action, is recorded and uploaded to—"

"I know about dust," Charles breaks in. "But I thought you solved that."

Yandre nods. "Our spy in Shreve is creating identities for us. But real citizens are recorded from the day they're born, and you can't fake a whole life's worth of data. If the city AI flags us as suspicious, anyone looking closely at our files will know we're bogus. We have to be model citizens from the moment we arrive."

"In Shreve," I say, "model citizens don't walk across the border."

"Do model citizens *fly*?" Charles asks.

Yandre turns to the airscreen again. "Nanocams are tiny—we'll leave them spinning in our wake. We'll be a glitch!"

"And the city AI won't notice seven glitches crossing the border?" Charles asks.

Yandre shakes their head. "The dust is disrupted all the time by wind, rain, flocks of birds. It isn't designed to detect humans flying without hoverboards. My guess is, it'll ignore us completely."

Col and Boss Charles frown, like they don't want to rely on guesses.

For me, though, the thought of being invisible in my father's city, even for a few seconds, is thrilling.

Growing up, the dust surrounded me, recording every lesson with my tutors, every murmur in my sleep. I breathed it for sixteen years. It settled on my food and in the pores of my skin, glittering in slants of sunlight, ever-present. It made the sky a different color.

At night, I dreamed of being free from it.

Every city has some kind of surveillance; even privacy-worshipping Paz uses traffic sensors and retina locks. But the dust in Shreve isn't in the air to prevent crime or accidents. The city AI watches everyone, its algorithms always searching for antisocial behavior.

While we're in my father's city, we'll have to watch our words, actions, gestures. Even the motions of our eyes.

Of course, I've spent my whole life pretending to be someone else. This is the mission I was born for.

"Okay," Col says. "So wingsuits are the way in. But how do we land without splattering?"

Zura waves another image onto the screen.

"That's the scary part," she says.

SPLASH

After a few minutes of falling, we reach the denser stratosphere.

A wind starts to build. My wings flutter, then fill. On the readout in my helmet, the numbers ticking off our descent begin to slow. Buffeted by currents of air, we arrange ourselves into a V formation, angling toward Shreve.

Zura takes the point, with me, Col, and Yandre on her right. Boss Charles is on the left wing, along with two commandoes I've never fought beside before.

One is Riggs, who was once the boss of Rafi's crew. When my sister took over, she somehow managed to keep Riggs as a second-in-command. Riggs is like a battle-worn version of Tally Youngblood, fierce and charismatic, wearing her scars proudly. Even now, surged into a smooth-faced citizen of Shreve, she looks dangerous.

She's the only commando who doesn't know my real name.

The last member of the team is Lodge, here to keep an eye on us for the free cities. He arrived from Diego already surged into his Shreve identity, so we don't know his real face.

He's a Special, like Zura, his strength and speed enhanced beyond any normal human's. But muscles and reflexes won't matter much if we get into a firefight with the whole Shreve army.

Our best chance is if no one knows we were here till after we're gone.

At forty kilometers up, the locator in my helmet display shows us still a hundred klicks from Shreve, which is nervous-making. If the wind doesn't carry us all the way to the landing site, there aren't any hoverboards or parachutes to fall back on.

We'll splatter.

The minutes pass. We keep falling.

Thirty kilometers, then twenty, the air is growing denser, the wind stronger, till it's like a mag-lev roaring past. Our wingsuits start to angle our fall toward Shreve.

From eighteen klicks' altitude, we see a suborbital taking off from Orlean. It breaches the clouds and arcs silently toward Tokyo on a bright lance of flame.

At ten thousand meters, we finally catch a real tailwind—the subtropical jet stream. The terrain is visibly sliding past beneath us, and I can make out the familiar shape of Shreve ahead. The border is outlined by searchlights, the greenbelt dark, and the city center glowing with hover traffic.

Beside me, Col is testing out his wingsuit, altering his course with waggles of his fingers. He wavers back and forth through the air, then slips up beside me to take my shoulder.

"How's it going, Islyn?"

"Uh, you know," I yell over the wind, "plummeting!"

His mad laughter buzzes through the suit connection.

"You can turn off your oxygen now," he shouts. "Just for a minute—the air's still pretty thin."

"Why would I do that?"

"The air's different at every level. I could *smell* the ozone layer!" His wind-rippled shoulders shrug a little. "At least, I convinced myself I could."

"Regular oxygen's fine with me," I yell.

Col starts to respond, but Zura is furiously flashing her lights at him.

He gives me a grin, then zooms back into formation.

We continue to fall, Zura keeping us on course. My helmet display shows our glide ratio climbing. Soon we're slipping forward through the air three times as fast as we're descending.

I'm getting used to this. Like I was born to fly.

Or born to fall.

One kilometer from the ground, my helmet display dims. The forest is zooming past below, and I glimpse moonlit streams and waterfalls, the somber lights of Shreve housing complexes.

At last I have a sense of my own speed, faster than any hoverboard or jetpack—but still slower than a diving peregrine falcon, Col told me yesterday.

At least falcons know how to stop themselves.

One minute from the landing zone, an alarm sounds. Time to spread the formation out so we don't all hit the lake too close together.

It's not exactly a lake anymore. Ten days ago, a flurry of nanos landed on it, disguised as snow. Like us, they fell from the stratosphere, each snowflake breaking into millions of machines.

Since that night, the nanos have been reconfiguring the H_2O molecules in the lake. It still looks like water from above, but it's been transformed into carefully calibrated layers of crash gel. Foamy on the top, then denser and denser, designed to gradually arrest our momentum as we dive through them.

Unless we come in too steep and break our necks. Or too shallow, and bounce off the surface like a flung rock and crash into the trees along the shoreline. Or we could hit a fish that woke up early from hibernating in the cold depths, swimming up to suffocate in the foam.

There are a dozen other ways this can go wrong, but I've forgotten most of them.

With ten seconds left, my display says I'm right on target. I stop watching the numbers and focus on the rushing world around me.

This feels like real flying—the roar of the air, the parkland hurtling past beneath me, the *tick* of bugs splatting against my helmet.

Like a wind spirit, invisible to my father's eyes and ears.

The lake shimmers ahead, alight with the moon.

Growing bigger . . .

I press my hands together like a diver.

My fingers smack against the surface, and the world transforms— I'm crashing through a sudden tempest, a jet-engine roar filling my helmet. Twisting downward into the denser layers, the pressure builds like a fist around me.

But the crash gel is working. My bones haven't snapped. My suit hasn't ruptured. I didn't hit a bird in the air or a windblown branch floating on the surface.

I'm not splattering.

My momentum slows, the rumble in my helmet subsiding. The weight of my half-depleted oxygen tanks pulls me gently down to the bottom. It's normal water down here, cold and heavy around my pressure suit. My feet settle onto soft mud.

The rushing, hurtling world has downshifted to slow motion. From a diving hawk, I've turned into a sluggish creature slinking along the bottom of the sea.

The cold water starts to leach the feeling from my hands and feet.

I check my oxygen tanks—eighteen minutes left—and orient myself with my helmet display. We're gathering on the western shore of the lake.

I start walking through the cold.

I'm home at last.

RECOVERY ROOM

Three weeks before the jump, doctors cut us into pieces and put us back together.

It's serious surgery, beyond the skills of any medic in my sister's rebel army. So Diego sends a military craft with bone-rattling jet engines to collect us commandoes.

Col and I sit next to each other on the plane, making jokes about how boring our new faces are going to be. Shreve surge is famously art-missing, as if my father just wants everyone to look the same.

That's when it starts to sink in—I'm going to be a different person tomorrow.

When we land in Diego, a cheery guide takes us on a tour. We see the infinity waterfalls, a wetlands reconstruction, the EverCarnival. Like tourists, not commandoes here to have our skin peeled off, our bones broken and remade.

As night falls, they stick us into surge tanks.

Claustrophobia hits as my tank starts to fill with fluid. I press my palms against the transparent sides, my teeth gripping the breathing mask.

They're going to take away my face.

Our face.

The happy-making chemicals fill my blood, and my panic turns soft and fuzzy, like a warm rain is soaking me.

And then I'm dreaming pretty dreams.

The next morning, I come out of the tank raw-skinned, unsteady on my feet. My old clothes don't fit, and my voice sounds wrong in my ears. This new body feels like some clumsy costume a kid would wear, a shell wrapped around my real self.

Breathing feels wrong too.

There are no mirrors in the room, not even shiny surfaces, and the psych doctor warns me not to look at my reflection until I'm used to this body. Camo-surge can be confusing the first time you get it.

She guides me to a recovery room and leaves me there—soothing music, orange juice, a huge picture window. The view is Diego's famous climbing wall, formed from a single sheet of vat-grown diamond, perfectly transparent. I suppose it's beautiful, but to me the climbers look like spiders swarming a fragile sheet of glass.

I flex my fingers. It feels like someone else's hand.

The door slides open, and a woman with a blandly pretty face walks into the recovery room. But it's not a person; it's the avatar of the sovereign city of Diego.

That aloof expression makes me twitch—the Diego city AI once took me captive for a month, trying to determine if I'll be fit to rule Shreve when they get rid of my father. I passed their tests, but I'll never forget that they held me against my will.

"How do you feel?" the avatar asks.

I shrug, not wanting to show any weakness. "Nothing hurts."

"Have you seen your new face?"

"Last week, with one of those mirrors that shows what you'll look like. But I haven't seen the results yet."

Diego sits down, smiling gently. Impassive, but connected to a mind that's the sum of every processor in this city of four million.

"Take your time," they say. "Dysmorphia can be tricky."

I give the avatar a frown. "You're a machine, wearing a body like it's a suit of clothes. You don't know anything about it."

"True, we have no practical experience with dysmorphia," the avatar admits. "But your mental state is important to us, Frey."

"As always," I mutter. The free cities want the next ruler of Shreve to be stable, predictable. "Are you here to test me again?"

"No. Only to say hello."

This makes me roll my eyes, which feels particularly weird.

Fresh out of the tank, my cheeks seemed to intrude on my vision. A doctor did a scan to make sure my eyeballs still fit inside their remade sockets. She said everything was fine, and that I'd get used to my new "visual field."

But my world has a different shape now.

"You may find yourself obsessing over small flaws with your new body," the avatar says. "That's a sign of dysmorphia. If you start to feel ugly, ask for help."

I frown at the word *ugly*.

Lots of people get surge. Rafi's rich friends, the staff in the tower—all of them altered their faces every few months. But hardly anyone transforms completely anymore, like an old-time ugly on their sixteenth birthday.

"How is this so weird?" I ask. "Back in the pretty regime, everyone *loved* getting surgery."

The avatar shrugs. "Uglies spent sixteen years preparing to change. They were told every day that no one would listen to them or love them until they were pretty. They were taught to hate their real selves, so losing who they were was easy."

I swallow. Maybe that's the problem. After impersonating my sister for so long, I barely have a real self to lose.

"You've never worried about your looks, have you, Frey?"

"My looks always belonged to Rafi, like our clothes, her friends." Even my name is hers, jumbled and misspelled. My face has always been my sister's, not mine to throw away.

And yet that's exactly what I've done.

"Dysmorphia by proxy," the avatar says with a smile. "Perhaps you can ask Boss X about that when you see him."

"X isn't confused about who he is," I say.

His surge is truly radical, as close to a wolf as human can be. If anyone knows what it means to get a new body, it's him.

31

I've never had the nerve to ask X why he chose to change himself that way. But I've always wondered if it had anything to do with my brother.

"Perhaps because he's one of a kind now," the avatar says. Then their face goes motionless for a moment, as if that vast mind, sprawled across a whole city, is choosing their words carefully. "Maybe this distance from your sister will be good for you," they finally add.

And suddenly I'm convinced that they planned this whole conversation.

Every subject we've discussed—dysmorphia, my sister, Boss X—was guiding me to this point. Anger makes my heart shuddery in my chest.

"When we were planning this mission," I say, "Col thought you wouldn't let me go. That you'd try to keep me safe in Rafi's mountain, ready to take over Shreve when my father's gone."

"But we did not object," the avatar points out.

"Because for this mission work, I'd have to get camo-surge, which means looking different from my sister. You wanted this!"

"An interesting theory," they say.

"Is it *true*?"

A soft sigh. "Our mind doesn't work like yours, Frey. You tell your-self a simple story about your motivations, your desires. We model millions of possible outcomes, weighing each in terms of value to the world. Then we pursue the path with the most positive sum total."

My annoyance is building. "I get it. Your brain's bigger than mine."

"Merely different. Our motives can't be reduced to something simple, like wanting Rafia to reject your new face. Like wanting you to be free to embrace your own destiny."

"And yet it sounds like *you've thought about it*."

"We think about everything, Frey. Especially when it comes to you."

I let out a groan. I haven't even told Rafi about this surge yet, because she'll be more angry than I want to imagine. And while I worry about my sister, the free cities are busy making their plans for me.

It's like playing chess against a dozen demigods at once.

Maybe it's time to stop playing.

"When are you going to kill my father?" I ask.

"No date has been set."

"A brain that big, and you can't make a decision?"

"Twelve cities are involved in this alliance, Frey. Each with its own agenda and decision-making processes."

"So it's never going to happen!" I shout.

"Frey," the avatar says. "You were born to guide Shreve going forward, and you shall. Your father's days are—"

Diego's voice shuts off as a door slides open. Into the recovery room comes a tall, handsome boy in hospital whites.

I take a slow breath. The doctors told me to stay calm while my body settles. I roll up my sleeve so the boy can check my vitals.

But he just stares at me.

"Frey?" he asks.

There's something about him.

Then I remember last week, when Col showed me which face . . .

33

But it's not the same as on a screen.

Fresh confusion rushes through my new body. My cheeks press up to crowd my eyes. My legs feel tangled, my hands like loose gloves.

It's him, but not. His eyes shatter me.

Col's gaze is the mirror I've been afraid to look into.

The doctors didn't change my heart, but it's beating slantways in my chest. Askew, along with every muscle, every gesture, every centimeter of my skin.

I'm used to being an impostor—that's what I've always been—*but Col can't be wrong.*

He was the first person to see the real me, the me that exists separate from my sister.

What if he can't see me anymore? What if I can't see him?

"Frey," he says again, more certainly. He takes my hand, and for a moment, I'm okay. He smiles a little. "Isn't this *weird*?"

Of course—for Col Palafox a new body is something wild and exciting, a science experiment bubbling up from a beaker.

He's always known who he is.

Col's confidence steadies me, even if the questions are still racing through my head.

What if my new face is something more than camouflage? What if I've lost myself for good?

What if every disguise changes me, just like every lie?

EMERGENCY

I can't let the Shreve AI see me in military-grade gear, so before my head breaches the surface, I take off my helmet. On that signal, my wings dissolve into the water around me.

I walk out of the lake in a modest Shreve bathing suit, trying not to think about the dust all around me, watching. It won't be long before—

"Good swim, Islyn?" comes a voice in my comms.

I breathe deep, keeping my expression steady. I've heard the voice of the Shreve city interface before, but the sound of it still sends a shiver through me.

It's too much like *his* voice.

My father likes to be in every citizen's ear, all day, every day. Not an exact match, of course—when he gives an important speech you know it's really *him*. The Shreve interface sounds more like his younger, more approachable brother.

But it's close enough to cast my father's shadow on every interaction with the city, a constant reminder that no one here can escape his will.

And unlike the mind of Paz, which only comes when called, the Shreve AI talks to you anytime it wants.

"Yes, sir," I answer. "The water's lovely tonight."

"A forty-minute swim! That's eighteen merits, Islyn."

"Thank you, sir."

I walk out of the water, my backpack over a shoulder, like I took it swimming. Suspicious, or at least weird, but the Shreve AI isn't a person, like Paz or Diego. My father doesn't want his own city vying against him for control, so he keeps it deliberately brain-missing.

Instead of a fully self-aware neural net, the Shreve AI is just a galaxy of algorithms, all asking the same question a million times a second:

Is this citizen obedient or rebellious?

Productive or a miscreant?

Good or bad?

We're gambling on the AI's simplemindedness, hoping it sees seven people swimming together at midnight as healthy exercise, not a mystery to be investigated.

Zura is already on the narrow beach that runs around the lake, playing catch with Lodge—the two Specials out of the water first. Their camo-surge has downplayed their inhuman muscles, but they still look like bodybuilders in their swimsuits.

They wave at me, all of us acting like midnight beach parties are perfectly normal. As if being back in Shreve in a surged body wasn't weird enough.

Above the trees, the shed luster of the city makes the sky glow orange and pink.

The AI thought I'd been swimming for forty minutes, so we must have splashed down behind schedule. Our Shreve identities were supposed to have jumped into the lake just ten minutes before the landing—at least, that's when the records of our counterfeit lives end, waiting for us to take over.

Still, it's apparently close enough to fool the Shreve AI. And the longer swim means more merits for me—or for my alter ego, anyway.

Not that she needs them. Islyn likes hiking and camping, does volunteer cleanup on the park trails, and has never been arrested or shame-cammed. Like all our new identities, she has stacks of good behavior merits.

We're model citizens, above suspicion. Last week, Col asked Zura if our fake selves weren't a little *too* perfect, but she only laughed.

In Shreve, plenty of citizens are perfect. It pays to be.

Two figures are strolling down the dark strip of beach toward us. Riggs, already dry and dressed in her street clothes, and Boss Charles, who looks the most different of all of us. She chose a very pretty face, at the outer limit of what's allowed in Shreve—not what I expected from a rebel boss.

But now she's limping, a trickle of blood coming from her nose. Her forearms and elbows are scraped.

"You okay?" I ask.

Charles shrugs. "Bumped the bottom."

Shreve's voice comes again in our comms. "Do you need medical attention?"

"No, sir." Boss Charles forces a hearty smile. "Great swim!"

The last thing we want is a med drone showing up. One millimeter-wave scan of the Specials and we're done.

Boss Charles was lucky. At forty meters a second, hitting the bottom could've been . . .

I look both ways down the beach. "Anybody seen the others?"

Zura shakes her head.

Out on the dark surface of the lake, the floating fallen leaves are oddly still, untroubled by the breeze.

Crash gel is great for landing in, but deadly for swimmers—you can't breathe it, but it's not dense enough to float in. Zura regaled us with tales of Rusty-era sailors in flotation vests drowning in storms, their lungs full of sea foam.

The nanos have turned the whole lake into a death trap.

If Col's or Yandre's helmets broke on impact, they might be suffocating down there.

But I can't call out for them—any sign of distress will alert the city.

I switch my vision to infrared, but there's no heat glimmering on the surface of the lake. The gel is too good an insulator.

We can only wait.

"Let's play a different game," Zura says.

It's awful, but she's right. We can't stand here staring at the lake—the city pays attention to what people are looking at, to what their faces show.

We can't risk an emergency response team showing up.

Lodge and Zura start playing soccer. The rest of us pretend to be relaxing on the beach.

I try not to do the math, but my own oxygen supply had less than twenty minutes left when I landed. If Col and Yandre are still down there, what are they breathing?

If they never reappear, we have to keep going without looking for them. Without a word about our loss. Without shedding a tear.

Nothing that the dust might spot.

The spy has programmed our fake identities to self-erase the moment the Shreve AI wonders where we are, whether at the mission's end or anywhere along the way . . . Col and Yandre will simply cease to exist.

This is why Zura kept saying terrifying things about the jump—to prepare us in case the worst happened.

I watch Zura, searching for any emotion in her eyes. She's known Col since he was a child, Yandre too. But her new face, surged to the boring look of a Shreve citizen, remains expressionless.

I turn back to the lake, a cold fist closing around my heart.

The worst part is, I can save them.

In Shreve, all you have to do is say the word *emergency* three times, and the dust will hear. Med drones and rescue craft would get here in minutes. But when they dive into the lake, they won't miss that it's full of crash gel. Security would be on the scene before the rescue was complete.

We'd all be in my father's hands—not just Col and Yandre.

My father has hated me with a world-wrecking passion since I killed his son. Sometimes I think his invasion of Victoria was just an excuse to fire a missile at me.

What would he do if he caught me now?

I stare at the lake again, not caring if I look suspicious. This awful silence can't be true.

It would be so easy to say the words:

Emergency, emergency, emergency.

If we're captured, our friends can rescue us. The free cities will be here soon enough in force.

Is any of this worth losing Col?

I open my mouth, ready to betray us all . . .

That's when I see it—a thin stick jutting from the surface.

It's moving back and forth, like a signal flag.

I open my backpack as calmly as I can and pull out my survival kit.

"Going for a swim," I say briskly, and hurl myself into the lake.

FACE

Col gazes at me, and I try to look at him too.

I saw this new face last week, on an airscreen back in Rafi's lair. But here in the flesh, it's too much. Too real.

His eyes are blue instead of brown, his skin lighter than a Victorian's. The surgery didn't change his nose, but his new cheeks are like mine—classic pretty, high and sharp. He's still handsome, but in a generic way.

Every few breaths, I have to shut my eyes to reset myself. To keep from feeling like a piece is missing from my heart.

I've only ever kissed one face, and now it's gone.

When I open my eyes again, this new Col is still gazing at me, like an oddly intense stranger on a public train.

"Are you okay?" he asks. "Did you look at yourself too soon?"

"I haven't yet, but your new face is giving me . . . dysmorphia by proxy."

Col's wrong-colored eyes widen. "Points for terminology."

"Diego's words, not mine." I'm thankful that the avatar has left us alone. It was messing with my head the whole time. "Sorry. This is hitting harder than I thought."

"Tell me about it," Col gently encourages.

I open my mouth to explain, and even that simple motion makes the muscles of my face feel funny.

"Doesn't it feel *wrong* to you?"

He shrugs. "I always wanted to get surge. But my mother wouldn't let me. It wasn't the Palafox thing to do."

Of course. Aribella Palafox, indomitable ruler of Victoria, wouldn't want the first son getting frivolous surge.

But I can't imagine Col wanting to change himself. "You didn't like your face?"

"I didn't want anything permanent. But all my friends got to look however they wanted!"

"Rafi's friends too. But Father never let her." I point at my eyebrow. "Except when we got this . . ."

But the scar we shared, from the assassination attempt, is gone from my face.

I have to take a few deep breaths.

Col gently touches the place where it's missing. "I used to go out into Victoria without my minders, pretending to be normal. Not someone from a famous family, with everyone always watching me. Now I get to see what that's really like."

I look at him, trying to smile. "You do look pretty average."

"You don't want to know what it would be like? To be two random people?"

"Who live in a random dictatorship?" I say. "At war with all its neighbors?"

"But it won't be *our* war anymore. We're two kids who don't care about all that. Islyn and Arav, model citizens in love."

I have to laugh. "This is a side of you I haven't seen before."

"See? The surge is already working."

I turn away from Col's—or Arav's—enthusiasm. "Okay, I get it. People want to escape who they are, now and then. But being someone else was my *job* for sixteen years."

"Islyn is someone who never had that job," he says.

I close my eyes, trying to imagine what that would feel like.

I am Islyn, Random of Shreve.

Nobody's ever tried to kill me, and I don't know how to kill anyone else.

Nobody wants to put me in charge of a city.

But when I open my eyes, I'm still Frey.

Col reads my expression and laughs. "It might take more than ten seconds."

"But my whole body feels wrong, Col. Even my smile—the first thing I ever learned—is wrong."

He stares at me. "Wait. You *learned* to smile?"

"Had to. Whenever Rafi went out in public, a hundred cams pointed at her. Her smile was my first impersonation. I've never really had one of my own."

"But you do." Col reaches out to trace a curve around the left side of my lips. "A little sly twist, right here, when you think someone's being logic-missing. Rafia just rolls her eyes."

"Huh." I touch my new lips—thinner, more symmetrical, tingly and raw. "Rafi and I used to practice smiling for hours."

"Then maybe you weren't impersonating her." Col shrugs. "Maybe Rafia of Shreve was a character you two made up."

I don't know how to answer that.

My sister and I learned so much side by side—dancing, walking, giving speeches. She might have borrowed some of her habits from me.

But Rafi was my father's heir; I was only a shadow. If I added anything to our identity, it's because she let me.

"Maybe everyone practices their smile in Shreve," Col says. "With the dust watching, you have to watch yourself."

I shake my head. "I don't know what it's like for regular people. I hardly ever left the tower."

"It's still your city. Shreve is in your bones."

I have to laugh. "These don't even *feel* like my bones."

My new frame is full of implants—the surge added a full centimeter of height. It's a way of disrupting my movement so the Shreve AI won't recognize my gait, my way of walking that's as much mine as my fingerprints.

"Still, you're going home," Col says softly.

And I realize—he must wish we were sneaking into Victoria.

It's half a year since we ran from his home city, the night my father conquered it. Col wakes up gasping from nightmares of breathing dust. A nightmare that his people are still living.

I take his hand. "We're going to save Victoria, Col. The free cities are going to end my father—Diego just promised me again."

"Let's focus on saving Boss X," he says quietly.

I look at him, forcing myself to take in his new face. To confront the strangeness of this person I love.

This is *Col*, this stranger. And I owe him a promise.

"When I'm in charge of Shreve," I say, "Victoria will be free."

He squeezes my hand, believing me.

But then he says, "And what about Shreve?"

I shrug—we've already had this conversation. "We'll move toward some form of democracy, AI or human."

"Is managing a whole city through that transition something you want to do?"

I don't answer, because the answer is that what I want doesn't matter anymore.

The free cities don't trust Rafi. They won't help us topple my father if it means she'll be in charge.

I'm not sure if I trust her either.

Besides, Col's crew have always worried that I'm not a suitable match for him. Every day he's in exile, his claim to Victoria slips away a little more. Being with me, a trained killer, an impostor, a rebel, doesn't help.

45

"It's better for you and me, isn't it?" I ask. "If I'm a respectable ruler of Shreve?"

He laughs. "I thought you were a rebel. Is respectability what you want now?"

When he puts it that way, the question's even harder.

"I want to figure out who I am." My eyes fall to my new hands, the fingers longer, thinner. "Maybe getting a new body wasn't the best idea."

"Don't worry." He reaches out again, his fingertips following the line of my jaw. "You're still in there."

Col's touch tingles on my raw skin. Every pore is clean and new, like a steam bath has opened them. My muscles, stretched onto this new frame, want to test themselves.

I take his hand, pull him closer. This unfamiliar body of mine is suddenly hungry.

For a long, strange moment, our lips, our bodies fit together wrong. Like kissing a stranger.

But then a trickle of certainty cuts through the alarm bells in my head. My heart knows who this boy is, even if my stomach is fluttering.

We pull apart, staring into each other's wrong-colored eyes.

I try to smile, but the expression feels unbalanced. Like in that half hour after dental surge, my face half-numb.

"Frey," Col whispers. "We're still us inside."

"Easy for you to say. You've never been anyone else!"

"Neither have you," he says.

His words are logic-missing, but he says them with such certainty that for a moment I can't speak.

"You should look in the mirror, Frey. Nothing's ever as bad as your imagination makes it."

He's right. And a small, brain-missing part of me is madly curious about my new face.

"There aren't any mirrors in here." I turn toward the view of the city. "Maybe the window . . ."

We walk to the wall of glass. Reflected in it, translucent against the sky, is the face I chose from the possibilities the doctors sent me.

The small nose, the high cheeks. Nothing flashy, just boring Shreve-pretty surge. I test a few expressions.

"Do you still . . . like my face?" I ask Col.

He laughs. "I like it on *you*."

The answer is so sense-missing, as if it's a dress I'm not sure about.

But it's also exactly how Col thinks.

We kiss again, slipping into our familiar way of holding each other. My right hand drifts along his flank, his left cradles the back of my neck. The shapes and angles have all changed, but I still recognize them, like an old dance to a new song.

And I realize there's something that the surgery didn't alter.

"You taste the same, Col."

He pulls back a little. "I have a *taste*?"

"Everyone does. It's not something I usually . . . except the rest of you is so different."

"Huh." Col ponders this a moment. "Let me taste you, then."

He folds us into another kiss, a mix of warm and familiar and unexpected and strange, but this time easier, more certain.

Kissing is a kind of trusting. And I trust Col, whatever he looks like.

Even with our new faces, raw skin, wrong eyes, we start to become ourselves again.

COLD WATER

I descend into the cold lake, holding my breath.

When I force my eyes open, a steady blinking is visible through the murk.

My fingers scramble for my light, but the crash gel is too foamy to carry a beam. I stumble and crawl along the muddy bottom. This is more like clawing through a snowbank than swimming.

The blinking shows two silhouettes together. I'm almost there. My heart is pounding, my lungs already empty.

Yandre's and Col's faces loom in the foam. Their helmets are off. They're sharing one breather.

Why are they still down here?

Col shoves the breather in my mouth. As I gulp oxygen, he points at his feet.

I kneel, shining my own light. Yandre's boot is caught, tangled in an old plastic fishing net crowded with sticks and leaves.

I make a fist, my thumb on the inside. The smart plastic squirms, and a moment later, the variable blade is in my hand. It cuts through the net in a stroke.

My brain is still wavering from lack of oxygen. That's all I can do—I turn and fight my way back toward the shore.

For long seconds, it feels like drowning. My instincts are screaming to swim for the surface, but the crash gel is too thin to hold me. I can only stumble back up the slope of the lake bed.

Blackness leaks across my vision, something fading inside me . . .

But then strong hands grasp my arms, pull me up and out. My head bursts through the surface—I'm gasping, coughing, Zura and Lodge on either side of me. The others watch from the beach, trying not to look alarmed.

"Do you need medical attention, Islyn?" my father's almost voice asks.

"Just snorted some water, sir," I manage. My right hand is open, so the knife has hidden itself back in the rings. "Everything's fine."

At least, I hope it is.

As the Specials haul me toward the beach, I scan the lake for any signs of movement. I must have freed Yandre, but did they have enough air left?

The water's rippling farther down the shore. Two heads bob to the surface.

I make my way toward them through the waist-deep gel.

Col looks at me, like he's about to explain what happened. But he can't say anything with the dust listening.

I take him in my arms. He's shivering to his core.

"I love you," Col says.

50

For a moment, the words make me feel exposed, with the dust listening. But Islyn and Arav are registered with the city as romantic partners. We're allowed to say these words to each other.

The Shreve AI takes a dim view of cheating—it likes to know everyone's relationship status.

"Love you too," I say. "Let's get you dry."

We head up into the trees, wet and cold.

Our new identities have homes, of course. Our helpful spy assigned us apartments near the center of town, suitable for such upright citizens. But we don't plan to use them.

Our cover is that we're hiking for a few days, camping out here in the greenbelt. Security headquarters, where Boss X is imprisoned, is on the far side of the city. It's a long walk from our landing spot, but we couldn't risk flying past military sensor arrays.

Besides, a camping trip is an excuse to carry makeshift weapons hidden in our equipment.

And to build fires.

Half a klick into the woods, we make camp next to the main greenbelt path. Our two-person tents unfold into polyhedrons while we watch and shiver.

Zura has enough energy to gather wood and stack it into the pyramid shape we've all practiced.

I want to tell Col about those awful minutes on the beach, not knowing if he and Yandre were alive or dead. Wondering how I could lose him and show the dust nothing.

Staying silent sets the blank spot on my arm tingling. But my feels are still gone, my emotions still tangled inside me.

Zura lights the fire, and it comes quickly to life. Col and I huddle close, and sparks fly out and singe our mylar blanket. He hasn't stopped shivering since those long minutes in the lake.

I hold him tight until the shudders subside.

And finally it appears, a thermal plume of sparks and smoke rushing up from the pyramid of flame. I glance down at the badge on my lapel—a gift from Diego.

It's the emblem of a Shreve camping club, decorated with a tent logo, five stars in the sky. But the badge is a sensor. The dust is noisy stuff—every nanocam, every tiny microphone sends its data pulsing through a web of repeaters. The little stars above the tent show the strength of that signal.

Right now, four of the five are subtly reflective in the firelight, the dust's normal strength out here in the wild.

But as Zura's fire builds, it draws the air from around us and channels it up through the burning core, vaporizing the dust. Soon there are only three stars flickering on my badge, then two . . .

When the signal is down to one wavering star, our words are being burned away before they can be transmitted. A familiar calm settles over me, like when Rafi and I would go out in a rainstorm to hide our secrets.

"Thanks for the save," Col whispers.

"How'd you find Yandre?"

"Walking into shore, I saw their signal light flashing. They were almost out of air, but I had some left from turning off my oxygen."

I have to smile. Nothing could be more Col—saving his friend thanks to a sense-missing attempt to smell the ozone layer.

"Told you Rafi's blade would come in handy," I say. "And you thought it wasn't worth the risk."

"Happy to be wrong." He's staring at his hands, which are still shivering.

"Let me." I gently rub his fingers, drinking in the fact that he's still alive.

Somehow in this new place, Col's new face doesn't seem as wrong. Maybe the three weeks since the surge have gotten me used to it, or maybe it was the shock of almost losing him.

Maybe somewhere in my brain, his old face is being gradually replaced with this one. But I'm glad he's still here, either way.

"At least I got fifteen merits out of it," he says.

"That's weird. I got eighteen, and I wasn't in the water as long as you."

Col shrugs. "It's random, to keep people guessing."

Just like my father—one day he'd be loving to Rafi, the next day, cruel. The unpredictability of his whims kept her eager to please, always hoping that tomorrow would be better.

Until the day she realized what he really was, of course.

The first rush of the fire is starting to fade. The single star is solid now, which means it'll be dangerous to talk soon.

"Waiting for you was . . ." My voice fades. Now that I can finally speak, finding the words is too exhausting. "I'm going to have drowning nightmares. I'm glad we're past the landing."

Col laughs. "Yeah, the rest is easy. Just walk across Shreve, capture the head of Security, and stroll into her headquarters."

The mission has barely begun.

"Sunrise isn't far off," I say. "We should get some sleep."

"Okay, but . . ." He leans closer and whispers, "When we were stuck down there in the dark and cold, I knew you'd come."

My new smile, a still unfamiliar twist of muscles, comes across my face. "Rescuing each other is what we're good at."

The fire sparks a little, and Col smiles back. "Works for me."

On my camping badge, the second star is flickering to life.

The dust is back.

We crawl to our tent. But before exhaustion takes us, the voice of Shreve murmurs in my ear again.

"Thirty merits for today's exercise—hiking is healthy and fun. Minus forty for the fire. Sleep well, Islyn."

"Thank you, sir," I say.

SHUDDER

The world is shaking, and my lungs are full of dust.

I know this nightmare—it runs along well-worn channels in my brain. Buildings tumble, people spill from their heights. Dark clouds sweep across the sun, choking the sky.

I twist awake, struggling against my sleeping bag, trying to escape.

"Islyn," Col's voice comes. "It's okay."

The false name means nothing, and I keep fighting. My fingers press a chord of Calm and Grief where my feels used to be.

Col holds me tight, knowing what this thrashing means. As the shape and warmth of him surround me, I remember to take slow breaths.

My fingers unclench from my arm, releasing the shadow of my feels. The panic subsides a little. Until I'm certain—

I'm not in Paz, the city my father destroyed with an earthquake.

But the ground really is quivering beneath us.

"Do you feel that?" I ask.

Seconds later, we're scrambling out of the tent.

The others are up too, looking in all directions in the faint light of dawn. The pine trees shiver around us, sending down a cool mist of dew.

My heart is racing, all the trauma of that day in Paz surging inside me. I turn toward the city in the distance, half expecting the towers to be falling.

Have my father's enemies somehow turned his own weapon against him?

But the skyline of Shreve stands there, solid and unmoving, against the bloodred sunrise.

"It's not an earthquake," Col says.

I slow my breath again, and as the roar of panic in my ears fades a little, I hear it in the distance.

The rumble of machines.

"Good morning," the city interface says. "You mentioned an earthquake? There is no alert for seismic activity."

"But the ground is shaking, sir."

"Scheduled construction," comes the answer.

What kind of construction moves the earth like this? The Shreve AI doesn't sound in the mood to explain.

I look at Zura, trusting her Special-enhanced hearing more than my own.

She nods down the path. In the direction of Security HQ and the imprisoned Boss X.

"Let's go for a walk," she says.

The path climbs beneath us, steep enough that the trembling sends little streams of loose dirt past our feet.

I can hear them clearly now—huge engines toiling in the distance. The sound seems to come from everywhere at once, bouncing through the trees.

It's growing louder as we climb.

The sky is still half-dark, the last stars only now fading in the west. As the jolt of adrenaline from my nightmare fades, I realize that our coffee is back at the camp, along with my toothpaste pills.

When we crest the ridge, the valley spreads out below us.

There they are, a column of machines raising clouds of dirt as it moves. Excavators, wielding earth-cutting blades the size of Ferris wheels. Soil conveyors, big as cantilever bridges on tractor treads. A forest of mobile drills, their diamond bits glittering like jewelry in the sun.

Strip-mining machines, designed to tear down mountains and pull out their metal hearts.

I follow the column's path with my eyes. It's headed toward the largest section of the greenbelt, the last place in Shreve that my father hasn't plundered.

Since invading Victoria, he's been embargoed, shunned by the world's markets. His invasion of Paz failed. The ruins he stole from Col's family must be empty of metal by now.

He has nowhere left to turn except his own land.

Unless this is something more sinister than strip mining. I

remember Rafi's warning—our father is most dangerous when cornered.

"Weren't we planning on hiking this way?" I ask lightly.

"You mentioned hiking," the city interface cuts in. "I'm afraid all trails are closed in this valley."

No one says anything. Boss X is being held on the other side of that column of machines.

Our rescue is scheduled for three nights from now. The free cities' diversionary strike, our spy crashing the dust at the head of Security's house, it's all carefully timed.

And we have no way to postpone it, no way to get any signal out of the city.

"Excuse me, sir," I say. "How many merits would it cost to hike on a closed trail?"

The Shreve AI pauses, long enough that I wonder if my words were taken by the breeze.

But then it says reproachfully, "Islyn, that doesn't sound like you."

"I know, sir. But we've been planning this for *months*."

"Hiking is healthy and fun, but construction zones are dangerous. We can't allow you to compromise your own safety. It's not a question of merits, but of mindset."

I'm not sure what that last part means, but it sounds like I'm at risk of being flagged. Shreve is at war with the whole world, but the dust is worried about someone hiking on a closed trail.

"Sorry, sir. We'll go back into the city." I put on a pouting face, like a scolded child. "Maybe we can catch a train to the other side of the valley."

"That's the spirit, Islyn!"

I turn back to the others, scanning for any disagreement.

Zura is gazing through her field glasses at the column of machines. To skirt this valley, we'll have to go into Shreve itself. A million people, thicker dust, endless chances to give ourselves away.

"Back to Shreve, then," she says. "So much for taking time off from the crowds."

PASSENGERS

The nearest train station is an hour's hike away.

Col—of course—spent last week memorizing the Shreve rail system. He draws it for us in the dirt, a wheel with ten spokes.

"We have to ride all the way into Central to switch trains. We can eat lunch somewhere near the station. You know a place, right, Islyn?"

I don't know any places, of course—he's just reminding everyone to let me do the talking in town. The city AI has our new voices on file, but real people might wonder why everyone but me has a foreign accent.

They'll stumble over etiquette and rules, like any tourists in a foreign city. Except Shreve doesn't have tourists anymore.

Fooling algorithms is tricky enough, but in the city, we'll have a million pairs of eyes watching us.

Being reported is dangerous in Shreve.

When Rafi and I were little, we used to watch a show called *Shame-Cam* on the local feeds. Every week, someone who'd been reported for bad behavior would have it revealed to the whole city. Mostly it was simple callousness, like mistreating a pet, breaking a promise, or kissing the wrong person.

But the hate was real. I still remember a woman who shoved a hesitant child aside to get on a slidewalk. For a week, she was the target of all my training moves—every punch, every kick, every thrust of my pulse knife aimed at her face.

Until the next episode, when someone new came along.

Rafi loved the show, but it always made me queasy. I wasn't sure if being an impostor, a liar, would one day mean I would be on *Shame-Cam*.

As we pack up our gear, the trembling earth feels fragile beneath my feet. The sunrise is swallowed by dark clouds in the distance.

The free cities are trying to make it rain while we're here—heavy downpours to sweep as much surveillance dust from the air as possible. It looks like the cloud seeding is already working.

We start the hike. From our path along the ridge, the skyline of Shreve splays out before us. Solid buildings of steel and glass, no floating hoverstruts, nothing taller than my father's tower.

Closer to the station, power lines and windmills start popping up against the gray sky. It's been months since I've lived in a normal, functioning city. I've gotten used to sleeping in a cave, to waking up every day surrounded by the wild, by crew.

Maybe Boss X was right, and I was always a rebel at heart.

But Diego and the other free cities think I should be the leader of Shreve, someone who settles the world's conflicts.

How can I be both those things?

We reach the station, and a train pulls in after half an hour.

It's a single car, empty except for a few hikers and a couple of crumblies with bags full of shopping from the city.

All of them stare at us as they get off the train—for a moment, I think they're looking at me.

For years, I pretended to be the first daughter of Shreve. A hundred cams, a thousand faces watched me wherever I went. But now their eyes slip from my boring new face to our duffel bags.

We're carrying too much stuff, of course. Shreve's greenbelt isn't very big, and the wild beyond the border is off-limits. Even disguised as tents and camping gear, our bags of weapons and equipment look suspicious.

We're pretty weird too.

Zura and Lodge with their imposing builds, Riggs and Charles with their rebel air.

In Shreve, reporting anything suspicious is a citizen's duty. It's as easy as opening your mouth and saying three magic words . . .

This looks wrong.

I wait for one of the passengers to speak up, to accuse us all of looking like foreign spies. But they have bigger things on their minds, and soon disappear into the countryside around us.

We get onto the empty train and take our seats, spreading out so it won't be so obvious that we're all together. When Riggs leaves her duffel bag in the walkway, the city AI docks her five merits. She sighs and puts it on the overhead rack.

She slumps in her seat, daring the dust to correct her posture.

Riggs has never fully invested in creating a new self for this mission. She didn't let the surgeons change her gait; she's even using her real first name. That made the rest of us nervous, until a search of Shreve public records found 247 people called Riggs.

Still, it seems like tempting fate.

A screen on the wall counts down the minutes till the train's departure. Maybe we'll have the whole car to ourselves . . .

But with thirty seconds to go, I see someone out the window.

He's a middle pretty, his temples graying. He wears a raincoat and carries an old-fashioned overnight bag with no hoverlifters. He's hurrying, carried by long athletic strides.

Col turns to me. "The next train's not for three hours. It'll be pouring by then."

I shake my head a little.

The fewer people who get a look at us, the better. And keeping to schedule is sacred here in Shreve.

Model citizen Arav would know all this, so I don't say it aloud. Col reads my expression, frowns, and looks back at the hurrying man.

It's going to be close. As the man reaches the station path, a sequence of beeps sounds. The air tingles, the train's magnetics coming to life.

The doors start to close—

Col sticks his foot out, catching them just in time.

An angry buzz shakes the train car as the doors halt and rebound.

The man slides through the gap. He's out of breath, and drops his bag on the floor with a nod of thanks to Col.

Col smiles back, pulling his foot away.

The doors close, and the train glides into motion.

Col is muttering into his comms. "Sorry, sir. I know, sir. Sorry—I won't. Thank you, sir."

It takes a slew of apologies to the city, but the conversation finally comes to an end.

"Be good, Arav," I tell him.

He shrugs, attempts a Shreve accent. "Just thirty demerits."

"Happy to reimburse you, my friend," the man says from across the aisle. "That train platform suffers from a lack of diversion. Three hours might've been a trial."

Col shakes his head. "You don't have to pay me back."

"Something more interesting than merits, then?" The man leans closer to us, quickly scanning the car before speaking again.

When he takes in the rest of the commandoes, he hesitates.

"Ah. *You're* an intriguing assemblage, aren't you?"

In a single glance, he knew we were all together.

"Just hiking with friends," I say.

"Which is healthy and fun, I'm sure." He hands me a small rectangle of paper. "My calling card."

The card looks like something out of a pre-Rusty drama. There's nothing on it except a name in very small letters.

JAXON ALLIFLEX

"Nice to meet you, Jaxon," I say.

"Perhaps the type is too small." He hands me a pair of eyeglasses, like you'd wear if your vision implants were fritzing.

"I can see fine," I say.

"Are you sure? Have you been to the eye doctor lately?"

"Um, no?"

Jaxon gestures to the glasses. "Then I insist."

Without any change in tone, those last words sound almost like a threat. He knows there's something off about us, and that we don't want trouble.

So I obey, slipping the glasses on my face to look at the card again . . . and somehow, there's more.

JAXON ALLIFLEX
PRIVATEER
(CALL ME JAX)

"Did that help?" he asks.

I blink, turning the card to different angles. The extra words fade in and out, a little unsteady on the paper.

"It did." I look up at him. "Thank you, Jax."

He smiles.

Then I see the rest, revealed on the walls of the train around us—symbols, printed text, graffiti, and drawings scrawled across the bland pastels of Shreve Rail signage. A layer of meaning invisible to my eyes, even with my military-grade vision implants, suddenly visible in the eyeglasses.

It must be invisible to the dust as well.

For a moment, Jax watches my eyes dart about the train. Then he plucks the glasses from my face, a gentle reminder not to react too obviously.

"Nice to meet you too," he says, handing the glasses to Col. "You look as though you could use my professional assistance."

PART II

PALIMPSEST

Words persist: they collect in gutters;
they pile up and require sweeping; they
hang in air like morning fog.

—Dexter Palmer

BEDLAM

Jax gives Col a look through the eyeglasses, and amazement flickers across his face.

He hands them back to the man. "Please, join us."

"An excellent idea," Jax says, standing. "But I must warn you, I am spellbinding company."

As he gathers his bag and raincoat from the overhead rack, my eyes scan the walls of the train again. All those words and symbols are gone, leaving no trace. I wonder how the glasses work, whether the trick was in the lenses or some kind of transmitter hidden in the glasses.

Did they do something to my vision implants?

Or my *brain*?

"I make my living as a widget," the man announces once he's settled. "I was doing an overnight, out here in the greenbelt."

Col looks confused, but I nod to show Jax that I understand.

In Shreve, when you leave your house empty, any homeless citizen is allowed to move in while you're gone. The dust watches them extra carefully, of course. Widgets make repairs, clean up, water your plants, and feed your pets, accumulating a few merits if the algorithm deems fit. The dust tells them when you're headed back, and they disappear, like helpful elves.

In the stories Rafi and I watched growing up, widgets were always kind and wise and even a little magical. But Rafi's friends made jokes about them. They're my father's solution to poverty—turning homeless people into repair workers, moving parts that can be slotted in anywhere. They're also gentle reminders that in Shreve, not even your home really belongs to you.

"Has widgeting been tricky, since the war?" I ask.

Jax nods. "Not many people traveling, thanks to the embargo. Fewer empty houses to go around."

"That's rough," I say.

Jax doesn't look poor, though. His bright green suit and red raincoat are patched in a few places, but also made with skill. An average citizen of Shreve might not spot the quality, but living in Paz taught me to appreciate handmade things.

"Are you looking for a place to stay?" Col asks. "We're headed back into the greenbelt for a few more days. My apartment's free."

I resist the urge to glare at him. The apartments assigned to our fake identities aren't just free—they're *empty*. Jax has already noticed something off about us. The last thing we need is him seeing empty closets and drawers where a life should be.

With those glasses, he's an outlaw of some kind. But that doesn't mean we can trust him.

"A kind invitation," Jax says. "But I have business today on the farthest outskirts of this metropolis."

I wonder what kind of business he means.

His card said *privateer*—a term I remember from military history. Privateers were sort of pirates, licensed by one nation to make war on another and keep any spoils for themselves.

But I don't know what the word means in Shreve.

"I'm looking for a construction site," Jax continues. "Something on the water."

I frown. "You mean the city reservoir?"

Since the war began, Shreve's main water supply has been surrounded by defenses. Every time the Vics or rebels have gone after it, they've been repulsed.

You can't even hike there, much less build a house.

"Not as good as the sea," Jax says. "But water is still the birthplace of life. Our blood is as salty as the ocean. And our tears, expressing the emotions that make us human, a reminder of where we hail from."

Col smiles, like all this makes sense. "So you want a house on the beach?"

"Not a mere *house*," Jax says. "As a widget, I've stayed in more houses than I care to count. What comes next must be magnificent, a means of connection. An expanse between two anchorages!"

I stare at him. "You mean a *bridge*?"

"You seem astonished, my dear. Don't you have bridges where you come from?"

I'm speechless for a moment, captured by Jax's smile and the gleam in his eye—and his implication that we're outsiders.

Maybe the man is simply sense-missing. His brightly colored, hand-made clothes are oddball enough, but building his own bridge . . .

I wonder why the dust isn't correcting him—you aren't allowed to say things that aren't true in Shreve. Maybe he's being vague enough that the dust doesn't understand.

"We're from here," Col says.

The man lights up. "Yes! But in the springtime, it's Paris that sizzles. Wouldn't you agree?"

He gestures out the window, as if the Eiffel Tower were passing by instead of the glum low-rise housing of the outer suburbs. The tallest things are occasional dust chimneys, spewing their haze of nano-machines into the air.

"I've never been to Paris," Col says in a gently humoring way, like Jax is an older relative who's forgotten to take their Alz-blockers.

For moment, I doubt what I saw on the walls of the train.

"If you ever go, look me up." Jax's eyes twinkle again, and he says with perfect clarity, "I am an excellent tour guide. Especially if you want to see the places no one ever shows a visitor."

I tense. He's calling us outsiders again.

But the city interface stays silent in my ears. Somehow its algorithms haven't been triggered. As if the AI doesn't pay attention to anything this man says.

Maybe his sense-missing talk is a strategy. Out of two million citizens, a few thousand must have untreatable disorders of the mind.

They must say odd things all the time, things that get flagged by the algorithms—but when Security investigates, it's just babble, full of overblown words and logic-missing ideas.

The AI would eventually learn to disregard those people, wouldn't it?

Jax is unerringly polite, and useful with his repairs and house-sitting, so his odd behavior might not even cost him any merits.

It's a way around the spy dust that I've never considered before.

"Next time I'm in Paris, I'll ping you," Col says with a gentle smile.

The train slows, the signposts for the next station gliding past the windows. More passengers are waiting here, and our conversation changes distinctly as they get on.

Jax tells us about the houses he's stayed in, the dogs he's made friends with while their owners were away. If there's any hidden meaning in his stories, it's too subtle for me.

Maybe having all these people around makes his act trickier. The city's algorithms might have trained themselves to ignore Jax, but humans are relentless at sniffing out meaning.

At least the presence of a loud, brightly dressed widget on the train distracts the other passengers from us—the group of oddballs with strange accents and too much camping equipment.

Zura keeps staring across the car at me and Col, wondering why we're talking to this eccentric stranger. Without that glimpse through the glasses, I'd be wondering myself.

As the train gets closer to the city, more cars are added, more passengers get on. A few tip their hats to Jax or give him a smile. Do they know him? Or do most citizens feel kindly toward widgets?

Then I realize that some of them are wearing eyeglasses.

How big is this conspiracy of hidden signs?

I remember when Col's Victorians and the rebels attacked Shreve, shutting down my father's dust for a few hours. Rafi and I went on the feeds and told the whole world our secret, the way our father used us.

Within minutes, thousands of people were on the rooftops, celebrating, thinking his regime was over. Maybe they were already connected, already part of some kind of organized resistance.

But how would it get started, in a city where everyone is always watched? How do people write messages without the dust noticing?

If I'm going to understand my own city, I need to find out how it works, and whether these privateers are rebels, criminals, or something else entirely.

I make a show of squinting at the screen listing the upcoming stops.

"Jax, I think you were right about my vision implants. You don't have any of those glasses for sale, do you?"

"Certainly." His eyes rise to our stacks of our gear on the luggage racks. "But not for mere merits."

He suspects we're carrying contraband, of course. But I can't trade him our weapons.

"I'm not sure—"

"It's bad luck," Jax cuts in, "discussing business before lunch. Perhaps I can take you somewhere?"

I nod in agreement, not daring to glance at Zura.

I've just made this mission a lot more complicated.

The train is excruciating.

My father has always kept the local transport slow, to make his domain seem bigger than it really is. And I'm used to traveling in an armored hoverlimo, with no part of Shreve more than twenty minutes from home.

When rebels move, it's on hoverboards. Free and in the open air, not stuffed into a can.

At last our train arrives in town.

The city's towers rise up around us, and my camping badge shows all five stars of signal strength. The dust is thick here.

We step out onto the platform, trying not to look like newcomers.

In town, no one stares at us, which is strange for me. Back when Rafi and I came to this station for appearances, there were always huge crowds waiting for us.

Shreve Central, one of my father's efforts at magnificence. Fifty meters over our heads, the ceiling is made from a stained-glass window the size of a soccer field. The clouds in the sky are breaking, and multihued shards of daylight scatter across the marble floor. The lancing sun ignites sparkles in the air.

Dust, a beautiful reminder that the city is watching.

The station feels half-empty, though. Before the war, visitors and traders from other cities used to come here in the thousands every day. But the embargo against Shreve has held firm. Central is now just a glorified transfer station between local trains.

My father's greed has hollowed out his city. This station always signified the world beyond Shreve. But now it feels spark-missing, like a hoverboard with no magnetics.

"Spectacular, isn't it?" Jax says, looking up at the ceiling. "But to grasp the full effect, your vision must be unimpaired."

He hands me the eyeglasses again. I slip them on . . .

I almost gasp aloud.

Exploding across my view are countless scribbles on the floor, layer upon layer of messages covering the expanse of white marble. The signs for shops and restaurants are obscured by mysterious symbols. Even the wallscreens have been hijacked—wavering words shudder alongside the train departure times and track numbers.

It's a mess, but somehow beautiful, this scrawled barrage of meaning, even if I don't understand any of it.

My father's city is full of secrets.

SHREVE
CENTRAL

"Shouldn't we be getting lunch?" Zura asks.

"The next train out isn't for two hours," Col says. "Let's take a walk with our new friend."

Zura wants to argue, and the rest of our crew looks confused. None of them have worn the eyeglasses. All they know is that Col and I are putting the mission at risk.

Here in the dust, there's no way to explain.

"Trust me," Col adds. "It'll be fun."

So we wind up with Jax leading us through the station, regaling us with the history of its construction.

It's the first time since the war started that I've seen citizens of Shreve in these numbers. Their clothes aren't just bland—they look threadbare. Like the holes in the wall are recycling the same material for the tenth time.

Lodge scans the crowd like he expects an ambush, and Zura quietly seethes. Yandre is reserving judgment, and Riggs and Boss Charles seem to be enjoying themselves. Maybe they sense a kindred spirit in Jax.

Or maybe they just enjoy chaos.

Jax leads us deeper into the station, to the lower levels, where subway pods glide beneath the city. The tunnels down here are less crowded, the air rumbling softly from the heavy trains overhead.

As he delivers his oration, Jax keeps glancing around, as if looking for hidden signs. But he isn't wearing the eyeglasses—I am.

The walls down here are dirty—the war has chipped away at the city's famous order. There's even litter in a few places, which I've never seen before in Shreve.

The city interface hasn't spoken to us since we arrived. Maybe here in the center of town, it's harder to catch its notice. Or maybe being in Jax's eccentric orbit deflects attention.

He keeps glancing at the plastic ribbons stuck into the concrete every few meters. They hang in groups of three or four, of various colors and lengths.

Are they signposts for a secret path?

Jax brings us to a halt on an empty platform, pointing down at the tracks below.

"Observe! A disused track, for the Cobra mag-lev that once visited our fair city." Jax kneels at the platform edge. "It holds a secret."

I look through the glasses. No hidden marks down there.

"Centuries ago," Jax says, "Rusty trains used this tunnel. The width of those trains was based on the Roman roads in Europe, designed to hold a chariot. Even our latest tech is ruled by the dimensions of ancient war machines!"

The city interface speaks up. "Not strictly correct—this continent had several different railroad track gauges. It wasn't till after the Slavery Abolition War that things were standardized. The Romans were irrelevant by then."

Jax looks miffed.

"Always a pleasure to hear from a fellow ferroequinologist," he says to the air. "But I think you've missed the pith of my argument. It's not that . . ."

His voice trails off as a train rumbles past in some nearby tunnel, stirring the air around us. Jax's gaze drifts to the platform wall, where three of the mysterious ribbons hang.

They dance in the sudden breeze, lifting up one by one. When the longest begins to flutter, Jax's manner changes all at once.

"Who *are* you people?" he asks.

Zura steps forward. "What do you—"

"It's okay," Col tells her, pointing at his camping badge. "The signal's at zero. The wind down here's too much for the dust."

"You need that explained?" Jax frowns. "You aren't smugglers, are you?"

Zura looks like she's about to punch someone.

"How long do we have?" I ask Jax.

"Three trains, arriving in sequence. Two minutes and forty seconds, more or less."

Yandre gestures at the ribbons. "That chalk mark on the wall—it's the minimum, right?"

"We don't have time for that," I cut in. "Jax, you're right—we're not smugglers. We're here to rescue a friend in prison. Can we trust you not to turn us in?"

He looks a little offended. "I would never betray a customer."

"Okay," I say. "But what exactly are you selling?"

"Besides your silence," Zura mutters.

"You do seem well funded." Jax scans our bags with greedy eyes. "What is it you need?"

A thousand questions crowd my mind.

"Those hidden symbols," I ask. "Are they just for smugglers?"

"Hardly," Jax says. "Thousands contribute to the palimpsest, with as many purposes. A little smuggling, a lot of venting. And perhaps some small degree of treason."

"Thousands," I breathe.

"It can't be that many," Col says. "Somebody would've betrayed you by now!"

Jax nods. "That issue is often debated. Some say that Security allows the palimpsest to exist—to collect their own profits on the black market, or to let us blow off steam. Others contend that relying on machines has made the regime weak. What Sir Dust can't see simply doesn't exist."

"And you're a smuggler?" I ask.

"A privateer, as my card says." Jax bows a little. "A broker of privacy. Of which you have ninety seconds left. Use them well."

That freezes me. I want to know everything about my city.

Yandre speaks up. "We need help."

Zara turn to them. "No we don't. We can't trust him!"

"But a diversion—"

"We already . . ." Zura halts herself, her teeth clenching in frustration. "You realize this is a *secret* mission, right?"

"Zura, this is bigger than our mission." Yandre turns to Col. "Think of home."

A look passes between the two childhood friends.

"This isn't the plan!" Lodge speaks up.

Riggs shares a smile with Boss Charles. "It's *better* than the plan."

"Sixty seconds," Jax says. "And I need to be paid for this time, and those glasses."

Col raises his hands to silence everyone. "The next minute is yours, Dre."

Yandre pulls their badge off and hands it to Jax. "Those stars there? They show the signal strength of the dust. None of them are shiny; it's safe to talk."

Jax stares at the badge in his palm. "But this is worth . . . *millions.*"

"We don't need merits," Yandre says. "We need help. Introduce us to someone who can disrupt Security."

Jax smiles. "What flavor of disruption?"

"We need to overwhelm the system," Yandre says. "So much suspicious activity that the staff can't look at it all."

"Ah, a denial of attention attack. It's been a while." Jax slips the badge into his breast pocket. "There's someone who lives nearby—I can ask them to meet you. The lane behind this station is our usual spot."

"When?" I ask. "And what about the dust?"

Jax glances at the wall. The rumble of the trains is fading, the flutter of the ribbons wavering.

"One answer to both your questions—wait for the rain."

And then, without a pause, he's lecturing us again on the history of steam engines, rolling stock, and magnetic levitation.

My father's eyes and ears are back.

But for the first time, the dust doesn't feel all-powerful.

STORM

I take my crew to the covered markets, not far from the station.

Dark clouds pile up over the city, the coming rain like a weight shifting overhead. The markets are busy, full of transport and farm workers, and our gear doesn't stick out as much.

I order food from the city interface—badly. My Shreve accent might be native, but I've never had to order a meal before. In a rebel crew, you eat what everyone else does. Growing up, I ate what was needed to keep my body exactly like Rafi's.

But that's not an issue anymore.

"That's quite a lot of food," the city says with a hint of displeasure.

Wasting food is frowned on here in Shreve, especially in wartime. But we won't get another hot meal till the mission is over.

"We have lots of hiking later, sir."

The city doesn't comment, but four hundred merits rattle out of my account. Penalty rates for conspicuous consumption.

"Thank you, sir," I mumble, letting the clatter and roar of the market envelop my words.

Zura is still quietly furious with me and Col. When I hand her Jax's eyeglasses, she barely glances through them. But she passes them around the table, giving the others a look.

The conversation feels forced. Over the last weeks, I've gotten used to my friends' camo-surge. But facing everyone around this table, it's like we're at some awkward costume party.

"Rain's coming soon," Col says, staring at the dust chimneys across the street.

Here in the center of Shreve, the chimneys are smaller than in the country. But they're on every rooftop, like we've traveled back in time to some Rusty city burning coal to stay warm.

We're not the only people talking about the weather. Half the customers are standing at the edge of the covers, looking at the sky. The rest are concentrating on their food, pointedly ignoring the coming rain.

Every downpour must create this divide—the good citizens and the rebellious. With the dust swept from the air, there's space for black-market deals and secret conversations.

Maybe more serious crimes.

The food arrives, way too much of it, carried by a fleet of drones. The rebels tear at the corn bread with their fingers instead of cutting it into slices.

The workers around us don't care about our eating habits, though. They're more interested in the dark and heavy sky.

Then I smell it—the sharp scent of rain.

We all start eating faster. It'll mean demerits if we waste food.

But other customers are already slipping into the downpour, leaving behind empty market stalls, stray packages, uneaten meals. They don't care how odd it looks.

Of course, if enough people do something, it's normal by definition.

Col leans back from his food. "A stroll, anyone?"

A glance from Zura tells Lodge to stay and look after our gear, and Boss Charles seems happy to finish eating. The other five of us push away from the table and head back toward the station.

The rain is falling in sheets. It's one of those springtime deluges that I remember playing in as a littlie, Rafi and me dancing on our balcony, even before we grew to hate the dust.

The streets turn instantly muddy—a slurry of surveillance nanos washed down from the sky. All those tiny cameras, microphones, and batteries now a layer of mire beneath our feet.

Already my lungs feel lighter, cleaner.

I glance up. Security sends drones out to keep watch during rainstorms; there's nothing overhead yet.

The lane behind the station is blustery, channeling the storm into wet, billowing gusts. A few small groups already huddle along its length, having frantic conversations in the dust-missing air.

"While we wait, maybe you three could explain," Zura says. "Why are we risking this entire mission *for a diversion*?"

"For Victoria," Col says.

Zura just stares at him.

"We always thought that the people here had no freedom at all," Yandre says. "But they've found ways around the dust!"

"Maybe Victoria isn't as hopeless as we thought," Col says.

"That's no reason to throw out the plan!" Zura is fighting not to shout. "If Security finds that badge on Jax, they'll come straight to us!"

"He's been a crim for a long time," I say. "He can stay out of trouble for two more days."

"Look at them all, grabbing this little sliver of privacy." Yandre waves at the people around us. "Imagine the diversion they can create!"

"Something big," Col says. "Big enough for a dictator to feel."

Zura looks away, not wanting to argue with Col when he's thinking about revenge for Victoria.

But she's not happy. "I hope it's worth it. This may cost us everything."

"Enough," Riggs hisses. "Someone's here."

We follow her gaze.

A figure is approaching through the rain.

DENIAL OF ATTENTION

It's a girl. Younger than me, tall, skinny, frizzy-haired. No surge.

Somehow I was expecting someone older.

"Jax said there were seven of you," she says.

"Two of us are watching our gear," Zura says.

The girl frowns—nothing is ever stolen in Shreve, unless you're brain-missing enough to leave it out in the rain.

"Must be serious contraband," she says.

Zura doesn't answer.

"Jax showed me that dust detector. Got any more?"

Col pulls off his badge and gives it to her.

She squints at the logo, then adds it to her own jacket, which is covered with badges from two dozen different social clubs.

"I'm Sara. I guess we're all going to be friends."

Then she starts talking fast, her words spilling out in a race with the rain. I can't understand half of what she's saying.

"Jax told me you want a DOA? Major denial, multiple cliques? No one's tried that since the Battle of Shreve, you know?"

We don't know, but Sara doesn't let that stop her.

"There's a clique called Crime. You met any of them?" She laughs. "Right, you aren't from around here. Crime doesn't do real crimes; they just sit around planning murders that Sir Dust won't see. Not boring stuff, like stabbing someone in the rain. Slipping in the shower, say, or an accident on a train platform, so it's just: Oops, a thousand merits for being clumsy! Crime is perfect for this DOA."

"DOA?" I ask. "As in Dead on Arrival?"

"Ha! Denial of Attention, also known as swamping the dust. I can get you Secret Hookups too! They'd love one of these badges. But the *perfect* clique for you is Future. Lots of members, all of them ready to help with something historic." She hesitates, looking down at her new badge. "One of those stars is flickering. Is that bad?"

"Probably just a few cams drifting by," Yandre says. "Anything less than a solid star, it's safe to talk."

"Bubbly. How many of these can you get me?"

We each had two when the mission started, so we still have a dozen—

"Only four," Zura says.

Sara's eyes light up. "Not bad. Can't exactly cut them into equal shares, but . . ."

She falls silent as she calculates, and the sound of the rain rushes in to fill the gap.

I scan the alleyway. There are half a dozen other clusters of people around us now, talking about who knows what. I wonder if some are from the cliques Sara's talking about, secret cultures in the shadows of my father's tower.

All those years growing up, I had no idea how much was happening down here in the rain and shadows.

But Yandre is right—the people of Shreve aren't cowed by the dust. They resist the regime in ways no one's ever told me about, even when I was playing Rafi full-time.

If she didn't know about the palimpsest, maybe Father doesn't either.

It lifts my heart, and yet raises a question: Why does Diego want me to lead, when I have no idea how my people really live?

It's one thing to save your city, another to understand it.

Yandre speaks up. "Let's talk about this diversion. It has to happen two nights from now. Just after midnight."

"So specific," Sara says. "Whatever you're planning, no one's getting hurt, right?"

"Not if we can help it." Yandre hesitates. "We're only—"

"Don't want to know!" she cries, her hands up to ward off their words. "Just don't get us all arrested. The cliques are still recovering from the Revelation."

"The Revelation?" I ask.

She stares at me. "You *must* know about that—when our first daughter turned out to be twins? The two sisters gave this speech together, the Revelation, telling everyone how bad it was to be them. Little rich girls having to share clothes. They told us to rise up and

91

kick their dad out of power—and everyone believed it! But then they bailed on us."

For a moment, no one says anything. None of the commandoes looks at me, but I can feel their thoughts like heat on my skin.

When Col and the rebels attacked my father's tower last year, Rafi and I went on the feeds to ask the people to rise up. But then Col was captured, and we lost, and I had to stay behind to save him.

"We know about the Battle of Shreve," Col finally says. "It didn't go as planned. Most battles don't."

"Sure," Sara says. "But after the fighting was over, Princess Rafia stuck by her dad, leaving us to take the heat for her little rebellion."

That was me, not Rafi.

Col keeps trying to defend me. "Maybe she didn't have a choice."

"Tell that to the people who went on their roofs that night, celebrating the end of the dictator! A few days later, Security shows up at their door. We aren't talking about merits either. Some of them were my friends."

Were my friends.

Sara looks at me, like she can see straight through my camo-surge. If I was wearing my real face, she'd curse me on behalf of her lost friends, probably turn me in to Security . . .

She wouldn't risk her freedom to help us, if she knew the truth of me.

"Maybe you shouldn't do this," I say softly.

Sara narrows her eyes. "Why not?"

"Once it's over, Security might take a close look and realize that the cliques conspired with us. We'll be gone, and you'll be left to take the blame . . . again."

No one speaks up. Col and Yandre look uncertain, and Zura is staring up into the rain, like she's ready to walk away from all of us in frustration.

"Keep that badge," I say. "You don't have to do this."

Sara looks me up and down. "I thought you were rebels. But rebels wouldn't choke like this. So who are you?"

I'm not sure what to tell her. That I'm the second daughter of Shreve? The next leader of her city?

The betrayer of her friends . . .

"This is our fight, not yours," I say.

A chuckle slips from her, barely audible in the rain. "If you think that, you really don't know *anything*."

Riggs speaks up. "Don't listen to her, Sara. You're right; she's not a rebel. But I am, and we don't choke."

With her foreign accent and intense expression, Riggs is completely convincing. The last word turns in my gut like a hot knife.

Sara gives me another wary glance, then nods to Riggs. "Four of those badges for the biggest DOA ever. Deal?"

Yandre speaks up. "We also need some hardware. Whatever you use to write those hidden messages."

"Okay. When we meet up with Future, I'll bring you a sprayer."

"We have to meet them too?" Yandre asks.

"The other cliques have leaders. I can bribe the right people, and

93

it's done. But in Future, we make our own stories. You'll have to convince people face-to-face."

Col shakes his head. "We don't have time to wait for another storm. This is all happening the day after tomorrow."

"Don't worry," Sara says. "Future does their meetups out in the greenbelt, in dust-free spots. Is a little hiking okay?"

When no one else answers, Riggs lets out a sigh.

"Hiking is healthy and fun."

SPLASH

It's still raining when we get back to the markets.

Boss Charles looks up from her picked-clean plate, wearing a satisfied expression. "Nice walk?"

"A little soggy," Yandre says. "But it all worked out."

I'm worse than soggy. This new face no longer feels like a disguise—more like I'm hiding in shame.

We should have realized that any resisters here would be wary of me and my sister. Encouraging the people of Shreve to rebel put them at risk, and then I supported my father in exchange for Col's life.

Every choice I make these days feels like betrayal.

My lunch is cold and beaded with the rainspray gusting across the markets. I'm not hungry anymore.

"How long till the next train out?" Zura asks Col.

"Forty minutes."

"Waiting in the station might be warmer," she says.

We gather our gear and step back out into the rain. I walk quickly, staring down at the puddles, my shoulders hunched.

A sudden roar fills the air.

It's a groundcar—moving too fast, skidding through the dust-slurry. As it rushes past, a curtain of mud splashes onto me, almost knocking me down.

The groundcar roars away down the street.

"What the . . ." Col's voice comes.

I wipe the muck from my face, blinded and confused. Dangerous driving in Shreve can get you shame-cammed.

"Count your bags," Riggs calls out.

There's a frantic moment of checking. My three bags are all accounted for.

Then Lodge calls out, "My pack!"

"That way!" Boss Charles shouts.

At the end of the street, a figure is splashing away through the puddles, carrying one of our backpacks.

"You two, with me," I say to Zura and Lodge. "Everyone else, stay here!"

We run after the figure, feet sliding in the mud.

The thief must have spotted us the moment we walked into the covered markets. If they think we're smugglers, afraid to report a theft, they're not completely wrong.

We can't afford the Shreve AI to look inside that pack.

Of course, neither can they.

But they know this city, where to run and hide. There's only one thing the thief doesn't know—two of us are Specials.

Zura and Lodge put on a burst of superhuman speed. They take the next corner, leaving me behind.

Running in my new body is strange. The extra height makes the ground feel too far away, and the swing of my arms is wrong. It feels like making a marionette run—the strings tangling, wooden feet uncertain on the mud.

I round the corner and skid in the wet. The dust-slurry feels slick and silty underfoot, like campfire ashes after a rain.

Ahead of me, the two Specials have come to a halt in the middle of the next street. The thief has disappeared.

I pull the eyeglasses from my pocket.

To my right, a pair of six-story buildings are marked with hidden symbols. I run toward them.

There's an alley between the buildings. At the far end, a blob of heat flashes in my infrared. But it's not the thief—it's two people intertwined in the rain, flashing bare skin.

Secret Hookups.

But halfway up one of the alley walls, someone's climbing a drainpipe.

"This way!" I call, and charge into the alley.

Grabbing the drainpipe, I haul myself up. The pipe trembles with the downpour flowing through it, but it isn't slick. There's some kind of grippy surface on the backside.

It's been treated to make it easy to climb in the rain.

This is a marked escape route—palimpsest symbols clutter the wall beside me.

Overhead, the thief slips over the top, then reappears for a moment against the dark gray sky, looking down at me.

It's a man, I can tell. He's wearing a mask, his eyes wide behind it, like he's surprised that I'm chasing him. Maybe real smugglers wouldn't take the risk.

I keep climbing, hoping he doesn't decide to drop something heavy on my head.

When I clear the edge, he's off again across the rooftops. There are gaps between the buildings, more alleys. But through the eyeglasses, I see arrows marking the best spots to jump.

As he takes the first leap, there's something familiar about the thief's run.

Zura clambers up and bolts past. I stagger after her, dodging between solar panels and dust chimneys, wondering if I really want to jump across an alley in this unfamiliar body—in the pouring rain.

The first chasm looms before us. Zura leaps it without hesitation, and I don't give myself a choice, pulling off the rain-streaked glasses and running straight at the gap.

Reflexes take over. My grippy climbing shoes don't slip in the wet. I land on the next rooftop, alive and well.

Lodge lands beside me a second later, graceful as a panther, and bounds ahead.

There's no way the thief can escape these two.

I try to keep up, flying across the next alley at a run. I start to find my stride, growing reckless and exultant in the geometries of my new body.

Turns out being tall is good for distance jumping.

Ahead of me, Zura skids to a halt. She kneels to look under the wet and glistening solar panels.

She turns as Lodge and I catch up. "He's gone. You think he went inside?"

"Into the dust?" I put the glasses back on.

It takes me only seconds to spot it—an exhaust hood a few meters away, a spinning fan on top, flinging out a skirt of rain. The access panel to the hood is marked with a hidden sign, a stylized bunch of feathers tied together.

I remember a pre-Rusty drama that Rafi used to watch, set in the age of horse-drawn carriages, ballroom intrigue, and *lots* of servants . . .

Those servants were always cleaning with bundles of feathers—it was called *dusting*.

"He's in there," I say softly.

Zura covers the distance in two long steps and yanks open the panel.

Crouched inside is the man, folded up like a doll.

He takes off the mask with a sigh.

It's Jax.

THE RAIN IS THE RAIN

"You are disheartened by this turn of events, perhaps," he says, unfolding himself from the tight space and standing up.

Zura grabs the stolen pack from him.

I take the glasses off. "We trusted you."

"Why wouldn't you? I sent you Sara, and she'll deliver." He shrugs. "But if Sir Dust isn't watching, then . . ."

"Then you try to run over us and take our stuff?" I cry.

"I've worked with that driver many times. She wouldn't harm a flea. And as for that stuff, is it legally yours, when the items themselves are illegal?"

"Yes! That's why you *ran away* after you took it!"

"Sir Dust tells us what belongs to whom," Jax says with a philosophical air. "It opens the front entrance for the owner, the back for the widget. It counts the merits when we buy and sell. So when the dust is rained away, the concept of property is up for grabs."

I groan. "You said you'd never betray a customer!"

He waves a hand. "A statement in the context of betraying you to the authorities, not disappointing behaviors *in general*."

"Disappointing?" I ask. "We need this gear for our mission!"

"Which I truly hope succeeds. But I can't let sentiment interfere with *business*." He looks into the sky. "The rain won't last much longer. Shall we go down?"

I share a look with Zura, but there's no point in exacting revenge on Jax. We have to let him go.

Maybe that's why he tried to steal from us. He saw no downside except the risk of embarrassment.

"There's another pipe this way," he says.

Through the rain-smudged glasses, I see the mark, a pair of wings.

"A tactical error, selling you those," Jax mutters.

As we climb down, the rain is already slackening. I check my badge, but it's still at zero. I wonder how long it takes for the dust to come back after a downpour.

"Any chance we were spotted?" I ask Jax at the bottom of the climb. "Traffic cams? Motion detectors on the rooftops?"

"I stayed between the cams." Jax shrugs. "Security could put eyes into every brick, but they choose not to. The rain is the rain."

"Raining or not," Zura warns, "my own philosophy of property includes breaking people's fingers."

The man smiles. "You're Sara's customer now, not mine. She's a true believer, and her friends know how to bring the drama. But I should warn you, the Futures can be a little sense-missing at time."

I laugh. "Coming from you, that's distressing."

"My madness has method. I'm never sure about them." Jax bows deeply. "Good luck . . . and *try* to be mindful of your possessions."

As we walk back toward the station, the downpour fades to a trickle. No stars flicker on my badge, and the air still has a fresh, clean taste.

Lodge looks up. "You think he's right? None of these traffic cams saw us chasing him?"

"I don't know what to think anymore," I say.

But I remember the original crims, uglies who played tricks back in the pretty regime. The authorities always gave them leeway to find themselves. Maybe Security doesn't mind a little mayhem boiling over in the rain.

Growing up here, the feeds always said there'd never been a single unsolved crime in Shreve. But they lied about everything else, so why not that too?

Or maybe it's what Jax said—what the dust doesn't see doesn't count.

Zura glances at the sky. "We won't have time to explain this to the others. You and I have to make this choice, Frey."

"What choice?"

"Whether to meet Sara tomorrow. If we can't trust Jax, why trust her?"

I frown. "Because he's a crim, and she isn't."

"So he claims, but Sara knows we're carrying valuable gear." Zura shakes her head. "What if her real plan is to steal it?"

"If they're plotting together, then why would Jax try—"

"To test us," she says. "He can warn them that we're Specials now."

I let out a sigh. As the rain fades, a new smell is rising up from the muck in the street, like graphite. The dust is starting to dry out, and the chimneys around us are belching haze into the air.

The first star is flickering on my badge.

"We don't even know what *kind* of clique we're meeting," Zura says quickly. "Jax said they're sense-missing. What does *Future* even mean?"

"Maybe that they want a better future. You want to tell Col and Yandre we're giving up?"

"There won't be a chance. Just say you've picked a different spot to camp. They'll trust you."

Col is still the heir to House Palafox, and Zura his loyal soldier. She'd rather lay this decision on me than disobey him directly.

"This campsite." Zura taps her location-finder, where Sara put in coordinates. "It's close to that construction zone."

"The valley that's off-limits?"

"Not just off-limits. Dangerous." Zura's voice goes softer. "Those digging machines, their drivers were wearing hazard suits."

I come to a halt in the street. "What for?"

Zura checks her badge before answering. The first star is almost solid, and she whispers now. "Radiation? Chemicals? Nanos? Whatever's out there, I'm not letting Col anywhere near it."

She pulls me back into motion.

In the silence, Rafi's warning goes through my head again.

He'll be ready with something.

A little mutually assured destruction.

What's my father up to on the outskirts of Shreve?

I put on the glasses again. Almost every doorway is marked. Half with drawing of a hand, others with wide, unblinking eyes. People who'll help you in a pinch? Those who are spies for Security?

In the last few hours, I've learned so much about Shreve, all the shades of complexity that were invisible from my father's tower. But I still hardly know a thing.

Like the palimpsest itself, there are layers upon layers here.

By the time we reach the station, sunlight slants through the broken clouds, revealing that the dust haze has returned. The air has that heavy smell again.

Three solid stars on my badge.

The rest of our crew is huddled at the station entrance, in a vigilant circle around our gear. When they see the pack in Lodge's hands, they relax a little.

"Just a misunderstanding," I say.

"So no change in plans?" Col asks. "We're still trying that new campsite?"

I hesitate, feeling Zura's eyes on me. The sensible step is to go back to the original plan. Let Victoria take care of itself. Stay away from cliques and crims, and even farther away from anyone in a hazard suit.

Rescue Boss X. Let the free cities handle Shreve.

I open my mouth.

"You bet we are. It sounds like fun."

PART III

FUTURES

*What is history? An echo of the past
in the future; a reflex from the future
on the past.*

—Victor Hugo

PAST THE MACHINES

Our train is running on time.

We stand out even more now, seven muddy campers with a vaguely foreign air. Being soaking wet is noticeable in any city, but here in Shreve it tells a story—we went out in the rain to escape the dust.

We're not the only soggy passengers, though. The train is divided into wet and dry, rebellious and obedient. Glances travel across the aisles. Suspicion, even a little fear, but mostly a steady resolve to ignore each other.

Maybe the good citizens of Shreve just want to stay out of trouble until we've all gone our separate ways.

The real tension on the train is between Zura and me. Her cool expression reminds me of my tutors in the month before I went to live with the Palafoxes. When I used the wrong fork for the hundredth time, they sighed with what a disappointment I was. But they also knew that my missing manners weren't my own fault. My big sister was born for elegance and style; I was born for havoc.

To Zura, I'm nothing but an unlucky roll of the dice, a complication in Col's path back to his rightful place. Boss X once told me that I owed the world nothing but chaos.

Lately I've been paying my debts in full.

"End of the line's an hour away," Col tells me. "If we hike fast, we can make the campsite before sunset."

He leaves a question in his voice, like a friend seeking approval for vacation planning. He's sensed the tension.

With the dust listening, I don't know how to reassure him.

"That's great, Arav. We're all pretty tired." Before I can say more, the voice of the city interface is in our ears.

"Sometimes a change in plan turns a trip into an adventure! Sorry the construction got in your way. These two train journeys will be merit-free."

"Thank you, sir," we both say.

We're silent for the next few minutes, as if waiting for an unwelcome passerby to leave us alone. But the Shreve AI isn't going anywhere.

It doesn't ask us what happened during the downpour. Maybe it doesn't worry about the gaps in its omniscience.

The rain is the rain.

Soon the terrain begins to climb beneath us. This slice of the greenbelt is for real hikers, a string of rocky hills and heavy forest.

We'll wind up roughly where we'd expected to tonight—this detour hasn't put us behind schedule yet.

"Funny how plans never work out quite how you think," I say to Col.

He smiles. "Where's your sense of adventure, Islyn?"

I wonder how adventurous he'd feel if he knew that Jax tried to steal from us. Or about the hazard suits.

Col sees my disquiet. He takes my hand.

"Have I ever told you about my dog? When I was five?"

For a split second, I freeze—we don't want the AI checking the detail-missing records of our early lives.

But the dust is only ten years old. Col can say anything he wants about when he was that little.

"I don't think so," I say.

"His name was Teo."

I smile. Col's telling me a story about his little brother.

"Teo used to get in all kinds of trouble. Once I was chasing him, and he led me down into the basement."

My head spins, trying to decode Col's story. The two brothers grew up in House Palafox, more a mansion than a house. By the basement, he must mean the oldest part—built of ancient stone in the pre-Rusty days.

"We found some family heirlooms down there," he goes on. "Things I wasn't supposed know about."

"So Teo was a . . . bad dog."

Col smiles. "No, a good dog. One of those antiques turned out to be very handy later on."

Of course—the pulse knife that Col and I stole from his family's collection. Without it, we couldn't have escaped after my father's forces attacked Victoria. It kept us alive until we found what remained of Col's army.

"Since then," he says, "my philosophy's been simple. Sometimes the place you aren't supposed to be is *exactly* where you're supposed to be."

I expect the Shreve AI to reprimand Col for this unruly doctrine. But it remains silent. Maybe his story was too vague for the AI to understand. But the meaning is clear to me.

Col is happy to risk broadening this mission—reconnaissance, rebellion, whatever blows against my father we can land. He wants to double down.

I suspect that Riggs, Boss Charles, and Yandre would agree. Lodge and Zura, absolutely not.

As always, my allies are in disarray.

But Col is on my side.

I reach out and hold him, taking in the feel of his body, still new and unfamiliar. Our false identities might be registered with the city as romantic partners, but it's still strange, kissing with the dust watching.

Col seems not to care—he pulls my lips to his.

I remember what he said in the recovery room, when we first saw each other with these new faces. Islyn and Arya, two normal people in love. No armies, no allies.

The world at war around us, but not *our* war.

I try to switch off my reflexes—all those years of being my sister's bodyguard. Checking the exits, scanning the crowd for dangers. Islyn lets the dust worry about all that.

I try to feel small and safe, there in Arav's embrace.

And for a moment, I become part of Shreve—one ordinary life lived against the backdrop of bloodshed and tumult . . .

Until the city speaks softly in my ear. "Your public display of affection has made others on the train look away."

Because they're uncomfortable? Or simply polite?

The Shreve AI doesn't threaten us with demerits. Maybe so few people kiss in public here that it doesn't have the data to make a judgment.

Col and I pull apart, looking at each other.

What would Islyn and Arav do?

Maybe they wouldn't worry about it. This dust, this dictatorship, this war, none of it has to matter right now.

I kiss him again, daring the world to stop me.

HIKING WITH NEW FRIENDS

We make camp in the greenbelt, exhausted, uncertain about what happens next.

In the morning, I wake up to noises outside our tent. It's barely dawn—my brain is fuzzy.

Col is still asleep, so I leave him and crawl out into the rosy light.

Zura and Yandre are already up, but the noise wasn't them.

Out in the morning mist, three figures are making their way toward us. Kids, too young to have had surgery.

They halt at the edge of our camp, wary and silent. The one in the center pulls her hoodie down—it's Sara.

Col crawls from our tent, sleepily taking in the scene. He touches my right hand, and I realize that it's clenched into a fist.

I relax, grateful that I didn't summon Rafi's birthday present by accident. Zura is already intimidating enough in her camping thermals, her Special muscles unmistakable.

One of the new kids wears glasses—he's scanning the campsite, our tents, us. After a moment, he nods at Sara.

She steps forward, a sly grin on her face.

"Want to see something bubbly?"

Riggs, Lodge, and Charles are still asleep, but our new friends don't wait around. They head off into the woods without another word.

We follow.

"Hiking with new friends!" the Shreve AI exclaims. "Two merits per kilometer."

"Thank you, sir," we all say.

We head east, back toward the off-limits valley. Every step is bringing us closer to the construction zone, and those hazard suits.

The boy with eyeglasses is scanning our route. When I slip on my own pair, I see the hidden signs—arrows on the trees.

They lead us into the brush. Brambles tear at our clothes and skin, the ground rising steeper into the hills. Then a new path opens up, barely wide enough for us to walk single file. It's not signposted like the official greenbelt trails.

Soon we're scrambling up a rock face, using our hands and feet. Through the glasses I can see the marks guiding us.

Then a battered old sign appears.

RECLAMATION AREA

WARNING: DUST GAPS

I remember this place now—when Rafi and I were little, one of my father's strip mines was restored into greenbelt. He gave a speech here when the work began, with me standing next to him, sweltering in a lacy dress and body armor.

The sign is a warning. Up here, we can lie to each other. If we're hurt, no med drones will come. If thieves and murderers are lurking, we're on our own.

But my badge still shows two stars.

Our guides keep climbing.

The land bears the scars of strip mining. Huge machine-cut pieces of mountain are jumbled on each other, like a giant's discarded playthings.

The three kids scramble through the rocks easily, familiar with every handhold.

We finally stop at the crest of the hill, in a triangular passage formed by three slabs of stone. One opening frames the wild beyond the city.

Our three hosts clamber up to sit together on a high ledge, staring down at us like the judges on *Shame-Cam*.

On my badge, the dust signal is now zero—the passage is channeling a steady breeze from the unpolluted air of the wild.

"Check it out." Sara holds up her badge for the boys to see.

"So that thing really works?" the boy with glasses asks.

"It does," I say. "And we can get you more of them."

They all look at me.

Sara gives her friends a nod each. "This is Ran, and that's Chulhee. They're the founders of Future."

"We can't tell you our names," Zura says.

"Sure," says Ran, the boy with the glasses. "But you're rebels, right?"

"Mostly," Yandre says.

That sends a flutter through them. Excitement, curiosity, and a hint of unease from Ran.

"Are you here to sabotage the farms?" he says.

Col shakes his head. "We don't hit your food supplies anymore. Not since the earthquake in Paz."

"Tell that to my ration card," Ran says with a grunt.

"You're only hungry because no one wants to trade with Shreve," Yandre says. "Your city isn't very popular right now."

Sara and Chulhee burst into laughter at this, and Ran gives them an annoyed look.

"I'm not a bubblehead," he says to Yandre. "I know the score."

Sara gives the boy a thump on his shoulder. "Ran *loves* eating."

At those words, my empty stomach rumbles, and the laughter spreads. Suddenly we aren't two teams sizing each other up—we're just a bunch of people who haven't had breakfast yet.

Col turns to Zura. "Did you bring any food?"

She nods and pulls out a TogoBar, a precious gift from the free cities. It's flavored with hand-grown chocolate from an agricultural syndicate in Africa.

Col takes the bar and breaks it into quarters, handing them out. "You *have* to try this."

The kids each take a piece, and Col gives me the last one. When I bite, flavor flows across my tongue, crisp with hazelnuts and cashews, luxuriant with the dark flavors of chocolate.

For a moment, our new friends are stunned into silent chewing.

Then Sara speaks up. "How is this so *good*?"

"Do you have more?" Ran asks.

The other boy, Chulhee, still hasn't said a word. But his eyes are alight in the pink morning sun.

I could tell them that this is what the rest of the world has to offer. That there's a whole planet full of food and art and music out there. That not least of my father's crimes is cutting his people off from the rest of humanity.

But I keep it simple.

"Yeah, lots more. Maybe we can help each other."

CLIQUE

"Tell us about Future," Col says. "What does it mean?"

"It's a clique for people who worry about how history will see us," Sara says.

I smile—just what we expected. "So you're tired of war and conquest defining Shreve."

"What?" Sara shakes her head. "Don't be silly—the war's not our fault. We're talking about our *personal* historians."

We all just look at her.

"You have . . . historians?" Yandre asks.

Chulhee speaks up for the first time. "Everything that happens in Shreve becomes history. Other cities have privacy laws, but the dust keeps everything . . . forever. So when historians in the future want to study the past, they're going to look at *us*."

There's a pause before Yandre asks, "No offense, but why would they study *you* specifically?"

"Not just us," Ran says. "Everyone. One day there'll be a dozen historians studying every person in Shreve."

I must look dumbfounded, because Chulhee starts talking like I'm a littlie, every word slow and careful.

"Since the mind-rain, humanity's been growing—like back in Rusty days. In a century or two, there could be ten times as many people as now. And about one percent of all people are professional historians."

"Okay," I say. "So?"

"So do the math!" Chulhee's eyes are lit up again, like he's had another bite of chocolate. "That's one historian for every ten people alive today. Except they can *only* study the citizens of Shreve. Nobody else's lives are recorded!"

"Future historians can watch every moment of my life," Sara says. "Rewinding, fast-forwarding. Like I'm their favorite feed drama!"

"And we're not just talking about *one* generation," Chulhee says. "Maybe a century from now, only one historian's watching me, but in *two* centuries, another one gets interested. In a thousand years, maybe there's a whole committee, all specializing in *me*."

"And you really think that's . . . likely?" Yandre asks.

Chulhee shrugs. "It's just math."

"And it's *exhausting*," Ran says. "You have to keep your life historic."

Sara turns to him with a smirk. "Like when you spend the whole day eating in front of the feeds? Who's gonna watch that?"

He sighs. "Don't judge—we all make our own stories."

"And you have to balance good and bad," Chulhee says. "You don't want to be on *Shame-Cam* all the time. But no one's going to study you unless there's *drama* in your life."

Sara tugs at her climbing clothes. "Just getting dressed in the morning can be headspinning. How am I supposed to know what's going to look bubbly a century from now?"

My brain is somehow connecting all this, recalling how Rafi fretted before our public appearances. Hundreds of people in the audience, thousands more watching on the feeds, all with different tastes, different backgrounds.

Somehow she was supposed to please them all. Those decisions were something I never envied my sister.

If the imperious Rafia of Shreve worried about that multitude of eyes, how can these three deal with *centuries* of being seen?

And why should they care about us?

"Sara," I say. "Future wants to help us fight this regime, right? You were part of the protests, after the Revelation?"

"Kind of." She gives me a sheepish smile. "That night was more about being historic. Like that picture of a nurse and sailor kissing, after the Rusty Anti-Fascist War ended. One grainy photo, and they live forever!"

"She was a dental assistant, not a nurse," Chulhee mutters. "And that *wasn't* consensual, so it wasn't a kiss."

Sara laughs. "See? You know all that, *because she's historic!*"

"Do a lot of people believe in this stuff?" Col asks Chulhee.

"We have *huge* meetups, but only out of the dust. If the historians know you're anticipating them, they won't think you're real enough to study. That's called meta-Heisenberging, and only drama-missing people do it."

I close my eyes for a moment, trying to keep it all straight.

"That's why we come up here—to do our outlining," Sara says.

Yandre stares at her. "You outline your . . . life?"

"Of course. Some people improvise." Chulhee shakes his head. "But that can get logic-missing, fast."

"This is *all* logic-missing!" Zura cries. "You're worried about people in the future? You have a brutal police force watching you *right now*!"

Sara shrugs off the outburst. "Security hardly watches anything, unless there's a crime flagged. And Future doesn't do crimes."

"But you do," I say. "By sitting here talking to us, you're committing *treason*."

No one speaks, and it hits me that maybe I've said the wrong thing.

What if these three decide that betraying us to Security will make them famous in the future?

But Sara only shrugs again. "This is lost in the air, so it doesn't matter."

"Lost in the air?" Col asks.

"Not recorded," Chulhee says. "What Sir Dust can't see isn't real at all."

That's almost what Jax said. Except I wasn't sure whether he meant it or not, and Chulhee is dead serious.

Zura stands up with a sigh. "You'll have to excuse us for a minute, Sara. My friends and I need to talk."

LOST IN
THE AIR

We four commandoes huddle at the wild end of the Stone Passage. The breeze is steady here, the risen sun lighting up the trees below.

The three Futures are still up on their perch, outlining how their next love triangle should play out.

"They don't live in the real world," Zura says quietly. "How can we trust them?"

"They're just playing the hand they've been dealt," Yandre says. "And a whole clique of people who *live* to create drama? That's the diversion we need."

Col looks at me, but I don't know what to say.

When I first saw the palimpsest, it seemed like resistance was everywhere in Shreve. But the reality is something much stranger than rebellion. Jax is more a thief than a rebel, and Future are like littlies imagining they're going to be astronauts when they grow up.

They only need Future because my father has crushed their real futures.

Right now, Chulhee's proposing a fight with Sara that will drive him into Ran's arms—but Ran's arguing that the other way around would be more dramatic.

"They're just kids," I say to Col.

"Your father invaded my city when I was seventeen," he says. "And you were fifteen when . . ."

When I killed for the first time. My own brother.

"That doesn't make it right," I say.

Yandre puts a hand on my shoulder. "We can give them a *real* future. One without a dictator, without dust."

"We're here to rescue Boss X," Zura says, looking at me. "Unless anyone has bigger plans?"

I hold her accusing stare.

Zura thinks I'm only here because I want to be the next leader of Shreve. She's not completely wrong—I want to know my own city, and there's a part of me that always wants to hurt my father.

Another part of me wants to understand Shreve better than Rafi ever did.

I can't say that out loud, but Col answers for me.

"Zura, do you want our people in Victoria to wind up like this? Living their lives for an imaginary audience?"

Her eyes stay locked with mine. "No, sir."

"Then we should fight this war with any means at our disposal, right?"

"Yes, sir," Zura says coolly, finally breaking her stare.

Col puts his arm around me, and I feel his certainty again.

Whatever hurts my father's regime helps everyone.

"Everything all right over there?" Sara calls.

"We're fine," I say, walking back toward them. "But we don't have much time. Are you going to help us?"

"Tell us more about this mission," Chulhee says. "How historic is it?"

"We can't—" Zura starts.

I cut her off. "It's totally history-making. We're going to break into Security headquarters and rescue a famous rebel boss. Then we'll crash the dust Shreve-wide to make our escape. The free cities are helping us with a military attack. The whole world will be watching!"

Zura stares at me, appalled at this breach of secrecy.

But I don't care. They have to understand that this won't be like the Revelation.

The three uglies from Future are spellbound.

"Tomorrow night's only the start," I keep going. "The free cities are going to change things here—soon. You want to be studied in the future? Then help us *make the future*."

The three of them are staring at me, eyes wide and bright. Like this is the opportunity they've always dreamed of.

"The clique is going to love this," Sara says softly.

"Come to the meetup, tonight at sunset," Chulhee says. "There'll be a hundred of us there, at least."

"A *hundred*?" I ask. "How do you hide a meeting that big?"

"We're officially Forestry Club." Sara pulls off one of her social badges, a stylized tree, and hands it to me. "Our old hideout's in the new construction zone, and it's going to be demolished soon. Everyone will be there tonight!"

I try to hand the badge back. "We don't have time. You'll have to convince them yourselves."

"They need to see you in person!" she protests. "Tell them everything, like you just told us!"

Chulhee nods sagely. "In Future, everyone chooses their own story."

Zura sighs. "So this was all a waste of—"

"Okay," I say. "I'll go alone."

If anyone needs to understand the people of Shreve, it's me. After all my mistakes, I'm the one who owes them a victory.

"I'm going too." Col turns to Zura. "Maybe we can make it there and back before—"

"Just go," Zura says. "Both of you."

Col stares at his old ally, a little surprised.

She waves a hand, not looking at him. "You're safer talking to some clique than in a firefight." She looks at me. "And we're all safer without a loose cannon in the crew."

I want to argue, but I'm getting what I want. Bickering in front of the Futures won't help our credibility.

Sara is so excited, she doesn't even see how fractured we are.

"Fantastic!" she says. "Go ahead without us. Here's the meetup spot."

She taps Col's location-finder with her own and hooks a thumb back at her two friends.

"Love-triangle drama in the heat of battle! We've got some *historic* outlining to do."

WALKAROUND

Col and I part with Zura and Yandre at the far edge of the Reclamation Area. We're halfway down the hill of broken rocks, the wild visible in the distance.

The wind up here is almost as strong as in the Stone Passage. Our badges show a single flickering star, so we risk a last few words.

"Midnight tomorrow," Zura says. "If you aren't with us by then, just keep clear."

Col faces her. "Frey and I will be there."

It's the first time he's said my real name since we landed in Shreve, and it settles my nerves a little.

That name still belongs to me, even if my sister's taken it.

Yandre hands Col a slab of smart glass. "This scanner detects nanos, radioactivity, most bioagents. Keep it handy."

"What for?" he asks.

"The digging machines," Zura says. "Their crews were wearing hazard suits. Something's going on in the construction zone."

Col looks at me.

I shrug. There's no telling what my father's up to until we take a look.

"Anyone have any food?" Yandre asks.

"You brought a multiscanner and no food? Typical." Zura digs in her pockets, and hands three energy bars each to me and Col.

Not enough for two days.

"What are we supposed to tell the others?" Yandre asks. "They'll ask why you're gone."

"Say as little as possible," Col says. "We don't want the dust hearing our names, in case . . ."

We all share a look.

Col and I are marching into an unknown danger, with only each other and our new, logic-missing allies in Future. If something goes wrong, our comrades might never find out what happened to us.

Unless, of course, the dust records our fate, and we go down in history.

"Signal!" Yandre hisses, staring at their badge.

And I feel it—the breeze from the wild is dropping.

Col slips the multiscanner out of sight and buttons his pocket. We all look at each other.

It's too late for a real good-bye.

"See you both soon," I say, light and easy.

Yandre gives me a firm hug.

Zura looks at Col, and in her expression, I see the years of effort she's invested in training him, guiding him, keeping him safe.

Her sad smile cuts my heart.

"Have a good hike, you two!" she manages.

Col and I stay close to the border.

There are more signs about dust gaps, reminders to carry an emergency beacon. And more than once the city interface warns us that unmonitored hiking won't earn us any merits.

"That's okay, sir," Col replies. "Hiking is healthy, even if you don't get credit for it."

The Shreve AI doesn't know how to answer that. Maybe it's like the Futures, and thinks anything that goes unrecorded isn't real.

Growing up, my sister sometimes had the same blind spot. She would worry all day about the few seconds she'd be on the feeds, making a speech or waving from a hovercar. As if the rest of her life—*our* life—didn't matter.

I wonder if Rafi ever contemplates how the future will see her.

The dust's signal fades in and out, but we save our breath for hiking—except when Col tells me the names of the passing birds and trees.

Living in the wild with Rafi's army, he stays up late memorizing the local species, and he and Yandre are in a competition to recognize birdsongs. But for me, the wild is like a dream remembered on awakening—noisy, amazing, vital, but impossible to capture in words.

The sun climbs higher, the day grows hotter, and my determination starts to waver.

Every step is taking us farther away from Boss X.

Sometimes, I wonder if I'm nervous about seeing X again. He's had a month to consider the fact that I killed the love of his life. Has all that time in a cell brought him to terms with it? Or the opposite?

"Maybe they're not completely brain-missing," Col says out of nowhere.

I check my badge—we're in another dust gap.

"The Futures?" I ask.

"Think about it—the dust is an invisible presence watching us, judging us. That's a concept as old as humanity! Like a Rusty god, or a conscience. Your father just built it for real."

I swallow. Why would anyone need an extra conscience?

"My father built a dictatorship," I say. "And those kids aren't trying to be good. They're just trying to be some weird version of famous."

Col shrugs. "They want to be seen. The system here is designed to erase them, to turn every choice into a stupid game with merits. But those three are using it to turn their lives into art."

I glance back the way we've come. "A love triangle? You call that art?"

He smiles. "Yandre's dad says you can't write a novel without one."

"Novels must be weird." But Col's point stands—the Futures have found a way to escape from my father's rule. Maybe any life seems more meaningful if it's turned into a story for someone else.

The star on my badge starts flickering, and we fall silent again.

As we get closer to the construction zone, my location-finder beeps at me.

"Hang on," I say. "Are we too far north?"

Col shakes his head. "I'm sure this is right."

"Would you like nav assistance?" the city asks.

"No, thank you, sir. We're practicing . . ." I recall the phrase that allows you to wander in Shreve. "Pathfinding self-reliance."

"Be careful, then," the city says.

Col promises to, but he keeps edging us northward, out toward the border. My location-finder shows more hills ahead of us, full of windy channels.

Col clearly wants to tell me something.

It's probably not more theories about the Futures.

The sound of rushing water comes from ahead, and he guides me toward the noise, until we reach a creek swollen with yesterday's rain.

Maybe he's just thirsty?

We head downstream, until we reach a roaring waterfall. Col climbs down its banks, into the damp cool, stirred by the rush of water. The air tastes fresh and clean.

The dust's signal is down to a single flickering star.

"Get ready," he whispers. "We left plenty of footprints."

Footprints?

Behind the waterfall, there's a shallow indent in the rocks. We squeeze inside, letting the curtain of falling water hide us from view.

Does he think someone's following us?

Standing shoulder to shoulder with Col, I'm soaked in a few seconds.

I close my eyes to listen, and remember my first time outside the dust as a littlie—at my father's hunting lodge. Like all his homes, it was a fortress, with cams, sentry drones, soldiers all around us. But like every kid in Shreve, I'd been raised to think that only surveillance dust could protect me—and my sister.

At night, I would imagine defending Rafi from assassins, bears, and under-the-bed monsters. Back then, I wasn't allowed to keep my pulse knife between training sessions, so I stole a cleaver from the kitchen and hid it under my pillow.

Something in the air has brought back that skin-prickling sense of danger.

And finally I hear it—a scrabbling in the rocks above.

Col's right. Someone was following us.

I make a fist, calling my variable blade into being. The thrum of battle starts up in my veins, its heat driving away the cold.

A long minute later, a human form drops into view, landing with a splash in the pool before us. They ease into a crouch, scanning the trees around the clearing.

They're in a stealth suit, shimmery through the falling water. I can't even tell which way they're looking.

For a moment, they crouch there, absolutely still. The stealth suit glitters with daylight, until they've disappeared again.

Col taps a countdown on my wrist.

Three . . . two . . . one . . .

We leap through the sheet of water together. Col barrels into the stalker, but they react just in time—spinning aside. Both of them lose their footing in the shallow pool.

The direct sunlight is blinding, so I don't try anything fancy. I shoulder the stalker hard, my full weight sending them staggering.

With a splash, we go down together, me on top, my blade at their throat.

"Don't move!" I shout.

"Really?" She coughs, spitting out water. "You want me to just lie here and drown?"

I blink away the water, the bright sunlight.

It's Riggs, our comrade.

My sister's second-in-command.

BABYSITTER

"You didn't *really* think we were all asleep this morning," Riggs says.

"We didn't have time to ask." Col squeezes water out of his shirt. We're sitting on the bank of the pool, all of us soaking wet. "The Futures were in a hurry."

Riggs flicks the mud from her boots. "In a hurry to split us up. Lodge and Charles stayed behind, in case this was a trick to steal our gear."

"Why'd you keep out of sight?" I ask.

Riggs smiles. "Because I'm like an angel, watching over you unseen."

"Because my sister told you to spy on me," I say. "That's why she sent you in the first place."

Riggs has a laugh at this.

Of course, she thinks that my sister is Frey, the dangerous twin. Which makes me Rafia, the first daughter, who shouldn't be left to her own devices in enemy territory.

The sister who might be secretly working with her father, if the darkest rumors are true.

"You spent all day walking in the wrong direction," Riggs says. "Can't blame me for wondering why."

"We're headed to a big Future meetup," I explain. "Getting them on board is turning out more complicated than we thought."

Riggs throws a rock into the pool. "Just like everything in Shreve."

I open my mouth, searching for a sharp retort. But she's only speaking the truth.

Shreve has a multitude of cliques, crims, and smugglers, working almost in plain sight. Not what we expected from a perfect surveillance state.

"Yeah," I say. "None of it makes sense."

Riggs shakes her head. "It makes perfect sense—someone powerful in Shreve has been undermining your father. There were no drones after the rainstorms, not enough cams to catch unsafe drivers. Your dreaded Security isn't doing its job."

"Maybe they're sick of fighting the whole world," I say.

"Or maybe if your father falls, there's only one logical choice to replace him. Rafia of Shreve."

It takes a moment for a laugh to startle out of me.

"You think *I'm* behind all this? The palimpsest? The Futures? *Secret Hookups?*"

"Not the details. Anytime you put humans in a box, they'll wriggle out. But someone here has been cracking the lid, and you're the one who benefits."

I consider this.

We know one thing—the spy who created our Shreve identities is near the center of power in this city. But I can't have Riggs thinking that it's *me*. Or Rafi, since that's who she thinks I am.

I channel my sister. "If I could overthrow my father from inside his tower, I wouldn't be sitting here in a puddle with *you*."

"Unless you wanted to be the hero of the revolution," she says. "Gathering up cliques to make your own army—as big as Boss Frey's."

Riggs's voice has gone cold, and her eyes stay locked with mine. A pulse of battle frenzy passes through my body.

It's because she's partly right—I do want to lead the Futures into resistance against my father. Which means, in a way, that I'm pitting myself against my sister too.

Col stands up, walks between us, breaking the stare-off.

"If you're so smart about politics," he says to Riggs, "how did Frey take over your crew?"

I expect her to bristle, but she laughs.

"That's only temporary."

Col glances at me.

Only temporary.

Riggs thinks my sister will move on to bigger things . . . like a city.

I decide to change the subject. "You should go back, Riggs. They can't pull off this mission with only four people."

"Too bad," Riggs says. "My orders from Boss Frey are to stay with you."

I wonder if Riggs would obey my sister if she knew the truth—that

137

I'm really Frey, the dangerous one. That her beloved boss is the first daughter of Shreve.

But there's no telling which way the truth would turn things. Riggs might not believe me, or she could desert us completely. This mission is complicated enough.

So I say something safe, and maybe even a little true.

"My sister and I are more alike than you think."

Riggs chuckles. "I'm starting to get that idea."

WIND TUNNEL

We get back on the trail.

We've lost time with all these detours, ambushes, and debates—so we walk fast and silent, no stops for meals.

Once we're back in the dust, the city interface has words for us.

"Good to see you all together! Unobserved observation is anti-social, Riggs."

"Sorry, sir," she says. "You were right. It's more fun now that I've caught up with them!"

I frown at her. If the city AI realized she was following us, why didn't it say anything?

Riggs returns my confused look with a wry smile.

"Eleven hundred merits."

It takes a moment to believe her—that's more than most people save in a year. Step by step, minute by minute, Riggs spent a fortune stalking us.

And yet Shreve never made her stop. Stalking is a crime in most cities—why make it something you can buy?

Maybe the city AI assumes that everyone in Shreve is always

safe. So stalking is only a nuisance, like leaving your backpack in the aisle of a commuter train. If something terrible happens to you, it's your own fault for leaving the protective gaze of the dust.

Or maybe the threat of being shame-cammed by your victim is more effective than any law.

The noises of construction machinery grow louder. On the trees, the leaves are quivering, and the sky reddens with dirt thrown up by excavation.

We reach the edge of a plateau, and at last see the rumbling machines below us.

The city interface speaks up again.

"All trails are closed ahead."

"Yes, sir." I point to the social badge that Sara gave me. "But we're meeting with our club."

"Yes, the safety testing crew. But only two of you are registered members of Forestry."

I hesitate. Sara must have added me and Col to the rolls, but she didn't know about our stalker.

Riggs speaks up. "I'd really like to help, sir. I've been so antisocial today. Please let me make up for it?"

The interface doesn't answer for a moment, as if thinking this over. Of course, it would have made its decision in the first nanosecond. The rest is just for dramatic effect.

"Good idea, Riggs," it finally says. "Working together is healthy and fun!"

We find a footpath down into the valley.

My legs are sore from the day's hike—and every step is one we'll have to take on the way back tomorrow.

At last, Col looks up from his location-finder and points ahead.

There's a low, smooth-sided hill in the distance, half a kilometer long. It's covered with solar panels that glitter in the sun, and a muffled whining sound comes from inside it.

Riggs takes a drink of water. "We hiked all day for *that*?"

"Hiking is fun," Col says.

I can make out the shape of a building beneath the hill. Buried under all that dirt is a half cylinder, as big as an airship hangar.

There's a large entrance on the near side. As we approach, the stars on my badge fade out.

Something here is disturbing the dust.

From the entrance, we can see all the way through to the other end. A trio of giant fans spins there, sending a strong and steady breeze through the huge space.

The signal on my badge has dropped to zero.

"A wind tunnel!" Col pulls out his multiscanner. "Rusty tech, for testing aircraft. But perfect for clearing dust!"

The spinning fans are at least ten meters across, sending flicking sunlight through the huge space.

So this is how the Futures have meetups of a hundred in my

father's city. I'm impressed—starting up the ancient machinery must have been tricky.

Inside, there are signs of recent habitation everywhere—empty water bottles, discarded wrappers from self-heating meals, a few chairs. But nothing left over from Rusty days.

In the wind from the fans, I can smell the wild beyond Shreve's borders.

Col frowns at his multiscanner. "There's a hint of extra background rad."

"Radiation?" A little shudder passes through me.

Riggs calls from the shadows. "I need the scanner."

Col and I join her near the curved wall. She's kneeling next to a stack of black bricks, almost invisible in the darkness. As my eyes adjust, I can see hundreds of them piled along the wall.

I lift one up. It's as heavy and shiny as onyx.

On one face of the brick is stamped a symbol—a globe, the continents etched into the blackness.

"Don't touch that," Riggs says, and reaches for Col's scanner.

I put the brick down carefully.

As Riggs brings the scanner closer to the bricks, a pinging noise fills the darkness.

She takes a step back. "At least we know why your father's poking around out here."

My eyes widen in the darkness. "What are those?"

"It's complicated," she says. "But they're radioactive."

CARBON

I remember Rafi's warning—mutual destruction.

The Rusties used the term for nuclear wars. But the black bricks don't look like bombs.

"Are they made of uranium?" I ask.

"Carbon." Riggs looks closer at the scanner's screen. "About twenty times normal background. Not deadly, but enough radiation to mess with the dust."

"Carbon?" I shake my head. "The stuff in diamonds?"

"The stuff in carbon dioxide—the greenhouse gas." Riggs's gaze drifts across the stack of bricks. "Near the end, the Rusties had a plan to scrub CO_2 from the atmosphere. The quickest way to fix the climate."

"They had the tech for that?" Col asks.

Riggs shrugs. "The tech is easy. At four thousand degrees, CO_2 falls apart into oxygen and carbon. You slam the carbon into bricks and spit out clean air. But that temperature's like the surface of the sun."

"Or a nuclear core," Col says. "This was a power plant, wasn't it?"

A shudder goes through me, deep as my bones. "They tried to fix the world with *nuclear power*? That's the Rustiest thing I've ever heard! Why didn't they just *plant more trees*?"

"There wasn't time. They had a broken climate and ten billion people to feed." Riggs lets out a sigh. "Of course, they didn't have time for this either—only a few prototypes were up and running when the Crash came."

"How do you know so much about this?" I ask her.

Riggs takes a long look at us, as if wondering if she should reveal more. But then a thin sigh slips out of her.

"Because some of us want to do the same thing."

I stare. "Rebels? Who live in the wild and hunt animals for food, want to build *nuclear power plants*?"

"We're just building a prototype," Riggs says. "The cities get nervous about nukes."

"Of course they do!" I cry in the darkness. "Even the Rusties knew that nuclear power was a world-endingly bad idea!"

She ignores my outburst.

"The Rusties liked to burn carbon. Wood, coal, oil, they spilled it all into the air. Undoing that damage needs the same scale of energy."

"Right," Col says. "The atmosphere's like a big battery. The Rusties drained it—we have to recharge it. Maybe nukes are the only way . . ."

I can barely hear their words.

My whole life, rebels have been a symbol of unchecked chaos, of the wild itself. They wear skins and furs, eat meat, and defend the planet by stripping the gears of civilization.

Learning that they have nuclear ambitions . . . it's like finding out that wolves have started hunting prey with railguns.

I shake my head, all my certainties falling away.

"Does Boss X know about this?"

"Of course," Riggs says. "He says he wants to taste the wild one day."

"Which means?" I ask.

"The air in the wilderness now is like the middle of a crowded city a few centuries ago. No one alive today has *ever* breathed fresh air. We're all breathing the Rusties' dust."

I stare at her, then at the fans spinning endlessly at the other end of the giant space. I can still taste the wild in that breeze.

But the wild I know is full of the white weed and ancient ruins. What if the wilderness is as much a lie as my own face?

"No one ever told me about this," I say.

Riggs laughs a little. "You're not a rebel."

It takes a moment for the weight of those words to settle on me. X always treated me like a kindred spirit, like family. He thought I was *born* a rebel. He asked me to join his crew.

But I was too focused on protecting Rafi to ever say yes.

Then I realize— "My sister *is* a rebel."

Riggs nods. "The deepest tunnels in our base are full of those bricks. That's where the Rusties planned to store the carbon—in coal mines, where it came from in the first place." She gives me a slow smile. "But Boss Frey decided not to tell you."

So Rafi knew too. But when she stole my name, she also took any trust that the rebels would've had in me.

I'm silent, trying to focus my spinning brain.

Col turns toward the fans. "I still don't get why there's a wind tunnel here."

"Our design scrubs ten cubic kilometers of atmosphere a day," Riggs says. "All that air has to move through the nuclear core, fast."

Col takes the multiscanner back from her, waves it around. "Well, the Futures got lucky. The people who built this place weren't the usual ethics-missing Rusties. They cleaned it up, even while their world was collapsing."

"But there must be spent nuclear fuel somewhere," Riggs says, looking at the stack of bricks. "The question is, where'd the Rusties bury it?"

All three of us look at the entrance. The roar of machinery still manages to reach us here in the tunnel.

"No," I say. "The question is, why is my father digging it up?"

SAFETY CHECK

We climb to the top of the hill of dirt that has accumulated over the wind tunnel.

From up here, we can see the mining machines at work, the closest a few kilometers away, others rumbling and clanking in the blurry distance. It doesn't look like any construction site I've ever seen, though. They aren't preparing foundations, or burying hoverstruts.

It's more like they're digging at random.

Excavators dip into the earth, their spinning blades tearing at the topsoil. Tons of rocks are gathered up, carried away on conveyors as long as the bridges over the Bossier River. At one rocky face, a host of machines pound the stone with a sound like distant hail, their diamond drill bits glinting in the afternoon sun.

Abandoned digs dot the landscape—dozens of open gouges, as if the earth has been assaulted by angry, confused attackers . . .

My father doesn't know where to look.

It's been centuries, of course, since the Rusties shut down their doomed project. The nuclear waste could be buried hundreds of meters beneath the surface. Maybe sealed in concrete or lead.

Here on the hilltop the dust's signal is strong.

"Lots of holes out there," I say, pointing at all the distant gashes in the earth.

Col nods, but gives me an uncertain look.

What do we do next?

Once my father finds what he's looking for, he'll create something terrible with it. Nuclear waste in a warhead could leave a city contaminated for centuries. Or Shreve could smuggle suitcase bombs into the free cities, a threat that would leave the world in deadly stalemate.

"Hey, you three!" someone calls from below. "You're late! Come down here!"

Below us, on the far side of the wind tunnel, half a dozen people are gathered. They're dressed in hiking boots, work gloves, and sun hats. In the distance, more are headed out across the construction zone.

Forestry Club is here to earn some merits.

"This is your safety meter," a boy called Batro says, handing me a tube the size of a makeup sprayer.

He's as young as me and Col, like everyone down here. Maybe Future makes more sense if you've grown up with the dust.

We're with the other late arrivals, getting orientation and training.

Between us and the groups already out there working, our number is at least the promised hundred.

"Just tap it on the ground every once in a while," Batro says. "The safety meter records the data automatically."

"Safety meter," I repeat. "What's it measuring, exactly?"

He shrugs. "Safety?"

"I think we're looking for hollow spots," the girl next to him says, then waits for the city interface to contradict her. When it doesn't, she smiles. "Those digging machines are heavy—we don't want them falling into a sinkhole. If you tap the ground and your meter turns red, you should get out of there!"

I turn to her. "If it's so unsafe, why are they using *us*?"

"Someone asked Sir Dust," she says. "It's a rush job—no time to print a fleet of drones."

"And shared work builds community," the city AI speaks up.

"Lucky us!" the girl says brightly, then gives me a quick frown, like my questions are point-missing. She's here for the secret Future meeting later, not to learn about how safety meters work.

If he's using random kids to search for buried nuclear fuel, my father must be desperate. No one's wearing hazard gear, and these rad meters look like they were printed in a hurry.

"One more thing," Batro says to us. "For every tap that turns your light yellow, Forestry gets bonus merits."

Col frowns. "Doesn't yellow mean danger?"

"It just means you're *close*." The boy laughs. "Don't worry. You aren't a ten-ton machine—you won't fall in. Just keep away from red."

"Don't worry," Col says. "We will."

After a few minutes of training, the group spreads out across the landscape. Col, Riggs, and I stick together, making our way toward the nearest group of machines.

The city interface crackles in our ears. "Veer right. Check the crater just ahead."

We obey, angling toward a giant hole left by the machines.

From the crater's edge, we can see it's the size of a soccer stadium, steep-sided and strewn with boulders.

"You want us to climb down, sir?" I ask.

"Yes, Islyn. Be careful, though!"

Be careful—as in, beware of ancient nuclear waste?

The machines have left a spiraling road that slopes gently down. But the descent is hard going. The digging machine's tractor treads have furrowed the earth, like we're stumbling in the footprints of giants.

The dust's signal fades until, at the bottom, the last star on my badge flickers out. The meter in my hand still shows green.

"Is this your father's master plan?" Riggs grumbles. "A bunch of kids, bashing around in empty holes?"

We spread out, tapping our meters.

Nothing but green.

Here at the bottom of the crater, broken rocks and gouges from the jaws of excavators mar the footing. It's half an hour later that we climb back out, dirty and exhausted, muscle-sore from our day of hiking.

I'm about to ask the dust where next, when Col points.

Along the edge of another crater, half a kilometer away, a small crowd has gathered. Some are staring down into the pit. Others are waving for help.

Col frowns. "Maybe someone's hurt?"

"Or maybe they found something," Riggs says.

HIEROGLYPHICS

We run, pushing our tired legs across the rough ground.

About two dozen Futures are gathered at the edge of the other crater. They look excited, talking to each other with waving hands.

We arrive breathless, and I look down into the pit. A handful of Futures are down there, scrambling around.

"They're getting yellow hits!" a boy tells us happily. "We're not sure if more people should go down."

"We've been trying to talk to Sir," the girl beside him says. "But the connection's shaky."

I check my badge—the signal is down to one star.

It's not windy at all.

Riggs gives me and Col a look, and I remember what she said back in the wind tunnel.

Enough radiation to mess with the dust.

"Wait here," I tell the Futures. "We'll go see what's happening."

We make the descent as fast as we dare, checking as we go.

The lights on our safety meters stay green until we're halfway down. Then Riggs gets a glimmer of yellow and brings us to a halt.

"Are you there, sir?" she asks.

No answer.

Col pulls out his multiscanner for a quick check.

"Thirty times normal rads," he says. "We should get everyone out of here."

For the last third of the descent, all three of our safety meters glow bright yellow.

"Batro!" I yell, recognizing the boy who trained us.

"Hey, Islyn." He's pleased with himself. "We found a bunch of weak spots. Step carefully!"

"We are." I check my badge—no signal, so I dare a lie. "Sir said to go back up."

Batro frowns. "Sir, are you there?"

There's no answer.

"You've done a great job," I say. "But we'll take over."

He points at the bottom of the pit. "We found a passage in the stone. There's something really old down there—maybe a Rusty artifact."

"We know," I say with perfect confidence. "Sir sent us down to check."

Batro looks at the three of us. "He sent *you*? Wait, are you even in this clique? I haven't seen you before."

Col brandishes the multiscanner. "We're here to look for something, but it's secret. Don't tell anyone up there about what you found. This could be really important—*lots* of merits for your clique."

Batro hesitates, his eyes on the multiscanner, uncertain. But then a lifetime of being told what to do kicks in. He gathers the other Futures to lead them back out of the crater.

Riggs has already found the passage, a fissure in a rocky expanse left bare by the digging machines. It's clogged with sand and soil.

She taps her safety meter against the entrance.

Still only yellow.

Riggs scoots into the gap, her wrist light shining down into dark. "There's some kind of wall down there—with drawings on it. Like hieroglyphics."

I kneel, crawling into the gap beside her. About five meters below us is a smooth gray expanse of permacrete. A tableau of stick people is carved into it.

The pictures tell a story—first the people are digging with shovels, then they've fallen over, crawling on hands and knees.

In the end, they look dead.

"It's a Keep Out sign," I say. "For people who can't read?"

Col is just behind me. "For people in the future. Nuclear waste will still be deadly after all our languages have died out."

I shudder a little, staring at the pictures. The warning is easy enough to understand, but would anyone take stick figures seriously?

It didn't work on Batro. Not when merits were at stake.

Riggs gives us a dark chuckle. "So the Rusties also made art for a future audience."

Col sighs. "Somewhat grimmer than a love triangle."

"And it's leaking." I squeeze in farther, tapping my safety meter again—the light stays yellow. "Why didn't they seal it better?"

Col shrugs. "Maybe they didn't expect anyone to come digging for nuclear waste."

They have a point—my father has done something so sense-missing, even the Rusties didn't anticipate it.

"So what do we do now?" Col says.

"We take pictures." I pull out a wafer cam. "And let the free cities figure it out."

At one end of the permacrete barrier, there's a sequence of digits—like a serial number. Maybe the Rusties kept a record of their burial sites.

I slide a little farther into the gap, trying to get my wrist light to illuminate the digits. But the angle is wrong.

There's nothing to hang on to on this smooth slant of stone. The drop to the barrier isn't far, but I'd rather not get any closer to the buried waste.

I scoot in a little farther, but still can't get the shot.

"Riggs. Can you aim your light at—"

My voice drops away. I'm sliding.

I drop the camera, clawing for purchase. My fingernails grip the stone for a moment, but then I'm skidding again.

"Col!" I cry.

They reach for me, grabbing a handful of my shirt. But it's too late—my momentum tears the fabric, an awful sound, like a knife cutting muscle and skin.

I stop trying to arrest my fall, bending my knees for impact. And then I'm falling into the darkness . . .

"Frey!" Col calls.

I land hard, the jolt driving the breath from me. Rolling on stone, I find myself face-to-face with the pictures of dying stick figures.

Lights flash around me—the others are trying to scramble down.

"Stay there!" I shout, pushing myself to my feet. My left ankle twinges, but nothing's broken.

My foot brushes something, which rattles down the slanted permacrete. It's my safety meter, bouncing across the raised shapes of hieroglyphics.

It glows bright in the darkness, still yellow.

"It's okay," I call up. "It's the same down here as up . . ."

The safety meter jerks to a stop—captured by a defect in the permacrete barrier, a crack no more than a centimeter wide.

The light turns red.

RADIOACTIVE

I freeze—as if a monster is lurking in the dark.

But it doesn't matter how still I am. The radiation is leaking from that fissure in the floor, passing through my skin into my cells, my blood, my bones.

"You okay?" Col shouts down.

I stare at my hands, like they might be glowing. But that's silly. The meter didn't turn red until it landed in the crack.

Still, this is a small chamber, the ceiling only a few meters above my head. Who knows how long the radiation has been building up in the air I'm breathing.

"I'm fine. Just help me out."

Col and Riggs look at each other, but all our climbing gear is back at camp. The ledge isn't close enough for me to jump.

Then I see another way up. The far wall of the chamber is dotted with cracks in the stone, big enough for handholds. With time and patience, the climb would be simple.

But going slow isn't an option. Not with that open fissure between me and the old nuclear fuel, still glowing red with the safety meter's light.

With enough of a running start, I can parkour myself up—

Which means jumping over the fissure.

Is radiation like a death ray, shining up at whatever crosses that opening? Or is it more like smoke, coiling around me as I stand here hesitating?

Col sticks an arm through the gap. "Jump! We can grab you!"

"Forget it. I might drag you down. My meter's red."

"What?"

"Just stay back," I say clearly. "Give me room."

A moment later, both of them pull away, leaving a clear sliver of sky showing through the gap. In the rosy light of sunset, I spot my wafer cam where it fell on the permacrete.

I snatch it up and take a quick photo of the serial number. Then I slip the cam in a pocket and scan at the fractures in the wall, imagining every step of my ascent.

Right foot in that cleft, left foot on that outthrust of rock. Then grab the ridge along the top, and haul myself out . . .

One slip and I'll roll back down across the split in the barrier. My safety meter has started beeping there, an awful and urgent sound in the darkness.

Jump, jump, jump.

I reach for Confidence, but my feels are still gone.

With a run, I launch myself across the glowing crack and at the chamber wall. One hiking shoe grips the stone, then the other. My arms stretch out, fingers grasping for the rocky shelf near the chamber's ceiling.

Pain flashes through my palms—the ledge is sharp, like a stone knife cutting my skin. My feet scramble against the wall, fingers slipping . . .

Below me, the safety meter beeps.

Fall, fall, fall.

The sky shining through the gap goes dark, Col's hand reaching out to grab my left wrist. My fingers slip from the ledge, but my boots grip the stone, and I start to pull myself up . . .

With a combat scream on my lips, I strain every limb, and together we pull me up and out into the soft light of dusk.

I roll onto my back, facing a red sky framed by the crater walls. My knees are scraped, my palms bleeding. My shirt is torn.

But I'm out of the poisoned chamber, with battle frenzy sharp and perfect in my veins.

I look up at the others, laughing. "Thought I told you to stay out of my way."

"Yeah," Col says. "And we told you nuclear waste was dangerous."

My elation fades a little. "So . . . am I dead?"

He pulls out the scanner, testing me from head to toe. It clicks a little, but Col doesn't look upset.

Until he gets to my feet, and the scanner emits a wild clatter of sounds, like hail on a hard roof.

"Get those shoes off—now!" Col cries. When I reach down, he grabs my hand. "Don't *touch* them!"

I obey, kicking the boots off. Riggs grabs me under my armpits and drags me away from them. Col kicks the boots down into the fissure.

"How bad?" I ask.

"I don't know." Col hesitates, looking at the scanner instead of me. "It'll be fine . . . once we get you to a city."

"A city." So I need serious medical care.

I stare down at myself, and a familiar unsettledness passes through me. I've barely gotten used to my new height, my new skin. This new face.

And now my body feels wrong again.

"What are the symptoms?"

"You'll be fine for another day at least." His voice quivers. "Maybe a lot longer. Maybe you're okay."

I look at the scanner. "Doesn't that thing work?"

"Yes, but radiation's unpredictable." His expression looks more helpless than uncertain, and suddenly I want his old face back. Not Arav—Col. "The soles of your boots absorbed most of it."

The stone under my bare feet feels warm, as if the spent fuel buried beneath us is baking up through the earth.

"How am I supposed to hike now?" My only spare pair of shoes is back at camp, almost a day's hike away.

"We'll borrow some," Col says. "At the meeting, when we tell the Futures what these safety checks are really about."

Silence settles over us. Our task tonight just got much harder. We not only have to convince the Futures to help us, but that their city has risked poisoning them.

I look up at the ledge of the crater.

A handful of faces are up there still, peering down, wondering how many merits we're making for the clique.

If even one of them doubts our story, the worst could happen.

"We should get moving," I say. "The meeting starts at sunset."

"Sure," Riggs says. "But before we hit the dust again, I have a question."

We wait for the rest, but Riggs doesn't speak. She's looking me up and down, as if something's different about me now.

"What is it?" Col asks.

Riggs turns to him. "When Rafia fell down that hole, why did you call her *Frey*?"

FREY

"I called her what?" Col asks.

Riggs's words come out steady and careful. "When she fell, you called her by name. But you didn't say *Rafia* or *Islyn*—you said *Frey*."

Col glances at me, uncertain. But I can't help. Riggs heard what she heard.

"Yeah, Col," I say. "What was *that* about?"

He shrugs. "In the early days of the war, Frey fought alongside me. And then Rafia showed up, with the same face—sometimes I get them confused."

"But she's not wearing her sister's face now," Riggs says.

"That only makes it trickier." Col gives us a dry laugh. "It's weird, having the first daughter of Shreve out here on a mission."

Riggs stands there, her gaze jumping back and forth between us. When her eyes come to rest on me, it's like they're trying to pry beneath my skin.

But it's too much for her to grasp all at once. Because then she'd have to realize that person she knows as Boss Frey is really Rafia.

"Just call her Islyn from now on," Riggs says. "That's why I didn't change my name—one less thing to remember."

"Sure," Col says. "You know what would help that, Islyn? If you don't fall down any more radioactive holes."

As the sun sets, over a hundred Futures meet in the wind tunnel.

They're abuzz with stories—hard climbs into craters, close scrapes with crumbling rocks, and meters flashing yellow. Apparently, two more ancient storage sites have been discovered.

The thought makes my skin crawl. My father will soon have all the nuclear waste he could possibly want.

The meeting starts with an older Future giving a history of the wind tunnel—how the fans were repaired, how this became the clique's meetup spot. There's a moment of respectful silence, because the new construction will raze the wind tunnel to the ground.

What the Futures don't realize is that this whole area will be contaminated, maybe for centuries.

While the meeting drags on, I try not to look at Riggs. But I can sense her gaze on me. She must still be wondering why Col called me Frey. It can only be so long before she guesses the truth.

Luckily, there are more important things for her to worry about.

The stage passes to Chulhee. He looks tired, a little sunburned from the long hike here. But once the group's attention falls on him, it's easy to see how he founded Future, convincing all these people to believe in something as sense-missing as their own historic destinies.

His voice rises above the whine of the fans, echoing from the ancient walls of the tunnel, filled with the confidence that he will be remembered for all time.

"Greetings, people of the Future. We make our own stories."

He waits for them to repeat the words back to him, then continues.

"It's sad, this last meetup here in this hallowed and secret place. But it doesn't have to be an unhappy ending. Tomorrow night, Future has the chance to be part of something more important than our clique—the end of an era."

He pauses, letting his words stir the crowd for a moment. They don't know what he means yet, but they can tell it's bigger than merits and love triangles.

"I'm talking about something *so* historic that if I told you myself, you wouldn't believe me. So I'll let someone else explain—someone from outside our city."

His eyes light up, as bright as in the Stone Passage.

And they fall on me.

When Chulhee told us that we had to convince the clique to join us ourselves, I thought he'd give me more of an introduction.

I also didn't think I'd be barefoot, radioactive, and wearing a torn shirt.

But the crowd is excited. In Shreve, the fact that we're from another city already makes us mysterious, dangerous.

I'll need all the help I can get—my big sister was always perfection at giving speeches, cutting ribbons, and charming crowds. This performance has to be magnificent to convince her that I'm Rafi.

"You'll do great," Col says, giving my hand a squeeze.

For the first time since we arrived in Shreve, I channel my sister, straightening my posture, wearing my torn hiking outfit like it's a ball gown.

The crowd parts for me, expectantly silent as I stride up to the stage . . .

Which is a neat stack of the carbon bricks. As my bare feet step onto them, I remember Col's warning not to touch them.

But everyone's eyes are on me. If I jump off this platform like a littlie from hot pavement, my credibility will be shot.

Surely a few minutes of standing on these bricks can't make my radiation poisoning worse.

Rafi always said that the best speech was a short one.

It takes longer than usual for my sister's posture to settle into this new body. But the grooves in my mind are deep, and soon I feel her imperious expression on my new face.

"Chulhee's right," I project above the whine of the fans. "My friends and I are here to make history. We're freedom fighters, part of an alliance of rebel crews and foreign cities, poised to strike a blow against the dictator of Shreve."

I pause, waiting for a reaction from the crowd. But they're silent, looking a little confused. I've rushed this.

Maybe if I make it personal.

My voice softens. "An old friend of mine, a rebel boss, is here in prison. We plan to save him. But not in some secret operation no one ever hears about. The free cities are helping us, with a diversionary attack that will light up the skies!"

Whispers move through the crowd. The energy feeds back to me, and I start to pace back and forth, half forgetting that I'm barefoot on a pile of radioactive bricks.

The spirit of Rafi starts to move in me again.

"You can help us by creating a more subtle diversion. Just do what you're best at—drama. Make Security notice you so they have less chance of noticing us."

The mention of Security brings looks of concern.

I hold up my hands. "Don't worry, though. You won't be abandoned, like you were after the Revelation. This regime won't be around long enough to punish you for anything you do tomorrow night—the free cities have promised me that. Everything here will change. History will be made."

For a moment, there's no sound except the steady drone of the fans. Just like Rafi taught me, I let the crowd absorb my words.

Then a girl steps forward, a hand raised. When I nod to her, she speaks in a hesitant voice.

"So when things change here, they're going to get rid of the dust?"

"Of course," I say. "We'll make Shreve a free city."

"Why would we want that?" the girl asks. "Without dust, nothing we do will ever be historic again."

I stare at her, remembering Zura saying that the Futures didn't live in the real world. Maybe some of them don't.

So I humor the girl. "It'll take some getting used to. Freedom can be strange at first."

"Freedom has a way of destroying things," she says.

The crowd murmurs its agreement.

LOVE OF DUST

The old words from Tally Youngblood have ignited something in the Futures.

It's not just the girl. Lots of them are worried about their lives being lost in the air.

"You don't need the dust," I say. "No one has to be watching your life for it to mean something. In a free city, you can be yourselves."

"This *is* ourselves," she says, growing in confidence. "Being historic is who we are, and you want to take that away."

She's right—we want to change everything here. Their dreams will fall apart once freedom comes.

I have to switch gears.

"You can still record yourselves, of course."

"That isn't the same," a boy speaks up. "If you're just another kid with a cam, the historians know you're meta-Heisenberging. The dust makes us *real*."

That's not something I can argue with, because it doesn't make sense to me.

I scan the crowd for Chulhee, hoping he can help. But he's way in the back, his arms around Ran and Sara. All three of them gaze at me smugly, as if pleased with how things are going.

That's when I realize—the founders of Future must also love the dust.

Did they invite us here to set us up? If just one person reports us, the mission will fail spectacularly, leaving my father's regime stronger. The founders of Future get what they want, without going down in history as snitches for a dictator.

I glance at Col again. He makes a fist—*stay strong*.

It's not that easy. I don't know how to win this argument, and my feet are itching to leave this poisoned stage.

Rafi could do this, but I'm not her.

It's a nightmare I had a hundred times as a littlie—pretending to be my sister, and the crowd seeing through me. Turning on me.

Then Riggs steps forward.

"So what does that mean, anyway?" she asks the girl. "Being historic?"

"It means being remembered," the girl says carefully, as if reciting from a textbook. "So that even a thousand years from now, you're alive somehow."

Riggs jumps onto the stage next to me, wearing a grin.

"Sure, I get it," she says to the crowd. "Us rebels want to be remembered too. We get killed in battle all the time. And nobody wants to die and be forgotten, right?"

The eyes of the crowd lock onto Riggs. Suddenly, her rebel swagger is showing, and I realize how she's been hiding her charisma, her bluster. She was a boss, after all, until my sister came along.

And she's not talking about mere drama, but the reality of war and revolution.

Historic stuff, compared to love triangles.

Riggs gives me a pat on the back.

I leave the stage to her and stand next to Col. He puts a comforting arm around me.

"When we rebels die," she says, "our friends remember us. People we fought beside to save the planet, closer than blood or marriage. That's how rebels pass into history. We don't need dust—we have crew."

She gives them a long look, weighing the Futures with her eyes. I can feel them cringing a little under her judgment.

Then she shrugs. "But, hey, you've got your own way. You've taken what this sad excuse for a city gives you and made something of your own. But unless you want to go down in history as fools, you have to remember one thing . . ."

Riggs leans down and lifts up one of the carbon bricks with a flourish.

"You might love the dust," she says. "But the dust doesn't love you."

The Futures stare at the black brick, spellbound, utterly confused.

Col steps forward, handing Riggs the scanner. She kneels to wave it across the pile, letting the click of the radiation reading ring out across the room.

"You must have wondered what these bricks are," she says. "They're leftovers from a Rusty nuclear plant. Not too dangerous, because the deadly stuff is out there. You've been looking for it all day."

A bewildered, nervous noise scatters through the crowd.

The girl speaks up first. "Why would Sir do that to us?"

"Because his enemies are coming for him," Riggs says. "And he's run out of ways to scare them."

The crowd's unrest is growing fearful now.

"So he sent you to look for nuclear waste, because drones would take a few more days to print." Her voice turns cold. "A rush job, the dust told you, right?"

They stare at the pile of bricks, unwilling to believe.

But before their doubts can take hold, Col takes the scanner from Riggs and walks out into the crowd.

"Hold up your hands!" he cries.

Most of them do.

There's a spellbound silence as he moves from person to person, waving the scanner across their palms. For long seconds, there's only the soft scrape of his footsteps through the crowd.

Then a clicking comes from the scanner.

Col takes a step back from the boy who set it off.

"Let me guess—you got a yellow light out there."

The boy nods, his eyes wide.

The fearful sound bubbles up again, turning to anger.

The Futures are starting to understand that their city has betrayed them.

Chulhee's making his way from the back, the smug grin gone from his face. I think he's going to argue against us. But he takes the scanner from Col and holds it against the bricks, staring at its screen.

I remember them arguing about the couple at the victory celebration—for the Rusty Anti-Fascist War. That was when nukes were first used. Those two cities in Japan, their names made historic.

Chulhee turns to the Futures, ashen-faced.

"We make our own stories, as always—it's your choice. But I think we should help them."

The girl who argued against me doesn't say a word.

KISS

"Thanks for the save," I say to Riggs as the meeting breaks up. "Should've let you make that speech in the first place."

She nods. "I was a boss, remember? I've had tougher audiences than that."

Of course—rebels vote on every mission, like pirates in pre-Rusty days. And I bet those crowds aren't afraid to heckle.

The moment someone argued with me, I choked.

Riggs checks to make sure none of the Futures are nearby. They're clearing out the wind tunnel around us, taking mementos, saying good-bye to their old meeting place for the last time.

"When Col called you Frey," Riggs says softly, "I thought you might really be her. But clearly you've never been a boss."

I smile. "That's true."

"But you've never been a first daughter either," Riggs says, her voice going hard. "Rafia of Shreve is famous for her interviews. She could've handled that crowd. So *who are you?*"

My mouth falls open, but nothing comes out.

"Rafia went away to get camo-surge," Riggs says, "and *you* came back. Different face, different voice, and we all just believed you were still her. But maybe Diego decided to send someone else in her place."

A laugh forces itself out of me. The thought that I'm not myself has crossed my mind so often since the surge, it's almost a relief to hear someone else say it.

I give her one of Rafi's eye rolls. "They wouldn't *dare* replace me."

"She asked them to replace her—the real Rafia's hiding in a luxury hotel somewhere, while you lead us off mission. It's obvious you don't care about X!"

The accusation stings, but I keep my voice level. "Don't you think Col would notice if I was a different person?"

"He's a city boy. He's in on the whole thing."

"This is brain-missing. I'm Rafi!"

Riggs cocks her head. "What did you just call yourself?"

My breath catches—I forgot to say *Rafia*, the name the world uses for my sister. No one but me leaves off the last letter.

Maybe it's the long day's hike, or the radiation leaking into my bones. Or that my father is planning another war crime to add to his list. But I can't make any more excuses.

I'm tired of hiding myself.

I've been tired of hiding myself for a long time.

"You were right the first time. I'm Frey."

She takes a step backward, half a dozen thoughts warring on her face. Then she does something unexpected—she reaches for my shirt collar and pulls me closer . . .

And kisses me.

The pressure of our mouths, my heartbeat in my lips, the salt of the day's hike—all of it torrents through my head, wild and curious.

A moment later, she pulls away.

"No," she says. "You aren't Boss Frey."

"Um, okay, it's not . . ." I try to gather myself. "You're right, I'm not *Boss* Frey. That's my sister, Rafi. She stole my name months ago, then went looking for a crew. She found yours."

My words run down. Too many random things, mostly that kiss, are buzzing in my head.

But I manage, "Um, so you and Rafi are . . ."

Riggs waves her hand—for her, that's not the revelation that matters here. "We were. And we kept it quiet. Old boss-new boss is messy."

So there's such a thing as rebel etiquette.

But Rafi never told me. I lived in her lair for weeks, and she never gave me a clue that anyone was important to her.

Sometimes I think my sister is a stranger to me.

"She was lying from the start," Riggs whispers.

"Since the Battle of Shreve. I was the one held captive in the tower, back when Col and I were supposed to get married. At first, Rafi was pretending to be me to keep my cover, but then she *wanted* to be a rebel."

175

"She took my crew," Riggs says. "And even after that, I still . . ."

I shrug. "That's Rafi for you."

Col appears beside us, looking a little concerned.

"Everything okay here?"

Riggs turns to him, angry. "*You* knew."

"Of course," I cut in. "Along with Charles's and X's crews. But that's it."

"Ah," Col says, understanding now. "Sorry we hid the truth from you, Riggs. It was complicated."

"To say the least." She shakes her head. "X too? So much for honor among bosses. Not that I'm a boss anymore—that spoiled brat took my crew."

"She's more than that," I say. "Maybe her name isn't the important thing here. She's still the person you . . ."

Kissed.

"If her name didn't matter, then why did she use a false one?" Riggs asks, but doesn't wait for an answer. She stalks away from us, out of the tunnel and into the night.

We don't try to stop her.

"My fault for calling you Frey," Col says. "I just—"

"This is my lie, not yours."

He shakes his head. "You didn't ask Rafia to steal your identity."

"Our father confused things in the first place," I say.

And we're still confused, both of us, caught in this dance of identities. But lately I can't tell whether my sister wants to be rid of me forever, or to turn herself into me.

She took my name, but then cut me out of her life.

Col looks out of the entrance into the darkness. "You think she's coming back?"

I don't answer.

When the Futures finish clearing out, Chulhee and Ran come by to say their farewells. Then Sara joins us to say that the other cliques have signed up to create their own diversions tomorrow night.

None of the three apologizes for setting us up to fail here, if that's even what happened. Maybe I was just being paranoid.

We all make our own stories.

This victory tonight feels hollow, shaky. On that stage, I felt that old gulf between me and my sister. She's the star, and I'm just in her orbit.

And then that kiss with Riggs . . .

Who I don't think is coming back. We're close to the border— maybe she plans on slipping out of Shreve and heading home to confront my big sister.

We wait in the wind tunnel until the last of the Futures is finally gone. They've taken all the solar panels from the hilltop, but leave the fans whirring, using up their batteries one last time.

Once the fans spin down, the dust will creep inside again.

"Should we spend the night here?" Col asks me. "In case Riggs comes back?"

"With a bunch of radioactive bricks?"

"One night won't hurt. But we can start hiking if you want." He smiles, reaching into his backpack. "You even have shoes."

A dark laugh squeezes out of me. I'd almost gotten used to being barefoot. "Where'd you find those?"

"That girl who argued with you, Terra, she wanted you to have them. She's hiking barefoot to the train station."

"That's . . . a long way."

"The Futures left us water and food too."

I take Col's backpack and look inside. More energy bars.

"Ugh. Is it okay if we start at dawn? I'm pretty tired."

"Me too, but we'll have to get up early." Col looks me up and down. "Is that all you feel? Tired?"

It takes me a moment to realize what he means.

"I don't know. What does radiation sickness feel like?"

Col's voice goes soft. "If you throw up, that's a problem. If your hair starts falling out, that's a bigger problem."

I stare at him. "My *hair*?"

"We'll have to surrender. You'll need treatment right away."

"No," I say. "We're not sacrificing the whole mission for me. With Riggs gone, the others are shorthanded. We have to make it to the rendezvous point in time!"

Col looks away. "Then I guess we should get some sleep. Any more questions? By the time we wake up, the dust will be here."

I close my eyes, searching my brain. It feels like being at the doctor's, wondering if I've asked enough questions.

There's only one thing.

"When Riggs gets home, what are the rebels going to do to my sister?"

Col sighs. "Boss Frey's got her own rep now. Maybe she doesn't need yours."

"So I'll *never* get my name back?"

"You're still Frey," he says gently. "I'd be more worried about what Riggs does next. It could get pretty intense between them."

I remember that kiss. "It already is."

We make a crude camp just inside the tunnel's entrance. No fire, no air mattress, one plastic blanket wrapped around both of us for warmth. We split the last TogoBar.

Col wraps my injured ankle in a compression bandage. He checks the skin carefully, and I realize that he's looking for radiation burns.

"Anything?" I ask.

"No. But let's keep an eye on you."

I nod and close my eyes, realizing that my toothpaste pills are back at camp . . .

It feels like only an instant before the dawn light spills into the tunnel, lighting up galaxies of dust. The fans are run down, silent and still.

We have a long way to go before the rescue starts tomorrow night, every step we hiked yesterday and hours more.

Riggs hasn't returned.

DELIVERY

The machines are already at work as we march away from the wind tunnel.

The battering sounds less furious this morning. Now that they've located the disposal sites, they must be carefully dismantling the radiation barriers, unleashing slow leaks of ancient poison back into the world.

The thought of it hastens my step—along with the fact that we have to be at the rendezvous spot by midnight. My muscles are already aching, and these new shoes are half a size too small.

As we leave the construction zone, Sir Dust speaks up.

"Thank you both for helping with safety testing yesterday. I hope it was fun."

"Definitely fun, sir," Col says.

Maybe not so healthy, though.

The ache in my muscles feels like more than fatigue. It reminds me of my camo-surge in the first days, a wrongness bubbling up from my marrow.

Is it my imagination? Or radiation sickness?

At least my ankle doesn't hurt, thanks to Col's compression bandage.

"One thing, Islyn," the city AI adds. "We'll have to charge you ten merits. You didn't return your safety meter."

I remember the red light of the meter glowing in the fissure of rock. Retrieving it didn't seem like a priority.

"Sorry, sir. I'll try to be more careful."

The voice goes mercifully silent.

Merits are new to me. I grew up surrounded by wealth, but I was a nonperson, with no money of my own. My rebel friends don't use credits of any kind.

And yet the system here has gotten under my skin—the merits in my account somehow matter to me. Maybe losing them is too much like my tutors punishing when I was a littlie—extra workouts, no dessert.

Maybe some part of me will always worry about my father's favor.

As the morning drags on, the wind dies. The warm air grows heavy, dizzy-making around us. The water the Futures gave us is running out. After two days, energy bars have gone from joy-missing to inedible.

But we have to keep walking fast. That's the deal I made when I went off mission.

With every step, I ask myself if it's worth it.

I may know more about the hidden forces at work here, but I'm not sure I *understand* the city any better than I did three days ago.

In some ways I'm just more confused.

It's almost noon when I stumble for the first time.

Col steadies me. "You okay, Islyn? Any nausea?"

I close my eyes, trying to feel what my body's telling me.

"You mentioned nausea," the dust says. "Do you need medical assistance?"

I give a hearty smile. "Just thirsty, sir."

"Water can be delivered by med drone," the AI says. "Two hundred merits."

Shreve charges merits for emergency supplies. I wonder what my old friend the Paz AI would say to that.

But Col's face lights up. "How much to bring us food, sir? Not hiking rations, but a real meal?"

"For wilderness delivery, splurge prices," the AI says. "What kind of meal?"

"Something high protein, with lots of carbs. Maybe sushi, and half a dozen onigiri for later. Two coffees, and lots of water!"

The voice takes on a disappointed tone. "Luxury food is not in the spirit of hiking."

"No, sir," Col says. "But in the spirit of . . . fun?"

"Very well. Six thousand seven hundred merits."

The number makes me dizzy again, but Col confirms without hesitation.

A few thousands merits won't dent our fake accounts. But a five-star meal in the middle of nowhere might ping the city's algorithms.

Noon is too early in the day for the cliques to have started their DOA attack—we can't afford to be flagged yet.

"Is this a good idea?" I ask Col. "We wanted to catch up with the others tonight!"

"We can't get there if we're too hungry to walk," he says.

Half an hour later, the sound of lifting fans comes hurtling across the wild. The drone follows us as we find a shady spot.

The meal is packed in bright plastic hexagons, specially molded to keep every sushi roll, every elegant triangle of rice intact. The fish is straight from the Gulf, as fresh as the delicacies Rafi used to smuggle me from her parties. After a few mouthfuls, I start to feel strong again.

Maybe my stumble was from hunger, not radiation.

At least for now.

As I thank the city AI for the food, another trick of my father's regime becomes clearer to me . . .

Anything can be yours in Shreve, as long as you play by Sir's rules.

With our bellies full, we hike hard and fast, keeping an eye on the clock.

My tongue rubs the extraction transmitter hidden in my tooth. If we don't rejoin the others in time, Col and I can still activate our transmitters to escape Shreve.

But the mission will be too shorthanded to succeed.

Failing Boss X would be too much to bear.

I quicken my pace.

It's still early afternoon when we pass north of the hills where we met Chulhee and Ran. At last we're in new terrain, the forest growing thicker around us. After a morning in the sun, the shade is mercifully cool.

The scent of pine needles reminds me of my father's hunting lodge out in the wild. Rafi and I had our first long secret talks hiking on those trails, but the signal here is two solid stars.

Our location-finders still say we'll make it to the rendezvous point thirty minutes late. So every step has to be faster than the city AI expects of us.

As the sun starts to set, we eat the last of our onigiri while walking.

"I feel like we're going to remember this vacation," Col says, still chewing.

A laugh rises out of me. "Too many diversions."

We wait for Sir Dust to add something, but he doesn't.

And yet he's still there in the silence.

Growing up, our father was ever-present in my life and Rafi's. But that was in his tower, his own home. I never realized how inescapable he was for everyone else in Shreve. Even out here in the trees, his AI is listening.

I remember what Col said about the Rusty sky gods, invisible beings who watched and judged everyone on earth. In the end, maybe that's what my father wants to become. Not merely rich and powerful, but a voice in everybody's head.

So what happens when that voice vanishes? How will the citizens of Shreve act when no one's forcing them to be good? How will the Futures feel, when their dramas are erased from the databanks in the name of privacy and freedom?

Hopefully, the vast minds of the free cities have considered all this. But I have a feeling they're just going to dump it all on me.

Col looks at his location-finder. "We're making up lost time. We can do this."

I don't even bother to look.

One foot in front of the other. Ignore the endless rub of Terra's too-small shoes.

"You think Riggs will be there too?" I ask.

"Hard to say."

That's the problem about living with the dust—everything's hard to say.

Then city AI speaks up.

"You mentioned Riggs, but I don't know who that is."

RIGGS

"You don't . . ." My voice sputters out, and I stumble to a halt.

The city AI doesn't know the name Riggs anymore.

Col and I stare at each other.

I haven't thought about it since we splashed down, when Col and Yandre went missing, but our Shreve identities are programmed to self-erase if we disappear.

Or if we die.

It was in case someone was lost in the lake full of crash gel. So the rest of us wouldn't have to deal with emergency services, med drones, and an investigation that first night.

But the programming is still there . . .

Riggs is gone from the city's surveillance systems.

"Islyn?" the city asks. "Who were you talking about?"

"My tongue slipped. I was wondering if any new friends will be there."

A pause. "You said *Riggs* instead of *new friends*."

I try to stay calm. "Yes."

"Interesting," the AI says.

The voice falls silent, but I can tell the conversation isn't over.

Our merit-missing behaviors have been adding up—random feasts, oddball conversations with a widget, our winding course through the greenbelt.

If the AI flags me, Security will spot in seconds what the algorithm is programmed not to see—one of my traveling companions has vanished.

We start walking again. There's no time to stand around.

But I can't help asking, "Sir, is there a problem?"

"Possibly. I have flagged the issue for low-priority review."

Flagged. A jolt goes through me at the word.

"The sun's almost down," Col says.

Right—the cliques have started their denial of attention attack by now. Hundreds of people across Shreve have thrown themselves into transgressions against the city's logic.

Maybe their host of dramas will protect us.

But the bomb is ticking. Sooner or later, Security will take a look at me. Everything depends on how distracting our allies in Secret Hookups, Crime, and Future can be.

"New friends are good," I say.

We start hiking faster, and soon our wrist lights are sweeping the dark ground.

Maybe Riggs found a way to slip across the border. She could be headed toward my sister to wrest back her old crew.

Not great for Rafi, but it's her fault for stealing my name.

Of course, there's another possibility—here in wartime, Shreve's border defenses are lethal. Riggs might be lying dead somewhere out there.

"You okay?" Col asks. "You look pale again."

I take a slow drink of water.

It's not radiation. It's . . . everything.

"Just anxious to see our friends," I say.

As we near the rendezvous point, barely on time, the wind kicks up.

Every rush of fluttering leaves is nervous-making. Like it's the roar of lifting fans in the sky—a Security detail arriving to question us about our vanished friend.

But no hovercars swoop down on us, and eventually we spot firelight flickering through the trees.

"Ten minutes early," Col says, and falls to his knees.

We made it.

Yandre, by the fire, looks up as I crash through the underbrush.

"Islyn!" They run to gather me in a hug.

We all converge by the fire. Boss Charles gives me a wink. Even Lodge and Zura look happy to see us. But their eyes are searching the dark trees behind us.

Someone's missing.

Col guides Yandre toward updraft of the fire, and I join them.

Its warmth envelops us, the air rushing past into its blistering core. The stars on my badge begin to flicker out.

No one speaks until the signal hits zero.

"Riggs followed you," Yandre says. "She didn't catch up?"

"She did," I say. "But she found out who I really was, and took it hard. She stormed off last night."

They frown. "To *where*?"

"Out of town, I guess. Her identity erased itself. We shouldn't say her name anymore."

Yandre's eyes widen.

"It gets worse," I say. "The AI flagged me a few hours ago. Low-priority, but Security could show up anytime. Maybe I should stay away from the rest of you . . ."

Yandre shakes their head. "The dust knows we're together. If they come for one of us, it won't matter how far apart we are."

Somehow the words are comforting. I don't have to leave the warmth of this fire, the strength of this crew.

We're all in this together.

"It's good to be back," I say.

Col holds me. "It's almost over—the hiding, the silence."

Nothing left but breaking and entering, kidnapping, and probably some shooting.

And in this moment of safety, my exhaustion comes crashing down at last. I've been hiking since dawn, worrying about the radiation in my body. Worrying about Riggs, and that the city will see my sins.

My sister was right. It's more than I can take, being watched every moment, being under his gaze, a littlie again.

But every person in Shreve has felt the same way for ten years.

My muscles burn beneath my skin, streaks of soreness down both legs and across my back. But it doesn't matter how tired I am.

This mission has to succeed.

I can't let my father win.

When we step away from the fire again, the city AI talks to me.

"You've had a long day, Islyn. Maybe you should get some sleep."

"Thank you, sir. But I'll be fine."

"You're going to have a long day tomorrow."

Why does the city think that?

I almost ask, but in five minutes, it won't matter what the city thinks. We'll be in a blind spot of crashed dust, courtesy of our helpful spy.

From then on, the rescue will unfold too fast for Sir to keep up.

"I'll be okay, sir." I have a rescue to get ready for.

I bend to touch my toes, stretching my aching hamstrings. The thrill of an upcoming battle starts to move in my veins.

No one came to arrest me while we hiked. Our new allies must have created enough drama to overwhelm the city's algorithms. I smile at the thought, hoping that every one of the Futures goes down in history.

But then the city AI speaks again.

"If you're staying awake, Islyn, you might want to check your messages. One came in while you were by the fire."

I freeze halfway into a stretch. "A message? From who?"

"City Counseling. Shall I connect you?"

"Uh . . ." City Counseling handles mental health issues. Do they think all this weird behavior means that I've gone sense-missing?

"We recommend you return the call," the dust says.

"Okay, sir. Connect me, please."

A moment later, a new voice pops into my comms—not an AI, a real human. "Islyn, my name is Dramond."

"Um, hi."

"I see you're up late. That's understandable."

"It is?"

"Of course," Dramond says, his voice filling with concern. "This is a very upsetting time. It may feel as though the whole world is against you. But don't worry—for the next few days, I'll be here for you, day or night."

"Uh . . . Dramond. What are you talking about?"

There's an oddly long pause, my comms going dead silent, and I almost think we've been cut off.

"Ah, I see you've been hiking. So you haven't been watching the feeds. You don't know, do you?"

I stare at the fire, afraid of what's coming. He sounds so worried for me, so reluctant to say the next words.

"I don't know *what?*"

"Well, here's the thing, Islyn. You've been shame-cammed."

PART IV

SHAME

Shame is the lie someone told you about yourself.

—Anaïs Nin

CAMMED

"This doesn't make sense," I say. "What did I *do?*"

Dramond's next words are stilted, like he's reading from a screen. "This afternoon at 16:45, you were reported for vindictive theft."

"Theft? Of *what?*"

"A pair of shoes, belonging to Terra Intyre. You stranded Terra in the greenbelt, dangerously far from the nearest transportation. Tonight's episode included images of her walking home in rough terrain. Her feet were bleeding, Islyn."

My mouth falls open. "But she . . ."

"The episode also included your meal this afternoon. When you celebrated your cruel joke on Terra with a luxury picnic at a cost of . . ." He pauses. *"Six thousand merits?"*

"Terra *gave* them to me!" I cry.

"She gave you six thousand merits?"

"No—the shoes!"

"We realize that this happened in a dust blind spot, Islyn, so we had no proof that you stole them. But then you *wore* the shoes."

"I never said I didn't have them—I said she *gave* them to me!"

"Terra has no reason to lie. And every reason not to hike three klicks barefoot." Dramond gives me a tired sigh. "Would you like to launch an appeal to the crowd?"

I swallow. A crowd appeal means that the whole city gets to weigh in. Every citizen of Shreve is allowed watch every second the dust has recorded of me for the last two days.

It never works out for the shamed—the crowd always finds something awful that you did.

Plus, I happen to be on a secret mission.

I take a deep breath. "No. I'll take the blame."

"That's the spirit," Dramond says. "Admit your guilt, and you'll get through this faster. You got lucky—*Shame-Cam* was crowded tonight. Lots of public fights, messy breakups. If it hadn't been for that luxury feast, you might not have made the cut."

"Well, that's good," I say.

"One last thing, Islyn. We suggest that you make a public apology. We've written one for you."

He waits for an answer, but all I can do is imagine the whole city glued to the feeds, watching Terra taking painful steps across broken ground. Then an image of me feasting like a queen.

All of them must hate me.

I stare into the embers, trying to clear my head of shame.

Why did Terra make up this story? To disrupt our mission? To protect her beloved Future from a world without dust?

Or was it was purely for the drama?

"Islyn?" Dramond prompts.

"I can't apologize tonight," I say.

"Understandable. Tomorrow, then?"

"Whatever. I mean, yes."

"Excellent," Dramond says. "Do you need anything else now? Any counseling?"

"I'll be okay."

"Very well," he says. "Take care, Islyn. Next week it'll be someone else."

The line goes dead.

And I'm standing here asking myself, why does being shamed even matter? I could get killed in a firefight tonight. Or die of radiation sickness.

Tomorrow, no one will care about Terra and her shoes. X's rescue will be the big news, along with the free cities' attack, and I'll be fifteen hundred klicks away.

Islyn won't exist. Her hateful face will vanish.

Still, part of me is withering inside . . .

Everyone in Shreve dreads being shame-cammed after a false accusation. An old childhood fear has come true out of nowhere.

And my new name—this person who was real for a while—is ashes in my mouth.

"You okay, Islyn?"

I look up from the embers—Col.

There's no point in explaining what happened. His face will have been edited out of my indulgent feast, to keep the hatred focused on me. And only someone born in Shreve can understand what a shaming means. How it feels.

"A little sore," I say.

Col frowns. "Are you okay?"

I shake my head.

In Shreve, you can't lie—and the truth now is that I'm a confessed thief. I can't say otherwise to Col with the dust listening.

"We're headed out," he says. "Yandre has your gear packed up. Make sure to tell someone if you feel sick."

Right, as in vomiting. My hair falling out.

But it's just a little shame-cam.

"Let's get this over with," I say.

HOME
INVASION

We keep to the darkened path.

After ten minutes' walk, Zura comes to a halt. Downhill from us, soft lights twinkle through the trees.

It's a large, old-fashioned house, made of wood and brick. The home of the head of Security, only a hundred meters from a public path. That's how much faith they put in the dust.

We head down toward it, swift and silent through the underbrush.

This was always the tricky part of the mission—will the city AI flag us now? Or have the cliques overwhelmed it with drama?

I watch my badge—with every step, the dust's signal fades. Before we reach the edge of the trees, it hits zero.

Our spy has done their work, at least.

Zura makes a hand signal—*spread out*.

We've practiced this part a hundred times in simulation, based on orbital photos of the house. The other commandoes are going in through the front door. Col and I are going in the back, across a terrace built from creaky recycled timber.

Kessa Shard is a Special. One stray sound will turn this into a firefight.

We stay in the shadows, skirting the swimming pool. Steam rises from its heated water. Tropical fish glint beneath the surface, caught in the floodlights bathing the backyard.

My breath cinches as Col and I pass the motion sensors that ring the house. But our spy has disabled the house AI. The comm links to the city should be down as well.

It's all of us against a single Special—and her daughter, I suppose, one of Rafi's rich friends. Too easy.

We reach the stairs leading up to the deck. I place a foot on the bottom step, testing my weight. A creaking sound, a gentle bowing of the wood.

We walk in slow motion, like on a frozen lake, listening for the faintest noise. How did the Rusties live in houses that creaked every time they moved?

At the top, the deck stretches out before us, its wooden planks ancient and water stained.

A scrabbling comes from above, and I freeze.

But it's just a squirrel flitting along the gutter.

My heart is beating hard now, all my battle frenzy pent up in my chest.

The back windows stretch the length of the deck, with a view of the pool, the forest, and me and Col. Glazed against the summer sun, they reflect us like an onyx mirror in the dead of night.

Anyone could be in there, taking aim at me.

A deep breath steadies my hands. I make a fist, thumb on the inside, so the variable blade forms. A hard squeeze sharpens it to nanometric thinness, the blade only a few molecules across, invisible in the moonlight.

The tip skids across the window for a moment, a noise like a diamond sliding down a mirror. Then the blade finds some microscopic flaw in the glass, and slips through.

I pull a piece of camping gear from my pocket. It looks like a water heater, but when I press it against the window, it grips the glass, a suction cup.

I draw a slow circle around the cup with my blade.

Col presses his face to the glass, trying to see inside. Not that he can do much if someone's in there—his weapon is a compressed air rifle, formed from one of our tent poles. It shoots low-velocity tranq darts that would bounce off this window like hummingbirds.

When my circle is complete, I tug the suction cup, and the glass pops out. I place it gently on the deck, letting the knife retract.

Col reaches through the hole and hits the window's manual override. The glass glides up into the ceiling.

We creep in, our footfalls soundless on the living grass carpet.

The orbital photos only showed the house's exterior. But infrared suggested that two rooms upstairs are warm at night—the bedrooms of the head of Security and her daughter.

We don't know which is which.

Down here, the walls are lined with shelves, full of old books, dusty wine bottles, models of Rusty aircraft—and antique weapons.

I glance at Col. Maybe we can borrow a few.

He gestures at an empty spot on a shelf, between two ancient sabers. One of the weapons is missing.

We head deeper into the house.

The front door is shut, but smoke rises from the lock—Zura and Lodge trying to get through.

I can smell the nanos breaking down the metal. If the scent wafts up to the bedrooms, it could wake someone.

We don't wait for the others.

Past a workroom, we find a wide staircase, the grass carpet continuing up it. A trickling irrigation system runs down either side, like two tiny waterfalls. The sound covers our ascent.

My own air rifle is out and ready now, also loaded with tranq darts. We can't risk killing Kessa Shard—we need her biometrics to enter Security headquarters.

At the top of the stairs, I freeze in a half crouch. A sound reaches my ears, barely audible above the trickle of water.

It's music, playing on tinny little speakers.

Someone is awake upstairs.

UPSTAIRS

I point at my ear. Col nods—he hears it too.

I peek over the staircase landing, like a cat slunk low to the ground, stalking prey.

Light spills from the doorway down the hall—one of the bedrooms. The rest of the upstairs is dark.

I steal up the last few steps, eyes trained on the open door. Whoever's up here might have that missing antique weapon.

Col takes position by the closed bedroom, covering my back.

I edge my way to the side of the open door, then step into the light, leveling my rifle.

Someone's on the bed, awake.

I fire twice—*pfft, pfft*.

"Take it easy!" the girl cries.

She's wearing body armor . . . in bed.

I aim for her legs.

"Stop it, Frey! I'm *helping* you!"

The sound of my own name freezes me.

I stare at her familiar face.

"Really?" she says. "You don't recognize your old friend Demeter?"

I squint, remembering my hundreds of hours spent watching Rafi's parties—Demeter was always there. We've even met a few times, like the night before Col and I escaped from Shreve, our engagement party.

"What are you . . . ?" I shake my head. "What's going on?"

Demeter sighs. "My mom's out cold in her bedroom. I used this thingy on her."

She gestures at the bedside table, where an old electric stunner sits. An intimidating black rod—crowd control from Rusty days.

"You're welcome," she says. "For *everything*."

"Oh," I say.

Demeter is one of Rafi's best friends, part of the inner circle of rich and powerful kids of Shreve. She's well connected, ambitious.

And also our spy, it seems.

We gather downstairs. It's almost midnight, eleven minutes before the military diversion begins.

Demeter starts tea on an old-fashioned flame stove and offers us cookies from a plate.

"I baked just for you," she says.

Zura stares at the cookies. "Nobody touch them."

"Hah!" Demeter sits down at the head of the table. "Like poison snickerdoodles would be my endgame?"

"Fair point." Col picks up a cookie, takes a bite, and talks with a full mouth. "If I die, at least the rest of you will know not to trust her. Wow, these are good."

Zura only sighs.

"One question before we start," Demeter says. "Did I see you on tonight's *Shame-Cam*, Frey?"

The others all look at me, wondering what she's talking about.

"False accusation," I say. "So *you're* our spy? All the way back to helping me and Col escape?"

"Not just me." A ping sounds, and Demeter stands, lifting the tea-kettle from the flame. "The other first families have had it with your dad's nonsense."

"We were starting to get that idea," Col says. "You're letting the system fall apart on purpose."

"We're loyal to our city, Col." Demeter pours the hot water into a teapot. "But we don't want to spend our lives under siege!"

It's strange, Demeter recognizing his new face. But she was the one who created these identities, I guess.

But that doesn't explain one thing: How does she know that I'm Frey, not Rafi?

I look at Zura, who's been coordinating with the spy—or spies, I guess—from the beginning. Why would she reveal my true identity to an anonymous source?

She looks back at me, holding my gaze as if I'm the one who needs to explain. I guess we'll have that conversation later.

The tea's orangey aroma fills the kitchen, mingling with the smell of the grass floor, the forest scents drifting through the open windows.

"If you're all against my father," I say, "then why knock Kessa out?"

Demeter gives me a tired look. "Mom's not going to let some rebel boss walk out of her jail. The crumblies don't want foreign intervention—they want to push your dad out gradually. They want Shreve for themselves."

"But you and Rafi's friends have other plans?" I ask.

"We don't care who the free cities put in charge. We just want to be normal rich people. We have parties to go to and *no one invites us anymore.*"

I fall silent, wondering if she would mind that Diego wants *me* in charge.

"You're missing a few parties," Col says. "Spoken like a true revolutionary."

"Don't be sense-missing, Col Palafox. You want the same thing we do—for the world to go back to normal, with you and your family in charge of Victoria!"

"I think we can do better than the way things have been," Col says. He looks like he's about to say more, but Zura cuts in.

"You did all this without help from your mother? She doesn't know anything about our mission?"

"She has no clue. All I did was borrow her software." Demeter pours herself tea, glancing at the shelves full of antiques. "Smuggling is *super* profit-making here—giving crims new identities is part of that. Mom also taught me how to crash the dust in this house. This table is where the families meet when they're treason-making. Tea, anyone?"

"Yes, please," Col says. "So you and your friends, you're a revolution within a revolution."

Demeter's eyes light up. "Yeah. That's the title for when they make us into a feed drama!"

It's like everyone in Shreve is thinking about their place in history. Which makes me wonder . . .

"How much does my sister know about you and your friends?"

Demeter sips tea. "You should ask her."

I stare at the girl. Does that mean Demeter isn't sure what Rafi knows? Or that she's not supposed to tell me?

"This is all fascinating." Boss Charles turns from Demeter to the rest of us. "But we've got three minutes till the next stage of our mission begins. So here's my question—does finding out that our spy is a useless rich kid change the plan?"

"Useless?" Demeter protests. "Beg to differ."

Zura looks around the table, waiting for someone else to make a point.

When nobody speaks, she shrugs. "We knew the spy was someone in the regime. We just expected someone older."

Someone not connected to my sister would be another way to put it. But I don't say a word.

"I'm a month older than Frey," Demeter mutters.

Zura ignores her. "So we follow the plan. Lodge, grab Kessa, take her to the garage. Yandre and Boss Charles, set a few charges around the house. Take out every cam and datapoint, just in case. You two are with me, up on the roof."

Col takes my hand. We're about to see some fireworks. The others spring to their feet, heading off to do as they're told.

"What about me?" Demeter asks.

Zura smiles. "That's easy."

She raises her rifle and, with perfect aim, shoots Demeter in the arm.

"*Ow*," Demeter says, dropping the teacup to the floor. "Rude."

"Long live the revolution," Zura says.

Demeter's eyes flutter, and she falls with a cringe-making *thud*.

"Well," Col says. "That's one way to forge alliances."

Zura shrugs. "Makes her look innocent."

"For now," I say. "But there's plenty of evidence in this house, if my father starts looking. Those smuggled antiques, the ID-making software . . ."

"Not our problem."

"Well, I'm taking this," Col says, standing up and heading to the shelves. From between two dueling pistols, he lifts a hunting bow.

Zura rolls her eyes. "All of military history, and you want a bow and arrow?"

My eyes scan the antique weapons, but there's nothing as useful as my variable blade.

Maybe Rafi knows me better than I know myself.

Then I see it—a pulse lance. Like my old pulse knife, but its blade can extend to the length of a spear. Boss X's preferred weapon.

I check the diagnostics and smile.

Kessa Shard keeps her antiques charged.

"Upstairs," Zura says. "The attack starts in three minutes."

FIREWORKS

The roof is as luxurious as the rest of the house—a fireplace, tall grass and a handful of trees, a second swimming pool.

It also has a view of my father's tower, and the solid, imperturbable skyline of Shreve.

"Where do you think they'll hit?" Col asks. He's busy with his arrows, rolling them along the roof parapet to test for straightness.

"Diego never gave us any details," I say.

Zura raises her field glasses. "We'll know in about thirty seconds."

A nervous shiver goes through me, and I reach for my feels, but for once, my fingers aren't sure which emotion to choose. Those reflexes are fading at last.

Zura lowers the glasses and looks at me. "I suppose you noticed that Demeter called you Frey."

"Of course. You told them my real name?"

She shakes her head. "Why would I do that?"

It finally hits me. "Because they're Rafi's friends. If they thought I was her, I could give them orders. You didn't want me taking control of their revolution!"

"That's ridiculous," she says. "I had no idea who I was communicating—"

"Let's figure this out later!" Col cuts in. "Three, two, one . . . "

The attack arrives with uncanny precision—a spray of light across the sky. Each bolt from orbit splinters into a dozen shrieking drones, leaving a dazzling trail, like pitchfork lightning.

The drones flare as their reentry shields fall apart, the sonic booms arriving a few seconds later, tardy thunder. The whole thing is magnificent and heart-shuddering.

For the first time, the free cities have struck at Shreve directly. This isn't some blockade, an embargo, or aid to rebel proxies. It's an unmistakable act of war.

"Those are underground factories." I point at the brightest fires on the horizon, then swing my arm from left to right. "That's the main barracks, and the *greenhouses* . . ."

A stray thought hits me—Ran was right to worry about his ration card.

The rain of orbital drones continues, until the night sky is zigzagged with fire. Every dust chimney around us goes up, struck with thermal warheads that billow burning clouds into the air. The free cities are blinding my father, killing his dust.

I wonder what the AI is thinking now. After a decade of fighting rudeness and littering, how is it coping with a rain of fire from the sky?

The Shreve fleet finally rises into the air, adding to the display.

"This is more than we expected," Col says softly.

Zura lowers her glasses. "A lot more. I'm starting to wonder if—"

There's a stuttering flash, and then the hovercraft pens near my father's tower ignite.

"Cover!" Zura cries.

I crouch behind the parapet, and seconds later, the air buckles. A vise closes tight around my chest, my ears, the liquid in my eyes. The shock wave isn't a mere sound—it's my skin transformed into the membrane of a drum.

I can't hear or think. The world takes long moments to pull itself back together around me.

Zura shouts above the ringing in my ears. "That wasn't a drone! That was a railgun, straight from orbit!"

I blink—the entry trail is still there, a glowing column in the sky, air turned to plasma by the projectile's passage.

Railguns fling down chunks of metal at a tenth the speed of light. The result is simple and cataclysmic, like being hit by a meteor.

This is a Rusty-style attack, using everything short of city-killers.

As far as I can tell, no houses have been targeted. But lots of civilians work at those greenhouses and factories . . .

My heart is beating wrong in my chest. This is my city, and it's burning before my eyes.

"This doesn't look like a diversion," Col says softly, ignoring his scattered arrows. "What if *we're* the diversion?"

I shake my head, uncertain of anything.

Would the free cities have committed to this attack if they knew my father was trying to build nukes? Or would they have hit him ten times as hard, so he never gets the chance to retaliate?

Maybe they found out somehow, and this is the result . . .

"Frey," Col says, taking my hand. "I'm so sorry."

We've watched a city bombarded like this before—Victoria, the night my father destroyed Col's home.

But the place where I grew up is still standing tall.

"If the free cities are going all in, why is the tower still standing?" I ask.

"They're worried about what happens if he dies," Zura says.

My breathing goes shallow—mutual destruction.

My father must have done something with that nuclear waste.

The free cities have not only started this war; they've pushed it to the brink of cataclysm.

"Down to the garage," Zura says. "Security will be calling in Kessa Shard."

No one says a word in the hovercar.

We all know what a full-scale war looks like. Something much larger than expected is unfolding, which means the free cities have hidden their true plans from us.

But there's nothing we can do except focus on our mission.

Boss X is still at Security headquarters, and there's no telling how long his prison will remain intact around him.

Most of us are back in the passenger section, hidden under the seats. Zura and I are in the front, with the unconscious Kessa Shard. I'm up here for my local accent, Zura for her reflexes, in case the ruse fails and we have to fly straight back out.

Hopefully, everyone at Security HQ will be too overwhelmed to give the boss's car a second glance.

The sky is still alight above us. The clouds flicker and flash, reflecting explosions on the ground.

The Shreve fleet has found its footing at last and is fighting back against the invaders.

I wonder if the Futures understand what's going on. Do they think we betrayed them? Or is all this destruction only sharpening their sense of historic drama?

"Set your clothes," Zura says.

"Right." I adjust the controls on my sleeve, and my hiking thermals turn the deep blue of Security. There are no campaign patches and my borrowed shoes are wrong, but it's close enough to fool a hurried glance.

Security HQ rises up before us, a giant hexagon, black against the forest. They've doused every light in the building, but hovercraft are streaming in and out of glowing entry bays, silhouetted against the flickering sky.

"Eye-scan," Zura orders.

I reach over and gently open Kessa Shard's right eye, then lean her toward the rearview monitor. The car's AI chirps, just like when we started up its engines.

The running lights on our car blink in a new pattern—*the commander is aboard*. As we approach an entry bay, the guards wave us through with a crisp salute.

But a few meters inside, an officer steps in front of us. The car's collision sensors *ping* and glide us to a halt.

Zura's hands tense on the flight stick.

"Hold on, everyone," she mutters over her shoulder. "We might have to back out fast."

I check the rearview. "Nothing's in the way."

The officer—two chevrons on his shoulder, a captain—comes around to my side of the hovercar. He has a data wafer in his hand.

He makes a sign with his fingers. The car's AI reacts, the window sliding down.

"Eyes-only data dump for the commander," he says, handing me the wafer. "Sent on a hard line from the tower."

"Thank you, Captain," I say in my crispest Shreve accent.

He leans a little lower, saluting Kessa Shard sitting motionless beside me, her eyes closed. When he frowns a little, I almost warn him that she hasn't had her coffee yet.

But he's not looking at Kessa—he's looking at me.

His eyes widen. "Were you . . . ?"

And it hits me. In the course of my city going up in flames, I've forgotten that my face was on all the feeds tonight.

"My big sister," I tell him. "An embarrassment to the family. But the commander is in a *hurry*, Captain."

He leaps back with a sharp salute. "Ma'am!"

The window slides closed as we drift ahead.

Zura drops the flight stick, letting the car fly itself into the commander's parking rack.

She looks at me. "Your *big sister*? What was that about?"

"One of the Futures decided to play a trick on me, on a feed show called *Shame-Cam*. It could be a problem, if anyone sees my face."

"*Shame-Cam*." Zura frowns. "Public humiliation, right? Does that mean you're a crim now?"

"Sort of." I sigh. "More like an ethics-missing rubbish person."

"Perfect," Zura says with a smile. "Car, open the dash."

A dashboard compartment pops open, and she rummages inside it for a moment.

She pulls out a pair of wrist cuffs. "You're my prisoner now, Islyn. Which means I need to take you to wherever prisoners are held."

I groan. "People who are shamed don't get *arrested*, Zura. It's worse to be free, where everyone can see you."

She shrugs. "The city's under attack. I'm declaring martial law."

"They think I stole some *shoes*. Why would anyone make me a priority?"

"A crim's a crim. This will work, trust me."

I sigh. We don't have time to argue, and maybe she's right—in this confusion, the story won't matter. All we need is for people to point us at the holding cells.

I set my hiking thermals back to civilian colors and hold out my hands, wrists together.

As the cuffs shut, an acid trickle of memory cuts through me. The *snick* of the lock is too much like the bomb collar my father made me wear the last time I was in Shreve.

"Take the key," Zura says, offering me a gray fob. "Just keep it out of sight."

"Don't need it. The variable blade Rafi gave me can handle these."

"Fine." She puts the fob away. "Your sister gives interesting presents."

"It's weird," I say with a smile. "All I ever get is weapons."

When X rescued me and Col, he presented me with a pulse knife, exquisitely wrapped. I'm glad I've brought him something in return, the lance heavy in its hidden holster.

X is somewhere in this very building, and soon we'll both be free again.

The car slides to a halt. Instead of a parking rack, stacked with the rest of Security's craft, Kessa Shard's space is in a quiet corner of the bay. Beside it is a door marked with the three stars of her rank.

Hopefully, an eye-scan from our sleeping passenger will open it.

Zura turns to the back of the car.

"Everyone ready?"

A cheer comes from the others as they pull themselves from hiding.

We're going in to get Boss X.

ENEMY OF THE CITY

We pile out of the hovercar, our two Specials carrying Kessa Shard to the door. Boss Charles, Col, and Yandre take up positions around me, their clothes and hiking boots turned Security blue.

I stand among them, my wrists bound, staring at the floor.

As the door opens, the two Specials bolt forward, dropping Kessa like a sack of recycling. Yandre barely catches her before she hits the floor.

The rest of us crowd through, into a small anteroom with a desk facing a dozen wallscreens. The officer who was waiting to greet Kessa is on the floor, out cold.

I look around for cams, my vision implants set for any flicker of reflection.

Nothing, and my badge shows zero dust signal.

As we suspected, Security doesn't want what happens in their headquarters to go down in history.

Zura has her ear pressed to the other door in the anteroom. She turns to us with a shake of her head.

"Soundproofed. Kessa likes her privacy."

I scan the wallscreens—the HQ is full of chaos, people running, loading into hovercars. They flinch at every rumble coming through the walls.

"There," I say, pointing with my bound hands.

One of the screens shows a large room, two dozen Security officers seated at a long table, focused on shimmering airscreens. A bigger version of the dust control room in my father's tower.

In the background is a door with three stars on it.

"Yandre," I say, "we could crash the dust citywide from in there, right? Like at the Battle of Shreve?"

They don't answer.

"Frey," Col says. He's kneeling beside Yandre, both of them staring at the screen in the lower right corner of the wall.

It shows a small room—a bare cell.

Pacing the floor is Boss X.

I drop to my haunches. I've never seen X look nervous and twitchy before. But he can hear the barrage coming down around us, and he's helpless.

I throw away my thoughts of crashing the dust.

We have to save him first.

"Can you tell where that is?" Col asks me.

I shake my head. The cell is featureless, no numbers or symbols on the door.

A rush of anger goes through me—none of the other screens show prisoners. Kessa Shard only wanted to watch Boss X, with all his lupine grace and strength, sealed inside that tiny space.

"We go through the control room," Zura says. "Just me, Yandre, and our prisoner. We'll get someone to guide us to the cells."

I shake my head. "Real Security officers would *know* where to go."

"We'll be visitors," she says, reaching for her sleeve. Her uniform changes from deep blue to black and gray—Shreve military colors.

"You think *soldiers* would bother with a shoe thief?" I ask.

"They'll think the shaming was cover for something bigger. You're a saboteur now, Islyn—look the part!"

I don't argue, but something in me doesn't trust this plan. Maybe it's just my revulsion at being paraded around with cuffs on.

Somehow I feel shame for a crime I didn't even commit.

"What about the rest of us?" Col asks.

Zura points at Boss X. "Watch that screen. If we get in trouble, storm the control room, then come find us."

Lodge grumbles about being left behind, but Col and Boss Charles nod their heads. Yandre grabs everyone's explosives, their control jacks, all the gear we brought to force a cell door.

Col kisses me. "We're almost home."

Not really. But maybe my real home is a battle.

Yandre and Zura stand by the door in black and gray. Their fake uniforms have no rank stripes, no campaign patches. But that only makes them look more intimidating, like they're in some secret unit with no insignia.

I hang my head, letting everything I felt in those moments talking to Dramond show on my face.

The door opens with a gentle push.

As we walk out, everyone in the control room snaps to attention, expecting Kessa Shard. They look baffled to see two soldiers leading out a prisoner.

Someone steps forward—a full colonel, the ranking officer in the room.

He salutes, glancing past us. "Is the commander . . . ?"

"Busy with an interrogation," Zura says. "We need an escort to the cells."

The colonel hesitates. Zura's accent is shaky, but her military air is unmistakable.

Then he sees me, and recognition flickers across his face.

In that expression, all the contradictions of Shreve tangle before my eyes. My city has killed tens of thousands with its wars but saves its righteous hatred for people who don't pick up their trash.

I am the enemy. Not the dictator in his tower. Not the free cities catapulting fire and metal from the sky.

The girl who broke the rules.

"Corporal!" the colonel barks. "Escort them to the priority cells!"

CELLS

As we walk, the stone floor shudders underfoot.

Every few seconds, another barrage convulses the headquarters. No alarms are ringing, but the whole structure feels unsteady.

I wonder how long before the free cities reduce it to rubble over our heads.

How important are a few rebels? Or the exiled heir of a conquered city? Maybe only my presence stays their hand.

And in the end, how important am I? The free cities don't seem to be leaving me much of Shreve to lead.

It takes only a few minutes to reach the first row of cells. But that's just the start—hallways of locked doors reach out in every direction, spokes on a giant wheel.

A stack of wheels, it turns out. We descend one, two, three flights of stairs. There must be hundreds of prisoners here.

Or thousands . . .

In Shreve, you're only shamed for small crimes. If you do anything that threatens the regime, you simply disappear. All those faces in my father's portrait gallery—the politicians he supplanted, the resisters he erased, the protesters who were foolish enough to believe Rafi and me.

What if they're all still here?

We walk for long minutes past rows of cells, the young corporal taking quick, nervous steps. He locks eyes with me once, but his gaze isn't hateful. He feels sorry for me.

He suspects this building is falling down tonight, and thinks I won't be leaving before it does.

"She's one of the vandals, isn't she?" he asks.

Yandre and Zura glance at each other.

The corporal goes on without prompting. "The AI was lighting up all afternoon. Flagging someone every minute. Like all the cliques in the city were messing with us!"

I find myself pleased again that the Futures came through.

"We should've known an attack was coming," he mutters, then falls silent.

Our pace is slowing at last. We're on the lowest level, on an offshoot of one of the longer spokes, a row of cells with heavier doors. The floor here is bedrock stone, painted a dark, dull red.

"Where do you want her?" the corporal asks.

"With the rebels," Zura says.

He frowns. "Only one rebel in the priority cells."

"Okay, then," Yandre says. "Put her next to the wolf-man."

The corporal's eyes go wide. "You know about him?"

"We're old friends." Yandre grins. "We were with the unit that brought him in."

"Whoa." If the corporal notices their accents, he's too impressed to care.

He leads us farther down the bloodred hall.

"Is it true, he brought down a heavy battle drone with a pulse lance?"

"Two," I say.

All of them look at me.

"Two drones, not two pulse lances." I give them a shrug. "I was there too."

The corporal stares at me. "But . . . you're just that girl who stole the shoes!"

"Don't believe everything you see on the feeds," I say.

He slows to a halt, still frowning. Then he nods at a door. "They're real careful with him, no contact allowed. I've only seen him on the screens."

"You mean, you never open the cell?" Zura asks.

The corporal nods. "Only the commander's authorized."

Zura swears in elegant Spanish—we've left Kessa and her retinas behind—then punches the corporal in the stomach.

He keels over, and she pulls a dart from her pocket and sticks him.

Yandre is already kneeling at Boss X's cell door, a control jack in hand. Its tendrils snake into the wall, searching for the mechanisms of the lock.

I make a fist, my variable blade flitting out to snip the handcuffs, and kneel to take the corporal's sidearm in my left hand.

Zura sighs. "A pistol and a sword. You look like a pirate."

"Like that's a bad thing?" I ask.

Yandre is staring at the jack's readout. "This door needs two commands to open it—one from out here, another from the control room."

"Just blow it up," Zura says.

Yandre takes a moment to answer. "Maybe the outer door, if I use everything we've got. But there's an inner layer—designed to fragment in an explosion."

"Like a grenade." I close my eyes, seeing my father's fingerprints. "If we blow the door, all those fragments fly into the cell."

Cutting Boss X to ribbons.

Zura swears again. "You mean, we have to go back and take the control room?"

A deep rumble goes through the building, rolling the bedrock beneath us. For a moment, it's like standing on the deck of a ship.

"We might not have time," Yandre says. "Maybe if I do it in two steps—a small charge first, to shatter the inner layer."

"And risk killing a rebel boss in his cell?" Zura asks. "Better to walk away."

"We aren't leaving," I say.

All three of us stand and listen to the distant battle, helpless.

"Finesse, not power," Zura finally says. "That knife your sister gave you."

"It's just smart plastic. It can't cut through solid . . ." My voice fades.

My gift for X.

I draw the antique pulse lance. It whirs to life, the blade extending. That familiar buzz in my hands, but a hundred times more intense.

Squeezing the weapon to full pulse, I place its tip against the door. The metal rings out, vibrating in sympathy with the lance.

If X hears that tone, he'll know to stand back.

I swing the lance straight down, cutting top to bottom.

The buzzing blade slices through the door, flinging out an angry cloud of pulverized metal. The particles swirl around me, the air aglitter, the taste of steel in my mouth.

Two more roaring strokes, and a chunk of the door crashes inward.

The opening is a ragged triangle, its edges glowing.

Boss X steps through, his dark coat shiny with metal dust. His lupine nails are long, his fur unkempt. He's hardly wearing any clothes, like his captors wanted him to look less human in that cell.

His eyes scan me up and down, taking in my stance, my expression, and the way I hold a pulse weapon.

"Camo-surge?" he asks.

"Yes, Boss," I say, breathless.

A grin crosses his face. "I thought it might be you. From the first explosion—*sounds like Frey*."

Something breaks apart inside my chest.

X knows me, even with this lie of a face. Even though our last conversation was the worst I've ever had.

He gently takes the lance from my hands. "How kind of you."

I hold him in my arms, taking in the strength, the heat of him. His coat smells like rain somehow.

He squints at the others through the swirl of metal dust.

"Yandre, obviously," he says, and then, "And the Palafox Special?"

"You got it, Boss," Yandre says, as a distant explosion rumbles the floor.

"Can you run?" Zura asks.

"Of course," X says. But he doesn't move.

"Come on, then," Zura says. "This whole place could come down any second!"

"I know." X's eyes travel down the row of cell doors. "That's why we have to let the rest of them go."

ESCAPE

Yandre is the first to speak.

"We can't blow the doors, Boss—they're booby-trapped. But there's a control room, maybe twenty officers on duty. If we can capture it, we can open the cells."

"Is it just us four?" X asks.

"Three more," Yandre says. "Boss Charles, Col Palafox, and a Special, standing by near the control room."

The two of them ignore me and Zura, speaking a shared tongue of certainty—ally or stranger, rebels don't leave anyone in a cell.

I realize again that I'm not one of them. (Would my sister, Boss Frey, pause to rescue them all?)

"We can't save hundreds of people," Zura says, not realizing that arguing is pointless. "We're in the middle of a war!"

"The perfect time." X checks the charge on his pulse lance. "And the perfect place—surrounded by the enemies of our enemy."

He takes a few steps down the corridor, the lance buzzing back to life in his hands.

With one elegant cut, he cleaves a perfect hole in the next door. A few steps later, the one after that.

Soon the hallway is full of choking clouds of metal dust. The roar of the pulse lance blends with the distant thunder of explosions, until it sounds like the world is crumbling.

Stunned, half-awake prisoners begin to step from their cells, discovering that they've been rescued by a half-naked wolf-man wielding a shrieking blade.

"You think the control room is seeing this?" I ask Yandre. There could be scores of Security officers still in the building.

"Yes." Yandre steps through the hole into Boss X's cell, looks up at the corner, and makes two rebel hand signs.

Back in Kessa Shard's office, Boss Charles has her orders.

X's pulse lance is running down. He decides to save what's left of the battery, waving us down the hall after him.

He's the boss now.

His crew is me, Yandre, and Zura, along with the motley gaggle of priority prisoners. I recognize a few—my father's political rivals from a decade ago, walking stunned through the rumbling corridors. A handful are Victorian army officers, who still look battle-fit. Yandre and Zura give them what weapons they can spare. I recognize a member of the Paz post-quake resistance and hand her my pistol.

As we move down the hall, the last prisoner in line is an older woman in a gray kimono. Her frame is slight, her movements elegant. She looks too frail to have threatened my father.

I take her arm, and she turns to me . . .

My heart skids.

It's Sensei Noriko.

When we were little, Noriko was Rafi's etiquette master.

She taught my big sister the tea ceremony, how to use a fan, how to wave to crowds. All the precise degrees of bowing, to greet the more and less powerful of our father's business partners. And also subtler arts, like how to graciously apologize.

I copied many things that Rafi learned from Noriko, but I only met the woman once. There was a curtsy I could never get quite right, so Rafi convinced me to take her place one day in etiquette class.

With her perfect eye for movement, it took only a few minutes for Noriko to see that I was an impostor.

The next day, she disappeared forever.

That was eight years ago.

"Thank you, young lady," she says, her weight leaning into me. "It's been some time since I've taken a walk."

I open my mouth, with no idea of what to say.

Do I reveal who I am? Blame my sister for the trick that cost

Noriko everything? Tell her that my father, her true tormentor, may soon be in a cell himself?

My only certainty is that I'm the last person she wants to see in her first moments of freedom.

"Lean on me all you need," I say.

There's a shout from ahead.

Gunfire erupts.

I cover Noriko with my body, but the firefight lasts only seconds. Then we're moving again, the two of us straggling behind the rest of the crew.

For a moment, I wonder why my father put her in with the priority prisoners, an etiquette master among soldiers, politicians, and freedom fighters.

But she knew his greatest secret—me.

I stare at the cell doors stretching out before us. How many other secrets will we unleash today?

The walk back to the control room takes longer than the way here. We're a crowd, negotiating stairways and blind corners, fighting stray Security officers in our path.

But there are no coordinated attacks, no sentry drones; there's no knockout gas coming through the vents. Col and the others must have taken the control room.

Security is a snake with its head cut off, writhing around us.

Or maybe not.

"Do you hear that?" Noriko whispers beside me.

I almost think she's joking, with a war in its birth pangs all around us. But then I hear them—running footsteps from behind me.

We've just passed a junction of two corridors.

"To the rear!" I cry out.

I charge back at the junction, making a fist to summon my variable blade.

They step into view before I can reach the corner, half a dozen Security officers. But they don't have shock wands or pistols—

Five of them are armed with autocannon, rotary machine guns as wide as firehoses. The staple of Shreve's crowd control, they can spray a hundred rounds a second.

Those five fall into line across the hall, ignoring me. Another officer stands behind them, ready to give the order.

This corridor has no cover, no bends, no place to hide.

Within seconds, they'll kill us all.

I skid to a halt, turning back toward the prisoners.

"Hold your fire! Everyone!"

Most of them freeze—they're unarmed, still dazed from the shock of freedom.

At the front of the column, X and the others turn to see. Our weapons are pitiful and improvised. Without cover, we don't stand a chance against autocannon.

The officer behind the others looks at me.

"You will surrender," she says. "At once."

I swallow. Boss X won't go back into his cell. But if he fights now, he's condemning us all to death.

"Give me a minute," I say. "I'll talk sense to them."

"A minute?" the officer says. "Don't be absurd. Cycle up!"

The guns whir to life, their barrels spinning too fast to see. The whine of it fills the air like a steam whistle.

The officer steps through the line, careful to leave the field of fire clear.

"Do you surrender?" she asks me. "Yes or no?"

"I'm not in command," I say. "Some of us are rebels, some Victorians. It's complicated!"

"No, it's simple. If you don't lay down your weapons and surrender, we will open fire—and you will all die."

I look back over my shoulder. Boss X is strolling toward us at a casual pace, pulse lance in hand.

One sweep of the lance will kill all six of the Security officers, and they know it. X is going to fight.

In his certainty, he looks magnificent.

The officer's eyes go wider.

"If your friend comes any closer, we will end every one of you."

I turn back and shout, "X, wait there—I've got this!"

He pauses in his stride, but all of us can see his muscles coiling, readying to strike.

X went into that cell to save me and the city of Paz. But he's not going back again. It's not something I can ask of him.

And I realize—it's not something I can let happen.

There are no more arguments inside me, no reasoning. Not with someone who still obeys my father's orders.

As I turn back to the Security officer, my fist tightens, my knife going long and thin, nothing but a shimmer in the air.

"Frankly," I say, "this surrender isn't happening."

"Unfortunate," she answers.

She raises her hand to give the order.

All at once, every cell door in the hallway opens.

OVERWHELM

They come stumbling out, scores of them.

These aren't rebels and terrorists, like the priority prisoners. Most have the bland surge of Shreve citizens.

So many of them look young. Maybe they were in the cliques that protested during the Battle of Shreve. Or maybe they just said the wrong thing while the dust was listening.

I try to smile, hoping Col in the control room can see me. However this turns out, our friends' timing was exquisite.

Some of the prisoners recognize each other, and for a moment, there are hugs and greetings. But when they see the dark blue uniforms of Security, the hallway goes quiet.

Surrounded now, the armed officers have lost focus. They're looking around nervously, guns pointed at the ceiling.

I manage to speak. "I'll accept your surrender now. You can't get all of us."

The officer hesitates.

"We've taken your control room," I say. "Your city will fall tonight. There's no point in killing anyone."

She swallows. "There's still a duty to be done."

"You don't have to—"

"Eyes forward!" she shouts.

Her officers gather themselves, leveling their autocannon at the crowd. I can hear Boss X just behind me.

It all happens in a flash—

The officer raises her hand again.

My variable blade sweeps across the space between us, high and fast, invisibly thin. I feel only the faintest *pings* when its molecule-width edge intersects flesh and bone.

Her hand falls first, spilling from her wrist. The stump is a clean and perfect cross section. She tries to look at it.

But her head turns wrong, slower than her neck. An awful sound, meat and jelly sliding. Her mouth still opens somehow, her panicked eyes staring at the sudden froth of blood at her wrist . . .

The hand lands on the floor with a muddy *slap*.

She goes down on one knee, and the hard *pop* of kneecap against stone seems to jar everything loose—vertebrae, muscles, veins and arteries, the skin and fat of her neck—all of it reluctantly, wetly disconnects.

Her head tumbles, *collapses* from her shoulders.

The other Security officers stare in horror, watching as her heart settles in her chest, spraying red across gray stone, each beat lessening a little.

Boss X steps forward to command their attention, his lance purring softly in his hand.

His voice is miraculously steady. "Cycle down your weapons."

It takes endless seconds, but one by one the autocannon spin to a halt.

For a second, I forget the blade in my hand, invisible and deadly. But finally I let my fist relax, and the plastic writhes back around my fingers.

Like this was all a magic trick, and the Security officer is about to stand up to take a bow. But she just lies there, her blood spreading across the floor toward my stolen shoes.

I stare at the rings on my fingers, but they're clean. The blade was too thin for any part of her to cling to.

Boss X places a hand on my shoulder. "Well struck."

I turn away from his praise, his pride in me.

This camo-surged body feels like it's falling apart, all its stringy tissues snapping. My bones are liquefacted, like the shock of what I've done is a fall at terminal velocity.

Dysmorphia by proxy.

Sensei Noriko is still beside me, and I expect to see horror in her gaze. But her eyes are calm.

"Young lady," she says, taking my arm. "Walk with me again."

She leads me away from the fallen officer, her steps measured, my weight leaning into her. He body is lined with iron, a dancer's muscles beneath silk.

In a soft voice, she tells me a story about a girl who loved a fish, and how its shining scales became the mountains and craters of the moon.

There is an etiquette, it seems, for beheadings.

The way Noriko holds my arm, it's like her fingers are pressing on my burned-out feels. I imagine Sublime and Philosophical passing through my veins.

All bodies fall apart in the end.

The escape is still happening around us. The former prisoners crowd the surviving Security officers into a cell, distributing their autocannon, sidearms, and body armor. X takes his place at the head of the line again. The shuffling throng around us has become formidable, the beginnings of an army.

But the battle frenzy has gone cold in my veins.

Col comes pushing through the crowd. He watched the beheading on a screen—I can tell from his face.

When Noriko sees him coming, she smiles and bows, withdrawing one elegant step.

Col wraps his arms around me. His breathlessness, the pounding of his heart, tells me that he ran all the way.

"You had to do it," he says.

I look at him—wondering if he knows how sad his words sound. They only make me feel worse.

I chopped off someone's head, like a mad queen from some littlies' story.

"What's happening to my city?" I ask.

"The tower's still standing. The Shreve feeds are claiming they've repulsed the invaders."

"But it's a lie?"

In answer, the building shivers around us.

"It's a work in progress," Col says.

I look at the prisoners filing past. There seems to be a never-ending supply of haggard faces, stunned by sudden freedom.

If you added up all the years they've been in those cells, how many lifetimes has my father stolen?

The eight years that Rafi and I stole from Sensei Noriko are unforgivable. Multiplying those years by all these people, unimaginable.

"How are we going to get everyone to safety?" I ask. "There must be hundreds of them."

"Six hundred and seventy-one," Cols says, "according to Kessa Shard. She's awake and cooperating—we told her Demeter was on our side. Or maybe she can see it's all over for your father."

I shake my head. Nothing can be certain until he's dead.

The battle above our heads is still raging. But I don't care if the sky falls in on us, as long as this attack ends my father once and for all.

"The free cities should have done this last year," I say. "The moment he invaded Victoria."

Col places a hand on the wall, as if to feel the vibrations of bombardment better. Shreve must have burned in his dreams a hundred times.

But he says, "This was never going to be simple."

I pull his hand away from the cold stone, keeping it in mine.

"Kessa gave the HQ evacuation order," he says. "Security's gone, along with most of the hovercars. But we found a few mass arrest shuttles in the bay."

Mass arrest, like the night of the Revelation.

I shake off the thought.

"We'll put one commando on each shuttle," Col says. "Our extraction transmitters will keep our side from shooting us down."

"But they're expecting to rescue eight of us—not hundreds!"

He shrugs. "Sometimes a change in plan turns a trip into an adventure, Islyn."

I turn away, watching the stream of freed prisoners filing past.

If my father's regime doesn't fall tonight, he'll be looking for someone to blame for this attack.

Who better than a bunch of old political enemies and crims?

"They might be safer in their cells," I say, "if this all goes wrong."

Col laughs. "Ask if they want to go back."

I squeeze his hand. "You set them all free at just the right moment, by the way. It saved us."

"Boss Charles did that. I think the rebels always planned to free everyone here."

"Of course." I remember X, a few moments out of his cell, taking command. "It must be nice, being so certain."

I must owe hundreds of these prisoners an apology, for leaving them exposed to my father's revenge after the Revelation. But I don't even know what to say to my first victim.

Or maybe I do.

I turn to Sensei Noriko, who's been listening to me and Col with quiet interest. Maybe it's been a while since she's heard a conversation.

"I'm sorry," I say.

She tilts her head a little, confused. "For rescuing me?"

"No—for getting you locked up in the first place." I lean close and whisper, "My face has changed, but my name is still Frey."

SENSEI

"You were the changeling," she says.

Genuine shame pours through me—something more real than the humiliation manufactured by a feed show. A rat in my chest that has gnawed at my heart for eight years.

Our childish prank cost this woman everything.

"I was a body double. We were just trying to play a trick. We didn't mean to get you in trouble."

Get you in trouble—as if a decade in a cell were twenty demerits.

"A body double is what I guessed, after I'd had some time to think about it." She looks me up and down, a little uncertain. "But you were only nine. And now . . ."

"Almost seventeen," I say.

Noriko can't hide her shock at how long she's been in that cell. She crumples a little before my eyes, and I have to look away.

"We're twin sisters," I explain to her. "When we were little, pretending to be the same person felt like a joke we were playing on the world." My throat is tight around the words. "Until we played it on you."

"A joke?" A flash of anger crosses her face—years of staring at blank cell walls, of betrayal bottled up and finally released.

"I'm sorry" is all I can say.

Slowly, as if controlled by a dial, calm descends on Noriko's face again.

"I made the choice to work for your father," she says. "I knew he was a monster, but I thought I could help his daughter gain empathy—which might help the world."

She looks at me questioningly.

I'm not sure if I have the answer Noriko wants. Rafi has empathy for *me*, but she also thinks I'm part of her.

"We knew right away we'd done something terrible," I say. "Both of us were sorry."

Noriko nods. "But you're not the same, you two."

It takes me a moment to answer, because the question has haunted me since I transformed my face.

"Not anymore."

"You were different then, Frey. That's how I knew something was amiss, when you came to my class. You moved like an entirely different creature."

"I took combat lessons; Rafi took ballroom dancing."

Noriko shakes her head. "It was more than that. The way you responded. The way you listened. Like a mirror image—the reverse of her."

After all these years, I realize something.

"You were the first person to see me." Before Col knew my real name. Before X saw the rebel in me.

And from that moment, part of me *knew* I was my own person.

"You must hate us," I say.

"For a long time, yes. But mostly I was worried for you. You were so young, with no one to protect you." Noriko looks at Col's hand in mine. "I'm glad that you're not alone anymore."

Something passes through my anguish, delicate but boundless, a ripple on a vast sea.

In Rafi's and my private language, the name *Noriko* was a muttered warning—a reminder that the truth of us was dangerous. A lesson we forgot before the Revelation.

All the people we betrayed that night may never forgive us, but at least Noriko has.

"Thank you," I say.

She answers with a small and perfect bow.

And then Boss X is beside us, abuzz with the havoc of battle.

"The first shuttle's being loaded. We need you aboard."

Col takes my hand. "I'll come too."

"Only one commando per shuttle," X says.

Right—our extraction transmitters are in demand.

"Let me stay a little longer, Boss," I say.

"You have to be on the first shuttle out. For you, the free cities will definitely hold their fire."

Col frowns. "I'm fairly certain they won't shoot *me* down."

X smiles and pats him on the shoulder. "That's why we're sending you second."

Boss X takes my arm, ready to get moving. But I resist, turning one last time to Sensei Noriko.

There's no etiquette for saying good-bye to someone you sent to prison for eight years.

She speaks first. "And your sister? Did she escape him in the end?"

Escape him? She's a rebel queen in the wild, with her own army, her own mountain, and my name.

But she'll never be free from him the way I am.

"She got away," I say.

A smile. "I suspected she would. Please give her my best."

I promise to, and Noriko's eyes release me at last.

SEANAN

Col and I surrender ourselves to Boss X's impatience.

We push our way through the crowd, into the control room with its host of flickering airscreens. Half the Security officers are cuffed and sitting on the floor. The other half are at their screens, under the vigilant watch of Yandre and Lodge.

I catch a glimpse of Kessa Shard in conversation with Zura.

How many people in my father's regime are making deals with the free cities tonight?

We don't have time to stop and listen. X hustles us through Kessa's anteroom and out into the parking bay.

A giant hovershuttle looms there in the dark, its row of windows reinforced with heavy ceramic mesh. It rests on the permacrete floor, its lifting fans churning the air.

"How many people does it carry?" I ask.

"A hundred seats." X's eyes are bright—a challenge is in front of us. "If we crowd them in, four shuttles can handle everyone."

"Through a war zone," I remind him. "And how do we get across the border?"

"We'll make an exit."

There's a line of prisoners already boarding. In the time it took me to apologize to Noriko, my friends have organized a mass evacuation.

Col gathers me into a hug. "I should get back to the control room. Stay safe. I'll see you in the wild."

We kiss, fitting together as if our new bodies are the originals. Col's surged face seems true now, like some side of him I hadn't seen before.

I'll miss it, just a little, when he transforms back into himself.

"In the wild," I say.

X and I go aboard. Cruel-looking restraints hang from every seat, and I recall military history classes about ancient warships rowed by slaves. The shuttle is only a quarter loaded but already has a scent familiar to me from fighting in the field—chem rinse.

My father didn't give his prisoners enough water to bathe.

X sits us down at the front, in the empty cockpit. A solid wall of metal surrounds it, to protect the crew from the prisoners.

"You're coming with us?" I ask.

"Of course." X shuts the door to the cockpit. "We have a conversation to finish."

I turn away, gazing through the front windshield at the parking bay. Through its doors, the battle rages, rendering Shreve's skyline in flickering silhouette.

Nerves flutter in my stomach.

The last time X and I spoke was on the Iron Mountain, my father's drones coming at us. That was when he learned that I'd killed the love of his life. Then he told me that lover's name—Seanan, my brother.

A moment later, I was running and X was captured.

And here we are.

It's too much to expect forgiveness twice in one day.

"I've been trying to figure out what to say," I begin. "It's been a month, but I'm still not sure."

"Did we save Paz?"

Right—X doesn't know anything that's happened since his capture.

"We restored the Paz AI. It's a free city again. And the backup was full of seismic data, proving the earthquake was my father's doing." I wave at the flickering skyline of Shreve. "The world finally turned against him—this is the result."

Boss X settles into his seat, a sigh pouring from his body. All this time in that cell, he was more worried about the mission than our shared past.

"I killed Seanan," I remind him.

X gives me a look, like I've insulted him.

"I suspected that all along. From the moment I heard there was another Rafia—a body double is always a bodyguard as well."

I stare at him. "But if you already . . ."

"Why do you think I allied with the Victorians? Because I thought they would *win*?" A short, pained laugh comes from him. "It was only to meet you, Frey of Shreve."

My fingers reach for my missing feels—Calm or Philosophical. Anything to help me understand.

Boss X has been my friend, my mentor. He asked me to join his crew. And yet . . .

"You always knew," I whisper. "So you hated me."

X bares his teeth, his fists clenched. Right—I'm trapped alone in a small cage with a rebel warlord twice my size.

"Why would I hate you?" he says through gritted teeth.

It takes a moment to speak. "Because I was my father's creature. The weapon that took Seanan from you."

"Yes," he hisses, and part of me shuts down, a rabbit going still in the presence of a wolf.

He reaches out one bared claw . . .

. . . and takes my wrist firmly, painfully.

"Seanan and I had said our good-byes already. It wasn't the sort of mission you back away from."

I close my eyes, trying to focus—X's claws are still in my flesh.

Of course. My brother had no extraction team waiting, no means of escape from the heart of Shreve. He'd come there expecting to die.

"Your father was only the first of many," X says. "If Shreve was allowed to ruin the earth, other cities would follow—the Rusties all over again. Seanan wanted to go down in history as a cautionary tale."

I shake my head. "A *what*?"

"A lesson for all tyrants in the future. With one speck of DNA, they'd know your father was killed by his own son."

"But Security kept it a secret. Even Rafi and I didn't know."

"Of course. But if Seanan had succeeded, the other first families of Shreve would've used him to blacken your father's legacy. Just as they're joining us now."

I glance at the anteroom door. Kessa Shard was plotting against my father all along. Rafi's friends too.

His rule was always hollow, however unshakable he seemed to me and Rafi.

I look out the side window at the prisoners lined up. They're still coming in, crowding the aisles.

If Seanan had succeeded, ending my father before the invasion of Victoria, how many of these people would never have seen the inside of a cell? That would've been worth dying for, I suppose.

But not everything makes sense yet . . .

"Why did you want to meet me, Boss?"

"To wreak my vengeance," he says gently, and releases me. "In a war, I knew there would be a chance."

"You had plenty of chances." A hopeful shiver goes through me. "When we talked on the way to the Battle of Shreve—me, you, and Yandre. Is that when you decided I wasn't so bad?"

"It wasn't anything you said, not at first." A slow laugh moves through him. "You have his eyes, is all."

"Oh," I say.

Strange, how that never occurred to me. I've never seen a decent picture of Seanan, but he must have looked like me.

Till now, all that mattered was that I looked like Rafi.

Growing up, there was someone else out there who shared the angles of our face. Our eyes. Maybe our smile.

"He never even knew about me," I say.

"No. But he loathed Rafia."

This stings for a moment—any judgment of my sister is a judgment of me, her mirror. But as Sensei Noriko saw that day, Rafi and I were never the same. Even when we were nine years old.

Still, my reflex is to defend her.

"Rafi hates our father more than you can know."

X's teeth are bright in the darkness. "Then she must hate herself."

I shake my head, but I don't know for sure.

My sister is a mystery to me. She had a whole revolution I didn't know about, ready to go. She sent a spy to follow me.

And that kiss from Riggs . . .

I make one last argument. "Seanan could've killed her that day. But he shot wild into the crowd."

"A decision in the moment. We had no backup plan, in case your father wasn't there."

The world tips a little beneath me.

" 'We'?"

X nods slowly. "I was supposed to be there too."

I stare at him.

X is the only one of us who isn't camo-surged. But since this conversation started, he's turned into a stranger.

"You were supposed to die *together*?"

"I loved him," he says simply.

"Doomed and in love." My lungs tear in my chest, and it takes a moment to speak again. "Did you think you were Romeo and Juliet?"

A dry laugh comes from him. "No, that's you and Col. From two warring families, equal in absurdity."

"Maybe so, but we never planned a mission we didn't expect to survive!" Suddenly I'm angry—with X, with Seanan, with the world for being broken in too many ways to count. "You helped my brother get himself killed!"

"Yes, I planned it all with him," X says, weary now. "And he slipped away without me. I woke up that morning to an empty bed— and every morning since."

My anger twists into something else.

"Why did you agree in the first place?" I plead.

"Your father seemed untouchable. His own people couldn't rise up because of the dust. His military was too powerful for us rebels to take on. The free cities were spineless."

I swallow. "But Seanan could hurt him."

"He could destroy the man, and also make him a lesson for all history—if you spoil the planet, your own children will despise you."

He intones these last words. Like that was the argument Seanan used to talk X into giving up his own life.

Because the whole plan was Seanan's idea. An obsession with a father who'd traded an infant son for power.

"It was his fight," I say. "Not yours."

"The planet is everyone's fight. And part of me thought we'd make it out alive."

"I'm glad my brother wasn't under that delusion." A flash of gratitude to Seanan goes through me, for sneaking out that morning without X.

He nods. "It took me a long time to realize that your brother didn't only betray me—he also saved me."

The hovershuttle is almost full by now, the nervous, joyful hubbub of freed prisoners all around us. We'll be leaving soon, heading into battle. Maybe we'll be shot down by the Shreve navy.

Maybe this is our good-bye.

I squeeze X's hand. "I'm glad he left you there. I'm sorry he's gone."

He's gone—when I'm the one who killed him.

But for the first time, I don't carry all the blame. Seanan expected to die; X could've talked him out of the mission. And, of course, my father is always at fault in the end.

"Seanan saved you too," X says with a smile. "Do you really think you and Rafi would've survived if I'd been there?"

I turn away, reimagining that day with two assassins, one of them the formidable Boss X.

A laugh bubbles up in me. "So . . . you were going to sneak into my father's ballroom as a *wolf*?"

"That was my old body. I went to the surgeons a month later."

The world skids beneath me again. Everything is connected to that day, the first time I saved my sister.

Something makes me reach out to stroke Boss X's fur. It's longer than I remember, unkempt from his month in a cell. But it's a beautiful chaos, a thousand fractious tangles intertwined.

X watches my fingers move.

"In losing him, I found myself," he says softly.

It makes perfect sense—the same thing is happening with me and Rafi, in slow motion. The more we pull away from each other, the more I become my own person.

X is part of the distance between us. He has his own gravity, drawing me away from her.

Toward being a rebel, maybe. Or maybe just being me.

"Are we really friends?" I ask.

"Family," X says. "You lost him too."

PART V

DEATH WISH

I could not love thee, dear, so much,
Loved I not honour more.

—John Donne

SHUTTLE

Zura sends us someone who can fly the shuttle.

"Navich," she introduces herself.

She has the long and shaggy hair of a freed prisoner. She squints at the controls, her hands running across them uncertainly. Her fingernails look bitten.

"How long since you've flown?" I ask.

"A few months, and that was a cargo truck." She gives us a sad laugh. "They brought me in on one of these shuttles. Should've paid more attention."

So she was arrested after the Revelation.

"Take your time," Boss X says. "My friend here will navigate to the border."

My friend—the words settle gently in my heart.

After a long inspection of the controls, Navich twists both flight sticks at the same time.

The shuttle lifts into the air, gliding forward on magnetics. But at the entrance to the parking bay, the lifting fans roar to life.

I bite down hard, crushing the false tooth that hides my extraction transmitter. It vibrates three times to tell me it's working. I feel the jagged edge of broken ceramic and taste blood.

I touch my cheek, wondering why city-level tech is always so painful.

We leap forward, a storm of leaves and dirt swirling around us. The maelstrom covers our view until we rise up, clumsy and newborn, above the treetops.

We lurch right, then left, holding on tight. Behind us, I hear the standing prisoners stumbling.

"Sorry! Got it now!" Navich calls, even though she doesn't.

We make a wide turn in halting stages, away from the bright and flickering center of Shreve.

"Are you certain you know how to fly this thing?" X asks.

"As long as we stay in the air." She points at a red button. "And for landing, there's always the emergency autopilot. But that'll send a distress signal."

I hook into my safety harness. "Manual it is, then."

More shudders go through the cabin, but these aren't Navich's fault—the battle is all around us now.

We're part of the air itself, trembling with every explosion, every roaring passage of armored hovercraft. On our right, two squadrons of minidrones are in a dogfight, their running lights twisting and coiling, streaks of tracer rounds skimming the black sky.

Navich's hands twist, and we bank hard, away from the skirmish. I hear shouts from behind as passengers stagger and fall.

"Easy," X says. "Neither side will shoot at us."

She stares at him. "You *sure* about that."

"Yes," I say—as long as the army of Shreve doesn't figure out this shuttle is in enemy hands.

Navich straightens our course, heading north. "What about the border defenses? This thing's too overloaded to get any altitude."

Boss X and I exchange a glance.

"We have friends at the border," I say.

As we fly away from the city's center, the fighting thins out. Ahead of us, smoke rises from a row of bombed-out greenhouses, but the battle out here seems over and done.

A few drones in Shreve livery are guarding a solar power field to our west. Navich angles us gently away from them.

In the rearview monitor, the Shreve skyline still has its familiar shape. The free cities haven't knocked down any skyscrapers.

Maybe the whole attack was really a diversion after all, more fireworks than bloodshed.

Lights twinkle into existence ahead, like stars on a dark expanse of ground. I realize where we are—not far from where Col and I woke up this morning.

I point through the windshield.

"Avoid that patch of lights—it's a restricted area." I don't mention the nuclear waste. Her hands are nervous enough at the controls.

As the lights grow closer, I remember the blinking red of my safety meter. My skin starts to itch.

The scratch in my throat might only be thirst. The ache in my bones, two solid days of hiking. My nausea, simply battle nerves.

But my bigger worry is, what has my father done with all that nuclear waste? Is one day enough time to create some kind of weapon with it?

Navich veers away from the construction zone. The pristine darkness of the wild beckons from beyond the border floodlights. Safety and freedom, if we can only get there.

"Something's trailing us," Navich says.

In the rearview, the pursuing craft are almost invisible. No running lights, just black silhouettes blotting out the flickers in the sky.

"Two heavy craft," I say. "Unmarked."

Are they Shreve drones, wondering what a Security shuttle is doing this far out? Or is this our extraction team?

"I can't outrun them in this bus," Navich says.

X leans forward. "Can you hail them? They're friends . . . maybe."

"*Maybe?*" Navich squints at the controls. "Let me see, the comm system should be somewhere."

The craft behind us draw closer, their shapes looming, too big to be drones.

All at once, their running lights flick on. Bright green, the color of the free city of Diego.

The extraction team.

I let out a sigh. "It's okay, Navich. They're friends."

That's when they open fire.

HARD
LANDING

Navich screams, twisting at the flight sticks.

The shuttle tips beneath us, banking at forty-five degrees. A tumult comes from behind, our dozens of extra passengers stumbling in the aisles.

Out the side window, the right-front lifting fan is smoking.

"They found out about the escape!" I cry.

"Then why the Diego colors?" X asks. "They'd just shoot us down."

"Right. But the extraction team wouldn't—"

Another volley hits, and the giant shuttle begins to yaw around us, spinning in the air. Here at the front, the centrifugal forces feel like being at the end of a whip.

I'm thrown sideways in my harness, and my face hits the metal wall of the cockpit. Blood wells in my mouth, and more cries come from the passenger cabin behind us.

The control panel glitters with a host of red lights. Alarms and acrid smoke fill the cabin.

I clutch my bleeding nose, waiting for a final barrage to end us—but it doesn't come.

The view is whirling past the windshield. The darkness of the wild, Shreve's bright skyline, the lurid green drones, again and again.

They could've burned us from the sky by now. If they haven't, it's because . . .

"Surrender to them!" I shout at Navich. "They're rescuing me!"

X understands and lets out a growled curse.

Navich stares. "They're doing *what*?"

I point at my cheek. "I have a tracker, and this is a Security craft. They think I'm your prisoner. Surrender!"

She stares at the control panel. "There isn't a button for that! And I don't know how to use the comm system!"

"Then land us!"

"With no stabilizers?" She waves at the world spinning in the windows. "We'll crash!"

"Hold on, then," Boss X says, and brings down his fist on the emergency autopilot button.

The lifting fans let out a shriek, and the landscape tilts in the windows. The forces pushing me into my harness turn slantways.

We're going down hard.

But then the awful spinning begins to slow, the view settling back into recognizable shapes. The world finally comes to a halt, the landscape rising up in the windows.

A *thump* rings through the cabin.

Then blessed stillness—we're on the ground.

"Great, Boss," I say. "But the ship's AI might—"

He pulls out his force lance, sets it buzzing, and stabs the AI panel. "Not to worry."

The warning lights wink off, the earsplitting alarms shutting down. In the windshield, one of the drones descends into view, weapons bristling.

I turn to Navich. "Open the door. I have to get out there and explain."

She reaches for the controls, opens the shuttle door.

Outside the pilot's cage, the freed prisoners are quiet, looking out the windows with scared faces, many of them bloody.

I keep my voice firm.

"Everyone stay calm. These are friends. We're all getting out of here tonight."

They look hopeful, which makes me turn away.

I walk down the ramp with my hands held up in surrender.

The craft hovers just above the ground. Its lifting fans are blowing a gale around me—my badge shows zero signal from the dust.

These must be allies. Except that the craft's primary weapon, a plasma gun, is aimed straight at my head.

"It's me," I call, pushing my hair from my face.

Nothing happens, as if the craft is some inscrutable alien visitor and I'm the emissary for all humanity.

But then twin landing ramps descend. A dozen soldiers spill out, wearing jump armor and moving with the insectoid twitchiness of Specials. They surround the shuttle, aiming their rifles up at the meshed-over windows.

Strolling out the door behind them is what seems to be a modestly dressed woman with a bland smile.

The avatar of the sovereign city of Diego.

DIEGO

"Are you injured?" the avatar asks.

I look down at myself—endless dirt, a bloody nose, and the grime of two days in the wilderness.

"Just the usual," I say.

"And the rest of the team?"

"On their way—the mission got complicated." I gesture back at the downed shuttle. "We have to get these people out of Shreve, along with three more groups. About seven hundred in all."

A pause. "Rather ambitious, don't you think?"

I gesture at the flickering skyline. "Ambitious? Like starting a war?"

"Not a war. An evolving situation." The avatar brightens, looking behind me. "Ah, Boss X. We meet at last."

X comes down the stairs. His eyes scan the avatar up and down, and he sniffs the air.

"You're not real."

"We are Diego—the sum total of every interaction in our city. The pulse of the power grid, the flow of traffic, every conversation, every purchase. We are very real."

"Don't get them started," I say to X. "Listen, we need to get out of here. That shuttle probably sent—"

"An alert," the avatar says. "Yes, you two should come aboard at once."

X plants himself. "We're not leaving these people behind."

The avatar regards the damaged lifting fan, then sighs.

Seconds later, three more crew come running from the Diego craft, carrying tools and parts. Two of them start working on the fan, the other checks the shuttle's underside.

"We did hail your craft before opening fire," the avatar explains. "But you didn't answer."

"Pilot issues," I say.

The avatar looks up at the shuttle. "And who are these people you want to save?"

"My father's political prisoners. Heroes of the resistance."

"Mixed in with smugglers and crims, no doubt."

X growls a little. "Have the free cities started sorting refugees into good and bad?"

The avatar gives him a look of disgust. "No need to be insulting. We aren't Rusties."

There's a roar from overhead—the second Diego craft opening fire at something in the distance. Answering explosions shake the air around us, and then a few pieces of burning wreckage fall from the sky, tumbling bright across the dark terrain.

Everyone takes cover except Diego.

"Scout drones," they say. "Shreve command is interested in us."

Boss X stands up from his crouch. "Then fix our shuttle."

"That seems doubtful, and even if we get it flying, the Shreve border defenses will be a challenge." The avatar hesitates. "Another signal is coming in—Col Palafox, on one of these overloaded shuttles. You really are making this extraction difficult."

I look back toward Security headquarters—if Shreve is coming for us, they'll target Col's shuttle and the other two as well.

"Get them an escort," I tell the avatar.

"Already done. But a war zone is not ideal for mass transportation."

"*You* made it a war zone!" I shout. "This was supposed to be a diversionary attack!"

The avatar looks at me curiously. "Your reaction confuses us, Frey. You must have known your message would escalate things."

"My message?"

"The one smuggled out by Riggs. We didn't believe her at first—her story was too convenient for the rebel cause. But then you confirmed it."

I shake my head. "I confirmed something?"

"With your appearance on *Shame-Cam*," the avatar says. "A brilliant improvisation."

My mouth opens, but I have no idea where to start.

"But I didn't . . ."

"Surely you did, Frey. Why else expose your undercover identity to the entire population of Shreve, if not to send a message to the outside world? Stolen shoes—*the ground itself is deadly*. Combined with orbital radiology, the truth was inescapable. You forced even the most cautious cities to face your father's nuclear agenda."

I turn toward the battle over Shreve. "So all this—is about my *shoes?*"

"It's about armageddon," the avatar says. "If your father is scrounging Rusty nuclear waste, he's building city-killers. Thus our escalation."

I turn to X, as if he can help me make sense of all this. But he's been locked in a cell for a month.

"I didn't send Riggs out," I say to the avatar. "But it's true—my father spent today digging up spent nuclear fuel."

"Which does complicate things," the avatar says.

"Or makes them simpler—just end him tonight. Then we don't have to evacuate anyone."

"Regime change: the *simple* solution." The avatar shakes their head. "Humans."

"He's trying to make nukes!" I cry. "Take him out from orbit!"

An infinitely remote expression comes across the avatar's face.

"We considered that strategy, and even sent recon drones flying over his tower. What they saw dissuaded us—your father has brought the nuclear material to his own home."

"He *what?*"

"He's created a dead-man's switch, of sorts. A decapitation strike against him will result in catastrophe."

My heart skids in my chest.

If the free cities railgun my father's tower, they'll spread a cloud of radiation across the whole city. They might as well nuke Shreve themselves.

Holding his own population hostage is exactly what my father would do.

Mutually assured destruction—not of his enemies, but of Shreve itself.

"Then we storm his tower," I say. "Take it in hand-to-hand combat!"

"Riggs's warning reached us mere hours ago, Frey." The avatar sounds disappointed in me. "A ground assault against a nuclear hazard will take days to prepare."

I curse, looking up at the shuttle. From its windows, scores of scared, expectant faces stare out at us.

"Then we have to get them out of here."

"Not tonight," Diego says. "That engine is beyond repair."

X claps me on the shoulder, his eyes bright.

"We can make a stand here—seven hundred of us, with orbital support from the cities. The Shreve army is already in tatters. We'd have a chance."

I stare at him. "They're civilians, truck pilots and kids from random cliques, unarmed. Throwing them into a battle is . . ."

A suicide mission.

X frowns. "A minute ago, you called them heroes."

"For protesting my father. That's not the same as fighting an army!"

He holds my accusing stare, with a darkness in his eyes I haven't seen before—X's bravery comes from the same place as my brother's.

"Not everyone has a death wish," I say.

He doesn't answer.

"Let them surrender, Frey," the avatar says. "The two of you can come with us. Your primary mission has succeeded."

"We can't," I say.

The three of us stand there a moment in silence.

Another roar comes from the sky, and I almost take cover. But it's the approach of a second mass arrest shuttle.

It settles heavily on the ground. Next to the sleek Diego warship, it looks clumsy and misshapen. It's taken fire, the scorch marks of projectiles lining its flanks.

"Last chance, Frey," the avatar says. "Come with us to safety."

It would be easy to fly away. But X won't go without the rest of the prisoners. And maybe if I'm here, a captive, the free cities will move against my father sooner.

"I'm staying."

"You still aren't your father's daughter, are you?"

I stare at them. "What do you—"

Behind me, the damaged lifting fan on our shuttle roars to life again. The mechanics run back aboard the Diego craft, the Specials following them.

It takes me a moment to understand.

"Are you kidding? You were testing me *again*?"

Alone now on the landing ramp, the avatar smiles. "The world never stops testing you, Frey. Why should we?"

Fury sweeps through me. My fist closes, thumb inside, and the variable blade slips into my hand. "You would have left all these people behind?"

"Only if you allowed us to, Frey."

I wish I could hurt them, but the knife won't do anything.

The AI is a *system*—I'd have to unravel an entire city, a million lives upended, customs and connections shattered. And yet I no longer find that inconceivable, if it wipes that smug expression away.

The doors of the other shuttle open. Col steps out.

"Why'd you stop?" he calls. "The others are just behind us!"

"Get us past the border defenses," I tell Diego.

They don't answer, but long seconds later, a curtain of fire comes down from the sky.

The streaks fall in parallel, choreographed diagonals of plasma. In the distance, the darkness ignites, a row of blinding pearls strung at the edges of the wild.

The sound arrives long seconds later, a shrieking chorus from the split-open sky—then a gentle warmth on my bare skin, like sunrise.

"Shreve is an open city now," the avatar says.

BORDERLINE

Six of us ride shotgun, four Victorian prisoners of war joining me and X on the shuttle's windy, shuddering topside. The repaired lifting fan looks shaky in its makeshift brace and whines like a drill in stone.

The other three shuttles keep station around ours, their top decks dotted with armed prisoners and commandoes. Col and Zura ride on the next one over. They've brought spoils from Security's armory— more autocannon, handy if any small drones come after us. The two Diego hovercraft are on overwatch, their dark shapes blotting out the stars above.

Our ragtag army has gained an equally ragtag fleet.

The night is cold up here. Even with our speed limited by the damaged fan, the fifty-click wind is a freezing gale. I'm huddled next to Boss X, clinging to the heat of him.

"Sorry things got awkward back there," I say.

A shrug goes through his frame. "Healthy debate is the rebel way."

"But what I said about having a death wish . . ."

He lets out a grumbling laugh. "I've been accused of worse."

I hesitate but say it anyway— "Do you think my brother did?"

X ponders this question for a while, looking back at the battle over Shreve. We can see the city much better from up here in the open, and the fighting seems to have settled. Dogfights and drone strikes streak the sky, but the orbital bombardment is over.

My father's tower still stands, a monument to self-preservation at any cost.

"Seanan didn't have a death wish," X says at last. "Just a firm grasp of how unimportant we all are, compared to the planet."

"But . . . you and he were important to *each other*."

X hesitates, turning to the wild now, its darkness drawing nearer. "The struggle was how we fell in love. We belonged to the fight against people like your father."

I try to understand, but erasing yourself to fix the world doesn't make sense to me. The world has been trying to erase me since the day I was born.

I grew up protecting my sister, but the whole planet is too big and abstract compared to her. Tonight may be historic, something that will echo down the centuries, but I'm only certain of the realities around me—the flashes of light painting the sky, the gunfire in the air, the warmth of X against my back, the bitter cold of everything that isn't him.

"I'm not sure I can be a rebel, Boss. I'm done with being selfless."

He laughs a little. "Your sister's a rebel, and she's managed to keep her sense of self intact."

"Except for pretending to be me."

"She's pretending to be both of you—the deadly sister *and* the charming one. Which is worrying." He turns to me with a grin. "Maybe she's trying to absorb you, as some twins do in the womb."

A shudder goes through me, even if he's joking. Which I'm not sure he is.

A rumble comes from behind us, and we turn to see fresh explosions fading in the sky, not far away. In my infrared, more sparkles scatter across the darkness, followed by the sound of metal being shredded.

The cold air seems to make the noises of battle sharper, brighter, like the glint from a freshly oiled blade.

"They're coming after us," X says. "We're wounded prey."

"And we've stolen my father's secrets," I say. "Every one of those prisoners may know something that can hurt him."

The flashes come again, and the rumbling reaches us quicker, like the thunder of an approaching storm.

Our pursuers keep closing, till I recognize the wide-set running lights of Shreve's flagship.

"The dreadnought." I hoist my autocannon, the metal cold and heavy against my chest. "Not much we can do with these."

"Maybe we can make them flinch," X says.

We set the barrels of our cannon spinning, adding their shriek to the damaged lifting fan's.

Overhead, one of the Diego ships unleashes a bolt from its primary plasma gun. A column of glowing air follows it into the darkness, heat prickling my freezing skin.

But the bolt spatters like a burning snowball against the dreadnought's armor.

"Diego appears to be outclassed," X says.

"They weren't expecting to start a war tonight. And that's my father's biggest ship."

A buzzing comes from our left, two small drones screaming out of the darkness. The shuttle trembles beneath us, projectiles rattling its metal skin. But they're shooting at the engines, not us on the topside.

We open fire, all four of our shuttles blazing with pinpricks of light. Both drones spark and shatter, tumbling into the trees below.

The two Diego craft above us fall back, trying to keep the dreadnought away from our convoy. But X is right—they're outgunned.

"In front!" comes a wind-torn cry from the next shuttle.

X and I spin around—another flight of drones is coming at our little fleet, dozens of microcraft the size of dinner plates. Too small to carry weapons, they're trying to ram us.

Our autocannon smash them like skeet.

The sky lights up behind us, the warcraft exchanging fire in earnest now. One of Diego's ships loses its stabilizers and goes whirling away into the dark.

"Uh-oh," I say.

Moments later, the other Diego craft lifts up and out of the battle, leaving nothing but empty air between us and the Shreve dreadnought.

"A pity," X says. "We almost made it to the wild."

The dark gap in the border is just ahead. But the dreadnought can destroy us just as easily out there.

Maybe X simply doesn't want to die in a city.

The Shreve ship draws closer, stately and unhurried in its pursuit. A miraculous orbital strike might take it out, but at this range, we'd all be pulverized together.

"Boss," I say, my heart sinking. "We have to surrender."

X sighs. "You may regret it, Frey, once you've been in a cell for a few weeks."

I wonder if I'll even last that long, but I can't tell X about the dose of radiation I took—he'll want to keep fighting for me.

He startles, his lupine ears twitching.

"Did you see that?" He peers into the darkness at our left.

Something flashes past in the corner of my eye.

Then another, and I recognize the shape . . .

People are tumbling from the sky.

Someone falls past right beside us, and we lean over the edge of the shuttle. The body doesn't hit the ground—retrojets flash to life, bringing it to a soft landing in the trees.

"Those Diego Specials," X says. "Were they wearing jump armor?"

"Yes." Somewhere overhead, they're abandoning ship.

I look up, just in time to see the wounded Diego hovercraft hurtling downward at us.

No—at the dreadnought.

Whirling end over end, its stabilizers blown to pieces, it somehow manages to spiral its way toward the Shreve craft. If they all jumped out, it must be the Diego AI itself flying, all those thousands of processors calculating wind speed, fan angle, lag time, and the air resistance of a thousand jagged, spinning surfaces.

I imagine the avatar at the controls, her face utterly blank in the hurtling, empty craft.

The two ships hit, the smaller breaking into pieces, the dreadnought's armor buckling at last. The shock wave hits us, hot and full of stinging debris, knocking me backward like a fist.

I skid across the shuttle's metal deck, sliding for a moment down the angled sides. My hands grasp a window frame, bringing me to a halt.

The lifting fan screams just below me—the hurricane of its airflow drags at my body, trying to pull me in. Maybe I should let go, and drop onto the grill protecting the blades.

Only instinct keeps me from releasing my grasp.

Then I look down—the mechanics removed the grill when they repaired the fan. Nothing's underneath me but naked metal spinning a hundred thousand times a second.

If I fall, there'll be nothing left of me but slush. I'll probably wreck the engine and bring the whole shuttle down.

My fingers cling in the cold, fighting the downdraft. The dreadnought's rolling crash is still underway, hurling out smoke, splintered trees, and shuddering air.

Caught in the shock wave, our shuttle starts to slew again. It spins into a slow turn, the angular momentum lifting my feet out into midair.

There's a meshed-over window just in front of me, one of the prisoners staring out of it. Face-to-face, we contemplate our imminent destruction.

Then the woman looks over my shoulder, her eyes widening.

What now?

Shouts come—impossibly—from behind me. Then I hear the buzz of smaller lifting fans and feel gloved hands grabbing at my arms, trying to peel me off.

I fight, kicking backward, clinging to the metal. Some furious part of me doesn't want to be captured, even if escape means tumbling into the spinning blades below.

But my muscles are spent, and I'm pried off, pulled away from the astonished prisoner staring at me through the window.

My feet hit a hoverboard deck, and strong arms wrap around me. I can't move.

"We got her, Boss!" the person holding me cries out.

"Get clear!" answer X's voice.

As we swerve away, I smell animal skins.

The air around me buzzes with hoverboards. I finally see them all swarming through the dark gap in the border.

The sky is full of rebels.

The city of Shreve is open, and my big sister is here.

REBEL ARMY

They take me to see Boss Frey.

She's down among the trees just beyond the border, surrounded by her rebel army. They swirl around us, hundreds of them, priming weapons and swapping out hoverboard batteries before the final push on Shreve.

Her name—*my name*—is on all their lips.

Rafi is the radiant center of the storm, her eyes alight. When she spots me and my escorts, confusion flashes on her face, as if she's forgotten my camo-surge. But a moment later, she reconciles my new and old selves, grabs me, and spins me in an ecstatic dance.

"You made it! You're going to be with us for the end!"

I pull away. "How are you here? I thought you were a thousand klicks away!"

She smiles. "We started mobilizing the moment you left, silly. Did you think I'd let you walk into Shreve without backup?"

I look around. This is too many soldiers for an extraction, and they're armed with city-wrecking weapons from my sister's secret cache—pulse bombs and plasma rifles.

"This isn't a rescue party," I say.

"Well, I knew *something* would happen." Rafi laughs, as happy as I've ever seen her. "And it did, Frey, thanks to you!"

My real name sends a start through me. At least a dozen people are in earshot, but everyone's too busy to notice.

Or maybe it wasn't a slip.

My voice drops. "Riggs found out about us switching places. Did she tell anyone?"

"First daughter, second daughter." Rafi waves a hand. "I don't care what people call me."

"It matters to me. I want my name back!"

"It's yours, Frey. But you'll need your old face for it to stick."

There, in her words, it hits me again—my dysmorphia by proxy. I'd gotten used to my camo-surge, but Rafi makes me feel like I'm in the wrong body again.

Maybe she always has.

"Don't look so glum, little sister," she says. "What matters is that Shreve is open and waiting for my army. The only birthday present I wanted, and you got it for me!"

Her fingers touch the rings on my right hand. Her deadly gift.

"I was only trying to get those people out of Shreve. I didn't even know you were here."

"Stop pretending, little sister." She gathers me into another hug, whispering in my ear, "I'm always with you."

It feels safe, here in my sister's arms. But her buoyant mood is almost wild, at the fragile borderline of manic. Maybe it's just that her lifelong dream is coming true.

Rafi steps away and gives me a long look, full of sympathy for my bedraggled state.

Then she does something sweet and simple—she hands me a canteen from her belt. I take a grateful drink of water.

"We can end this together." She speaks quietly, like we're littlies sharing a secret. "Tonight."

Her words almost disappear into the roar of lifting fans overhead, and I look up. It's my shuttle, repaired again, the last of the prisoners headed out into the safety of the wild.

Rafi follows my skyward gaze. "Don't worry—Col didn't go. Your whole crew's coming with us, plus a bunch of Diego jump troopers we found in the woods. We can trust them, right?"

"Yes. It was Diego who opened the border."

Rafi narrows her eyes. "They also kept you in prison for a month."

"For my own protection." I decide to change the subject. "Speaking of trust—this whole time, you knew who our spy was, didn't you?"

Rafi's fevered smile returns. "How'd you guess that?"

"She called me by my real name."

"Ugh, of course. Demeter's my best friend, but she's not the sharpest knife in the block."

Best friend. I take a step back.

"We've been plotting for years, since we were kids," Rafi says.

"You never told me about any of this!"

She takes my hand, drawing me near again. "You were part of it, Frey. Remember when you watched my parties? I said it was to make you a better impostor. But it was so you'd warn me if the cameras ever picked up us saying anything suspicious. You were protecting me, even if you didn't know it!"

"You mean, you trusted your bubblehead friends more than *me*?"

"Daddy watched you closer. He was scared of *you*, not them."

I take a deep breath. What Rafi's saying isn't completely logic-missing, but it goes against my whole understanding of our childhood.

We kept secrets from the rest of the world, not from each other. We *were* the secret.

"Rafi, the night before I left for Shreve, you said not to trust the spy. Why, if she was your *best friend*?"

"Because I didn't want you talking to her and getting yourself confused." Rafi turns away from me, dismissing my anger. "But I'll admit, you were perfect. You created chaos beyond my wildest dreams."

In confirmation of her words, a distant rumble shakes the sky.

I take another drink from the canteen, and the mineral taste of Rafi's mountain lair curls on my tongue. All the logistics of this invasion unfold in my head—water, food, weapons, batteries, everything needed to fly hundreds of rebels half a continent across the wild and then throw them into battle.

She must have been preparing for this trip for weeks.

"You've kept a lot from me, Rafi. You never even told me about you and Riggs."

She raises a single eyebrow, the one gesture of hers I've never managed to imitate. "How did *that* come up?"

"She thought I was you, just for a moment."

"How deliciously awkward." Rafi's tone changes all at once, sending a chill through me. "But you've kept a secret from me too, little sister."

"What secret?"

"The free cities want you to rule Shreve," she says.

BETRAYED

My anger twists in on itself.

Suddenly I'm the hidden sister again—curtsying wrong, tying a scarf badly, forgetting someone's name on a receiving line. Shame rolls through me like it's spilling from my feels.

"It wasn't my idea," I say.

Rafi nods. "But it was in your head somewhere. All those years in my shadow—maybe you wanted to be me?"

"No, it was Diego's idea! When I was their captive, they tested me, to make sure I'm not like Father—and they couldn't test you. That's the only reason they wanted me in charge. I only agreed so they'd help us fight him!"

But this whole mission, I've been studying Shreve. Preparing myself to lead.

Rafi seems to see the doubts in my heart.

"You never told me, though," she says.

The reasons for my silence fly through my head—Rafi's tantrums when she was little and didn't get her way. Her terrifying certainty, from age seven, that she'd one day kill our father.

But all those explanations sound like attacks on her.

She steps closer. "You thought I wouldn't trust you, little sister? If we're going to kill Dad tonight, we have to trust each other."

"I always trusted you, until . . ." Something becomes clear to me. "Until you stole my name. It was all I had."

"Ah." She puts her arms around me. "I'm truly sorry for that, Frey."

There, in her embrace, the last few days come crashing down. Not only my exhaustion, but the weight of the dust always watching. The city pressing close against my skin. Its voice, so like our father's, in my ears.

"You were right—it was hard, coming home. He's everywhere."

"Not for long." She squeezes me tighter. "Not if we do this right."

"You can have the city, Rafi. Shreve was always supposed to be yours."

"Thank you, Frey." She releases me at last. "But just so you understand—who do you think told me about your agreement with Diego?"

My brain spins through the possibilities. It must have been one of the other cities in the alliance. "Someone who wants me and you fighting each other so neither of us takes over?"

"Clever Frey," Rafi says, a smile playing on her lips. "Now look for a pattern."

A pattern. Of course.

"Diego told you," I whisper.

She nods.

Everything the city has done—testing me, offering me Shreve, changing my face—all of it was to drive a wedge between me and my sister. They admitted as much after my camo-surge.

"Everyone wants to divide us," Rafi says. "Because together we're unstoppable. Now come and see."

She leads me through the trees, her hand in mine, like we're littlies off to play a game. At the edge of the forest, we reach the border zone, where our father's defenses once bristled. Now it's a line of impact craters the size of radio telescopes, the awesome footprint of Diego's bombardment.

A fine ash covers everything.

Parked along the nearest crater's edge are dozens of hoverboards. Rafi leads me to one, sleek and black, and we stand on it together.

She snaps her fingers. We rise into the air.

Before us, Shreve's skyline still shimmers from burning fires and the last patches of fighting.

"A rebel army at our command, an open border, Shreve in tatters," she says. "This is the best chance we'll ever get."

"Yes." My throat goes dry again. "One problem—Father's turned his tower into a dirty bomb."

"So I've been informed."

I look at Rafi. "You're going to lead your rebels into hand-to-hand combat—inside a nuclear waste dump?"

"They know the risks. They'd rather face the nightmare now than let Dad fling it at some other city next week. There's a thing about rebels—"

"They love suicide missions," I say softly.

A smile. "You're starting to understand."

I turn away from her pleased expression. Does Rafi think her rebels are expendable?

But she's risking herself too. Maybe she's become one of them, with that same death wish as X and Seanan. Anything for the cause, even if her own cause is more personal than planetary.

One fact cuts through all these thoughts—my sister is in danger, which kindles something old and pure inside me.

"Don't worry, Rafi. I'll protect you."

She squeezes me. "I know."

SUCCESSION

The hoverboard gently descends, and a minute later, we're back in the thick of preparations.

A shout of "Boss Frey!" comes from the trees, and she heads off to handle something, leaving me alone in the whirlwind's center.

It's hard to stand up straight. Maybe it's the awesome fact that my father's life might end tonight, or maybe it's simple exhaustion—or that dose of radiation taking hold at last.

I wonder if there's somewhere to lie down, even for a few minutes.

"Need any gear?" asks a familiar voice.

It's Riggs, a pair of shoes in her hand.

I slip off the shoes I took from Terra, half a size small and coated with shame. Too bad there isn't a fire to throw them in.

Then I see why they hurt so much—

There are burns on the soles of my feet.

We both stare. The skin is red and blistering. The worst spot is the side of my left foot, which was closest to the fissure at the bottom of the crater.

"See a medic," Riggs says, but too softly for anyone else to hear. She knows what my choice will be.

"Tomorrow." I slip on the new shoes.

They're grippy, night-camo black, designed for hoverboarding. They fit perfectly.

Riggs watches me put them on. "We're all marching into a nuclear bomb, I guess. You've just got a head start."

She offers me a pair of ceramic greaves and shoulder pads.

I shake my head. "If my father blows up his tower, body armor won't do much."

"You'll regret it." She looks around to check that we're alone. "Just so you know, I didn't tell anyone your real name. Didn't want to cause trouble before a battle."

"I don't think she cares," I say.

Riggs nods. "Your sister will have what she wants, and I'll get back my crew."

"Still, thanks for keeping our secret." I offer to shake. "And for the shoes."

Riggs stares at my hand a moment, hesitant.

"Least I could do," she says, "after the shame thing."

"The shame thing . . ." Then it hits me. "You."

She looks away. "After I left you and Col last night, I heard some Futures talking. They said that girl, Terra, lent you her shoes. So I tracked her down and told her that you wanted to be reported for theft. A little extra drama."

"And she believed you—that I wanted to get *shame-cammed*?"

"Didn't take much convincing." Riggs finally meets my eyes, chuckling a little. "I don't think Terra likes you."

"You risked the whole mission, just because you were mad at Rafi? What went wrong between you and her?"

"Everything." She gives me an embarrassed half smile. "But I was just following orders."

"Whose?" I ask.

She laughs. "How do you still not know, Frey?"

Then she walks away, ignoring me when I call after her.

It doesn't make sense. Who cares if a made-up girl named Islyn gets shame-cammed?

My dizziness hits again, and I sit down on the crater's edge. The leftover heat from the bombardment rises up from the glowing depths, like the embers from a waning campfire.

My feet burn in their new shoes.

If Riggs wants to be mysterious, fine. After my conversations with Noriko, Boss X, and Rafi, the last thing I need tonight is another revelation.

As I sit there, the vanguard take their places on the hoverboards around me, all the rebels who'll ride into battle at my sister's side. The bosses of her assembled crews.

No one talks. We can all see Shreve in the distance, a wounded city under a sky of ash and smoke.

When Col arrives, he sits beside me.

"This is it, Frey. Shreve is free tonight."

"Victoria too," I say.

He kisses me, his heartbeat fast and nervous in his lips. I wonder if this is the last time we'll kiss like this—before a battle. Maybe this war will be over tonight.

What kind of world will that be?

"Shreve is lucky," he says. "You're going to make a good leader."

"I'm afraid not. It was never going to be me."

"They want to put an AI in charge first?" He shakes his head. "I should've known Diego would change the deal."

"No, Rafi did."

"Ah." Col faces me again. "But it isn't her choice, is it? The free cities want you."

"They want us fighting each other. It was all a setup, a way to weaken us."

He's silent for a moment, but he doesn't seem surprised.

Col, of course, has seen the free cities break a hundred promises. If Victoria is liberated tomorrow, it's only because my father over-reached one too many times.

"What do *you* want, Frey?" Col asks. "That's the question."

Maybe it is. But it's one I've never been much good at answering.

"All those detours on the mission," I say. "Trying to read the palimpsest, allying with the cliques—for me, it was to understand Shreve."

"So you'd be ready. So you'd know your people."

"It was to know *myself*, Col. I want to be someone who understands the world beyond tower politics and fighting a war—the way real people do."

Col takes my hand. "Real is all you've ever been, Frey."

"Then how come I can't tell where I begin and my sister ends?"

"Because that's how Rafia wants it," he says, anger in his voice now.

"What do you mean?"

"The more confused you are, the more you stay a part of her. You were *created* for her, Frey—a playmate, a protector, an extension, a spare. With you there, she can never be anything but important, beloved, magnificent."

A laugh comes out of me. "She's all those things already."

"*You* are all those things!" Col cries. "That's why she needs you as a mirror. That's why she stole your name."

I turn away and regard my sister's army.

Crews who were with us at the Iron Mountain. New ones I've never seen before. Yandre and Boss Charles meeting up with their old raiders, and X resplendent in battle armor and freshly oiled fur.

Everyone's here to see the end of my father.

"She did all this," I say. "Not me."

"You rescued her from the tower," he says. "You found the rebels first, and your name made them follow her. You allied with the free cities who opened the door to Shreve tonight."

I shake my head.

Col sees a strength in me that isn't there.

"I don't care if you lead Shreve or not," he says. "But you can't be your sister's shadow anymore."

A trickle of wariness travels through me. "Are you also trying to split us up?"

"I'm trying to fight for you," Col says, and rises up to one knee.

He takes out his sidearm and lays it on the ground between us.

"I always fight for you, Frey."

His wrong-colored eyes shine through the split in my heart.

"You have a city to save, Col."

"Victoria has known freedom since the mind-rain, except these last six months." He reaches for my hand. "Tonight you will too."

I can't speak.

Even if it's only him looking at me in this vast swirl of preparation, it's hard to be the center of attention like this.

Not as Rafi, but as Frey.

Maybe tomorrow—after I do this one last thing for her—I can tear myself away.

But tonight I fight for Rafia.

Zura comes over to break the moment, brusque, efficient. She ignores Col on his knee and starts handing us gear.

"Rebreathers, crash bracelets, rad meters."

I frown. "How did the rebels know to bring radiation gear?"

"They didn't," she says. "The cities air-dropped us supplies an hour ago. Paz sent this for you."

She hands me a pulse knife.

I smile, a silent thank-you to the sovereign city of Paz. The knife's charge is full, and it flits like a hummingbird when I test my gestures.

My sister finally joins us, some last detail attended to, and I wonder for a moment when she learned how to run an army. It's like Rafi became someone else when she stole my name.

She's carrying her own pulse knife, still pretending to be me.

We all rise into the air together. Five hundred rebels—a swarm, a horde.

Before she gives the signal, Rafi turns to me.

"You okay, little sister? You don't look as happy as you should."

I shake my head. She doesn't need to know about my conversation with Col. Or my dose of radiation. She'd probably yell at me for not taking proper care of our DNA.

"Just tired," I say.

"Maybe a battle will perk you up," she says with a smile. "Be careful—these boards are shiny new free-city tech. They're ridiculously fast."

We move out, the huge formation taking shape around us. It's the first time my sister and I have ridden side by side since just before I left home for Victoria, all those months ago.

That night, Rafi promised me that I'd never have to hide again, once she was in charge. Standing here beside her, I'm not sure why I ever let Diego's lies betray that vision.

She reaches out to take my hand.

"Let's go see Dad," she says.

TOWER

On fast boards, our childhood home is less than an hour away.

My father's army doesn't try to stop us. Skimming the treetops, we're below radar, and what's left of the dust can't see us at this speed. I doubt even the citizens notice us—after a night of earth-shuddering explosions, the buzz of our stealthy boards is nothing.

Below us, Shreve has transformed. The perfect surveillance state is now a sense-addled wreck, piles of smoking rubble everywhere, whole neighborhoods darkened by power outages. Over the city, the only presence in the air is firefighting and med drones.

It gives me an awful, hollow feeling, seeing my city broken.

I was only barely starting to know it.

When we draw close to my father's tower, what's left of his fleet comes into view.

It's a mismatched collection—border defense ships bristling with plasma cannon, patrol craft for hunting down rebels, riot control cars, a few blockade runners.

Rafi shouts a series of code words, and the bosses leave the vanguard, returning to their crews. The attack plan looks simple enough—no flanking maneuvers or skirmish formations. We stay in a single column, serpentine in the ragged wind, twisting at my father's heart.

Our anti-hovercraft weapons are up at the front, and soon the sky ignites with bolts from plasma rifles. My sister's rebels ignore the battle wagons, focusing on sleek patrol craft and Security cars. Once we swarm past them, the big ships can't turn their weapons around and fire back at the tower.

The first few bolts go wild, untrained rebels firing at will. But then a patrol craft ignites into a ball of plasma. Boss X's crew charges ahead. I spot Yandre among them, their buzzing pulse lance carving into metal hulls.

No one gave me a rifle. My sister doesn't want me shooting—my job is inside the tower, at the kill.

One of the big ships gets off a broadside, but the shrieking bolts simply pass through our formation, like bullets wasted on a cloud of mosquitos. Col and I pass though the column of ionized air left behind, and our boards shudder, the heat sharp on my face.

My sister is laughing. The Shreve navy is designed to fight another fleet, not rebels on hoverboards.

She calls out, "Cut it open!"

From around us in the vanguard, plasma rifles open up. These are better aimed, striking the tower square along its length. The walls blow open in six places, spilling out smoke and debris.

I veer closer to my sister.

"What are you doing? You'll poison the whole city!"

"Don't worry," she calls back, laughing. "We only hit Daddy's favorites!"

Adjusting my night vision, I see what she means. That smoking hole down on the eleventh floor, where a balcony should be—that's *our* room lying open. Rafi's and my beds, our clothes, all of it is spilling out into the night breeze.

A few floors below it, the wreckage of our father's trophy room is visible. All those paintings of his vanquished enemies, so lovingly mounted on those walls, must be in tatters. The image of Aribella Palafox, and that painting of me, the one he had ready for my death.

Near the top of the tower—the control room, where the data from every speck of dust is gathered, analyzed, and stored. The wine cellars, the kitchens, the ballroom where Seanan died.

Six places our father loves too much to sully with nuclear waste.

Rafi has struck at his heart, as no one else could.

If you spoil the planet, your own children will despise you.

I wonder how much Rafi will worry about the planet when she's in charge.

The main body of our column makes contact with the fleet. The air sizzles around me, small arms fire from Shreve patrol and riot cars. Rebels start to fall now, shot from the boards, twisting in the air. Their crash bracelets jerk them upright, arms spread like prisoners in ancient dungeons as they waft toward the ground.

I crouch low, yelling at Col and Zura.

"Follow me!"

I'm heading for my old bedroom. That has to be where Rafi's going first.

My father's probably in his study, two floors above the control room. But it'll be surrounded by elite troops in heavy armor.

Rafi and I don't need a frontal assault. Once inside the tower, we know every passageway, every hiding place.

Rebels and hovercars envelop me, the air singing with bullets, lifting fans, bolts of plasma. A patrol craft falls past, guns still shrieking, smoke belching from its open wounds. It spins in a lopsided tumble, two of its fans clawing at the air.

The wind of its passage sends me veering, my crash bracelets locking tight around my wrists. They keep me on the board, and Col swings in front of me, creating a slipstream of steady air.

"Thanks!" I call, regaining control.

He turns to face me, flashing a grin.

Without my new grippy shoes from Riggs, I'd have fallen.

The tower looms over us, the rebels spilling up its sides. The crews break apart, hitting every entryway at once.

As they fly past the smoke-filled openings, rebels leap from their boards, with nothing but crash bracelets to halt their momentum. The abandoned hoverboards swing around on autopilot, clustering at the smoking gaps in the tower walls.

My sister's crew must have practiced this—my father's soldiers waiting inside will be bowled over by incoming rebels.

Col and I follow Rafi, who's headed toward the eleventh floor.

At last, I'm going home.

BEDROOM

I jump from the sleek black hoverboard into the wreckage of my old bedroom, wrists crossed in front of me.

The magnetics in my crash bracelets grab the tower's metal, jerking to life as I pass through the ragged gap. But I'm still moving fast as my feet hit the floor. My grippy shoes skid on dust and debris. I smash sideways into Rafi's makeup table. Its wooden legs snap, the mirror shatters, pain shoots through my shins and left shoulder.

Col and Zura fly through the hole after me, arms linked. Her Special reflexes guide them into a skidding, gentle halt against my sister's closet doors.

Col stands up, staring at his bracelets with the expression of someone who's never crashed a hoverboard before.

Even with one wall blown out, the room is familiar around me. My bed next to Rafi's, our old photos scattered on the floor. Pictures of us together couldn't be stored in the datasphere—we had to print them out and stick them on the walls.

The images are irreplaceable, and now a rebel army is charging across them. I kneel and take one, slipping it into my pocket.

The bedroom door is open, and rebel shouts come from the hallway. No gunfire.

I wonder how many soldiers are stationed here in my father's tower. An attack by five hundred rebels probably never crossed his mind.

Col, Zura, and I move out into the hallway. It's full of rebels, breathing masks on their faces. Half of them are waving around rad meters.

No red lights . . . yet.

Rafi was right—my father wouldn't sully her old bedroom with nuclear waste. He hasn't changed that much in the months since we escaped.

"Islyn!" calls my sister's voice from ahead. "Up here!"

There are cams everywhere, of course, maybe some dust left in the air. Rafi doesn't want Father figuring out who I really am.

Which makes her the obvious target.

Why is she protecting *me*?

I run to take her side, my pulse knife buzzing.

A small crew of us head into the servants' stairwell. In these tight quarters, we climb two abreast, me and my sister shoulder to shoulder. The buzz of her pulse knife makes echoing harmonies with my own.

Three floors up, a cloud of tiny drones flutters down at us, carried on translucent wings like butterflies. I remember these from when a team of Shreve Specials tried to grab me in Paz. They're mounted with knockout needles.

Our pulse knives shred the air, turning them to glitter.

"Seriously?" Rafi mutters. "Is *this* all Dad has up his sleeve?"

"He didn't see a full-on ground assault coming," I say. "You outsmarted him, Boss Frey."

She gives me a grin for calling her *Frey*—or maybe *Boss*.

The way a shadow would do.

A few floors up, a cloud of heavy gas tumbles down the stairs, and we snap our rebreathers on. Riggs sprays neutralizer, and the gas does nothing but make my skin itch. If these automated defenses are all my father can throw at us, his tower will be ours in half an hour.

But the sound of shots rattles down from above.

We climb until the gunfire is shaking the stairwell. Rafi chooses a spot and sticks a wad of thermal nanos against the wall.

A roaring fire erupts from it, a wave of heat and brimstone smell.

"Go!" my sister shouts.

Through the eye-stinging smoke, we dive into a burning hole in the permacrete. A squad of Shreve troopers is in a firefight with rebels.

We've surrounded them.

Part of me watches my sister. Rafi fights hard and fast, her knife flowing through the air. I remember all those nights she made me teach her combat moves. It's not her skill that surprises me—it's the fury. She's channeled all her childhood anger into blood and mayhem.

Maybe I'm not the deadly sister anymore.

But if she is, then who am I?

After a quick and bloody struggle, the Shreve troopers surrender.

Our fellow rebels join us. With numbers doubled, we head for the main staircase.

In the hallway, Col looks down. "It's still there."

I look at the red line on the floor. Growing up, I couldn't cross it except when I was pretending to be Rafi.

"The boundary of my world," I say.

"Of *our* world," Rafi says, and spits on the floor. "He didn't even paint it over."

A reminder that he once had us in a cage.

We reach the main stairway. Rebels are already working here, slicing into the tower walls. As we climb, there are gouges everywhere. Exposed wires, data fiber, even the plumbing pipes—all torn out.

"You're cutting him off," Zura says to Rafi.

"In case he has a hard line to his dirty bomb."

My eyes widen. "What if you set it off by accident?"

"He wouldn't risk that," Rafi says. "He doesn't have a death wish, little sister. But he thinks *you* do."

Rafi's expression makes me realize—her Boss Frey persona isn't only to impress her rebels.

She's performing for our father. Ever since I killed Seanan, he's been scared of me. Maybe I always made him nervous, like a dangerous pet.

Maybe tonight is part of why she took my name . . .

His deadly daughter storming this tower is his worst nightmare, and delivering our father nightmares is Rafi's oldest desire.

The stairs end at the control room—the nerve center into which all the dust's data flowed. It's a wreck now, an entire wall blown inward, the wallscreens blank or frizzing. The half-darkened city of Shreve is framed in the ragged hole.

All that data, lost in the air.

The staff has run away—but there are bodies everywhere.

Dead rebels.

Zura moves protectively closer to Col.

The control room was always run by pensive, quiet people who saw the world only as data. So who killed these rebels?

Then I hear it—the whine of servomotors.

As I spin around, a squad of Shreve heavy troopers lumbers into view. Like broad-shouldered gorillas in their powered suits, they crowd the doorway. The rebels open fire, but their bullets bounce off the ceramic armor, flying wild around us.

The first heavy trooper lets off a burst from their shockgun, sending a wave of energy through the room. It catches Riggs and two other rebels, throwing them out the breached wall into the night sky.

"Fall back!" Rafi shouts, but she doesn't run—she dives at the heavies, her knife shrieking.

I follow her.

We duck beneath the shockguns' barrels just in time, my eardrums splitting as they fire again.

I ignore the cries behind me, thrusting my pulse knife into a heavy's ceramic knee joint, slicing at servomotors.

The leg freezes, and the powered suit loses balance, falling back against the wall.

Rafi's done the same—her victim is twisting in the doorway, hamstrung by her shrieking blade. We roll out of the way as both heavies crash to the floor.

But more of them are pushing through, peering down at us through faceless visors.

Rafi springs up, embracing the nearest trooper—too close for a shockgun to come into play. Her knife slips into a seam beneath the rib plate . . . a spray of blood jets out, covering her.

The scream, thin and muffled inside the armor, barely penetrates the din of battle. A servo-powered arm lashes out, flinging Rafi across the room.

She crashes to the floor beside a control panel.

As I scramble after her, the wounded heavy fires—too high. But the edge of a shock wave hits us both, sending us rolling. I cover my sister with my body.

We're exposed, about to be pulped by the next blast.

She sighs in my arms. "He had a last, perfect line of defense. Like you were for me."

"I was never perfect," I say, staring at my city one last time.

Out in the dark sky is a silhouette, a person floating in midair, taking aim.

FALLEN

The figure fires, a binding beam of light passing over me and my sister.

It scalds the air around us, sucking the oxygen from my lungs, scorching my exposed skin. A shredding sound comes from the Shreve heavy troopers.

Then more screams.

The flash illuminates the figure out in the darkness—it's one of the jump troopers we saw falling from the avatar's craft.

"Who's saving us?" Rafi asks.

"Dieg—" I start, but then the return fire hits.

As the jump trooper crumples in midair, the shock wave's edge catches me and Rafi, sends us skidding across the floor, through the hole . . .

And out into the night.

We're falling, tumbling, with only the slightest tug from our crash bracelets. They're battery-dead from when we jumped off our boards—you're only expected to crash once a night, I guess.

"Frey," she says. "You're magnificent."

I hold my sister.

Flares of light surround us—three more Diego jump troopers falling faster than we are, their retrojets inverted.

They fly beneath us and form a triangle, linking arms to catch us. We come to a gradual halt in midair.

"Are you injured?" one asks.

"No," my sister says. "Take us back to the fight."

We rise up again, wreathed in the white heat of the jets and the smell of burning fuel.

More troopers are overhead, clinging to the walls, firing in at the Shreve heavies. By the time we reach the control room, our enemies have fallen silent.

We glide up over the edge of the blasted wall, landing in the wrecked control room. Dead and wounded heavy troopers fill the doorway and the hall outside, like piles of armored parts.

There's still gunfire sounding from above, the ceiling rattling from shockgun blasts.

Col is huddled on the floor, and Zura, both with bloody noses and black eyes from the shock waves.

I run to hug him, and silence seems to fall around us two. All I feel is my heart beating against him.

Then I pull away. "How are you not . . . ?"

He points at an open floor panel, crowded with a tangle of exposed data fiber like glowing hair.

"We hid down there." His fingers gently touch my upper lip. They come away smeared red. "You okay?"

I nod, tasting the iron at last. We've all got bloody noses from the shockguns.

Except Rafi, somehow unhurt after being thrown across the room by that heavy. Or maybe she doesn't feel the broken ribs yet.

She's gathering the surviving rebels, getting a situation report from a Diego jump trooper.

My father's study is only two floors above. The fighting must be at his doorstep by now.

Col looks out the window. "Where's Riggs?"

My breath halts. She was thrown out by the first blast.

I hold up a crash bracelet. "The batteries are spent, Col, from when we jumped off our boards."

"Oh." He takes my hand. "Maybe she had some left."

"Maybe," I say.

Col clears his throat. "Frey, there's good news. No one's rad meters are pinging. Not even in the basement levels."

I shake my head. "The recon photos . . ."

"Maybe those transports were empty," Col says. "A bluff, to keep us from blowing up the tower!"

A little shudder goes through me. What if my father's survival instinct is too exquisitely refined to wrap himself in a dirty bomb?

Like when he sent me in Rafi's place as a hostage—he gives the illusion of taking risks but never exposes anything he really cares about to danger.

It was just me he was willing to lose, not his first daughter.

"Then we can take him out."

"No need," Rafi's voice comes from behind me.

I turn. Her eyes are alight. She looks almost feverish.

"They did it," she says, breathless. "Boss X's crew and the Diego squad—they got through the heavies."

I look up. The firefight above us has fallen silent.

Col takes my hand.

"Is he up there?" I ask.

Rafi nods.

"They have him. And he wants to see us."

FATHER

The stairs up to our father's study are a wreck.

Blood and bullet casings. Scorched and broken stone, fiber dangling from holes in the walls. The massive bodies of heavies shoved aside to make room to walk, like a burial ground for giants.

It smells like sweat and campfire.

A military history tutor once told me that pre-Rusties thought battle-grounds were sacred. Climbing past the carnage of this stairway, I wonder if he was serious.

My father's study is somehow untouched by the battle. The curved windows taking in the skyline of Shreve are unscratched. The leather chairs, with their soft animal smell, aren't even smudged.

The only difference from my last visit is that the huge fireplace isn't lit. A heavy piece of metal covers it—my father was afraid of rebels coming down the chimney.

Boss X and Yandre are already here. Field bandages are wrapped around X's arm, and his fur is matted with dust and blood. Yandre looks somehow unhurt.

Two Diego jump troopers stand to attention when Rafi walks in.

Our father is in his armchair, an empty glass in his hand. His army defeated, his city in flames, he still wears a contented smile. Like he's just eaten the *best* dinner and is thinking of bed.

My stomach clenches as his eyes drift across me—that old mix of fear, anxiety, and the pressure to stand up straight.

But he barely registers my presence. In my camo-surge, I'm just some random with a pulse knife.

He glares at Rafi in her leather and furs.

"You," he says. "Where's Rafia? I know she's here—she wouldn't miss this."

My sister smiles, staying in character. "Rafi doesn't care to see you. The truth is, she despises you."

"But I have something to give her—for her birthday. Did you forget? You used to enjoy those parties, from a distance."

My sister doesn't rise to his bait.

"You have nothing left to give, Father."

"Don't call me that," he says.

Her eyes flash. "You might be an obscene excuse for a parent, but I'm still your child."

"You were just a copy," he says. "A throwaway."

Rafi's knife starts rumbling in her hand. "And your own son tried to kill you."

A pulse of dislocation goes through me. It's like watching myself in a dream, saying what I've always wanted to our father's face.

He only smiles. "I wasn't there that day. Maybe it was your sister that Seanan wanted to murder. She took his place as heir, after all."

Boss X's hands twitch. I catch his eye, giving him the smallest shake of my head. This is Rafi's moment.

"I've met Seanan's friends, the people he loved," she says. "And he despised you, just like Rafi does."

Our father shrugs. "Brainwashed. Raised by rebels."

"Well, I was raised by *you*, Father." She steps forward, lifting the knife. "And I'm going to end you."

That's when I realize that Rafi isn't going to reveal who she is. All those years, she hated him on my behalf—for erasing me, for ignoring me, for keeping me locked up, friendless and invisible.

Rafi doesn't simply want to kill our father.

She wants to kill him *as me*.

I resolve not to move a muscle. This invasion was my birthday gift to her, after all. This kill goes with it.

Rafi takes a step forward, knife buzzing, and I half expect the Diego troopers to intervene. But they're just watching—one has a hovercam floating at his shoulder.

The city of Diego, always observing. Always testing us.

"Stop this nonsense," our father says. "Bring my daughter here, girl."

Col steps forward. "You don't give orders anymore."

"And who are *you*?" my father asks.

313

"Col Palafox." He gestures out the window. "I owed you a wrecked city. I trust the debt is paid."

"Ah, the knight in shining armor." My father stares at Col, looking bored. "Except it's camo-surge. Pathetic."

Rafi pushes Col back, looming over our father. "Did you miss the part where you *lost*?"

"I still have cards to play," he says softly. "Now get your sister—I need to talk to both of you."

"You'll never see her again," Rafi says, knife pulsing in her hand. "Never touch her again!"

Her eyes are alight, ecstatic. She gets to watch him die, without giving him the satisfaction of being in the same room one last time.

My father ignores her shouting, her raised knife. He licks his finger and rubs it on the rim of the glass, creating a soft hum.

"We'll see about that," he says gently.

The metal plate across the fireplace slides away.

Filling the hearth, stretching up into the chimney, are stacks of lead-covered boxes. Hundreds of them.

"Oh, crap," my sister says.

My father smiles, holding the glass like something precious and fragile.

"Now get me Rafia," he says. "Or I'll poison this city for a thousand years."

314

DEAD-MAN'S SWITCH

Yandre walks to the fireplace, multiscanner in hand.

It chirps an alert, flashing red.

They kneel, holds the scanner closer—stuffed between the boxes are slender red packets.

"Explosives," Yandre says.

"Enough to scatter a new kind of dust two thousand klicks downwind," our father says. "Powdered nuclear fuel. Now, bring me my real daughter."

Rafi doesn't even look at me.

"Father," she says. "This whole city is a monument to you. You won't destroy it."

"Hopefully not." He gazes with distaste at the fireplace, like it's something the servants haven't properly cleaned. "I just need both of you in the same room, and we can avoid disaster. Now bring Rafia here, *or I'll end this.*"

His hand is white-knuckled around the glass. Finally my sister looks my way, worried.

We have no Rafia of Shreve to show him. Even if she reveals herself, there's no way to convince him that both of us are here.

We have to go for the trigger, the glass in his hand.

I glance at Zura, wondering if she can move fast enough. But she's across the room with Col, as if she can protect him from a dirty bomb big enough to kill a city.

Beside her, Col catches my eye. He points at the fourth knuckle on his hand—his ring finger.

Of course.

I ease myself closer to Boss X and Yandre, out of my father's eye line.

My sister sees me moving and starts pacing in the opposite direction. "Why do you want to see Rafi?"

"To give her my city," my father says.

"It's not yours anymore."

"But I can kill it." He lifts the glass. "That's just as good."

I make a fist, my thumb on the inside.

"You always said nukes were beneath you," Rafi says.

"Many things I've done are beneath me. One adjusts."

She smirks. "What if don't I think you have the guts?"

"Then a million people die. And another million are sick for the rest of their lives."

The variable blade forms in my hand, and I keep squeezing until it's a meter long, thin as a wire. Then two meters, until it fades into a glimmer.

"No more stalling," our father demands. "Get me my daughter!"

"That can be arranged." Rafi nods at me.

The knife is invisible now, and I'm not sure exactly where its tip is. I'm squeezing so hard my arm is trembling.

But if I can slice off his hand—

"Stop," he says, turning to look straight at me. "Whatever you're doing, you'll kill us all. This is a dead-man's switch."

I stare at the glass and realize that my father's hand is trembling too. The fear in his eyes tells me the rest.

A dead-man's switch doesn't go off when you trigger it—it goes off when you let go. If he drops the glass, the world ends.

I almost destroyed a city.

I uncurl my fist, letting the knife snap back into the rings. I hold up my empty hands and take a step back.

But my father is still staring at me.

"Oh." His eyes widen. "I see it now. Of *course*."

For a moment, I think he recognizes me from shame-cam, but he's looking at the way I'm standing—the ready-to-fight pose flayed into me by a dozen combat tutors.

A wounded flutter of excitement goes through me.

My father has seen beneath my camo-surge, just like X did coming through his cell door. At last.

"*You're* Frey," he breathes, then throws back his head and barks a single, choked laugh. He turns to Rafi. "And what did you call me? 'An obscene excuse for a parent'? Hardly a guard dog's vocabulary."

The flutter dies in my stomach.

My father turns to me again, disgusted now. "You gave up your name *and* your face? A throwaway to the end."

I find my voice. "This face is temporary. Just like you."

He grunts and turns back to Rafi.

Once more, I don't exist.

"Congratulations, Daddy," she says. "You figured it out—we're both here. So say whatever you've been dying to and then *give me Shreve!*"

"Rafia." Our father sighs, rapturously, as if uttering her name was all he wanted. "I need you to understand this birthday gift. With me gone, the world will help you put Shreve back together. But they'll always fear and respect you, thanks to me."

"*Nothing* is thanks to you." She points her pulse knife at the window. "Look what you did to my city!"

"Yes, this is my fault." He stares sadly at the glass in his hand. "When I learned that Seanan had died in my own house, killed by my own creation, I lost control. But you'll do better, as long as you rid yourself of the weakness in your heart. Once and for all."

He looks at me. Rafi does too.

Her voice goes small. "What are you saying, Daddy?"

"I'll give you Shreve," he says, "if you kill your sister."

There's an endless moment of silence.

Then Rafi lets out a laugh. "Go to hell, Dad."

"Happy to," he says, raising the glass. "But a million people will come with me. Or you can just do this one thing for me."

"Why? What did *Frey* ever do to you?"

"She turned you against me." His voice is growing hoarse, ragged with grief. "She gave you someone to take care of, which made you weak."

"She *saved* me!" Rafi shouts. "Without her, there was only you!"

"She killed your brother," he says.

Rafi shakes her head. "*You* killed Seanan. You traded him for power!"

"My finest moment! That's what you need to learn, Rafia—give up your sister, and you can have this city!"

Of course. Letting the kidnappers keep Seanan is what made my father the way he is, and now he wants to cast Rafi in his own image.

One last lesson in the etiquette of dictators.

"With power comes sacrifice." He raises the glass over his head, ready to throw it to the ground. "Lose one sister, or kill a million people. That's a choice no leader can hesitate to make!"

"I'd rather die," my sister says.

"Not just you," my father says.

My eyes go to the skyline framed by the window—those Futures, so desperately trying to make sense of life in the dust. The cliques who just wanted some drama, some fun. The crims and smugglers scrawling on the walls invisibly, undermining the rigid order of the regime. The widgets cleaning houses, moving every night. The randoms breathing dust and hearing lies and telling themselves *this is normal*.

All of them are about to die . . . for me.

No one dies for me.

I step forward. It's the only way.

Neither my sister nor my father sees me, though. Their real struggle has always been with each other.

"You have thirty seconds to decide," he says, the glass high. "It's all the same to me."

"Wreck it, then!" Rafi brings her knife to full pulse, points it at his throat. *"You don't get to win this!"*

"Frey dies either way," my father says.

"Not by my hand." But there are tears in her eyes, and her voice is breaking. I think she knows the right thing to do.

"Save a whole city, Rafia," my father whispers, pointing at me. "All you have to do is *tear her heart out*."

She hesitates, just for a moment. Like she understands.

"That, I can do," Rafi says—

And throws her pulse knife into Col's chest.

PALAFOX HEIR

The world is screaming around me.

Our father laughing at the spectacle, hysterical and satisfied. Rafi walking into his embrace, gently taking the glass from his hand. Then the spray of pink mist as her pulse knife guts him, shreds him, halves him from bottom to top.

Zura and Yandre kneeling over Col, calling for the Diego troopers—for anyone—to go for help. But the troopers are too busy taking the trigger glass out of Rafi's blood-slippery hands.

Me, sinking to my knees, unable to help Col. Or my sister, who's howling now, in pain again, like she didn't want to hurt me this way. Or like she's realized that killing our father wasn't enough and never will be.

Boss X taking me in his strong arms. A piece of me knowing that he's the only one left who'll fight for me. And at first I think I'm sobbing—but it's X, like Seanan has died again today.

The hovercam from Diego, recording it all.

Within moments, a huge hovercraft in Paz livery looms in the ragged window. It blocks off the news cams behind it, swarming in the sky, wanting to come in and take historic pictures.

A dozen med drones scream through the door, descending on the bodies of wounded soldiers, a dictator cut in half lengthwise, a dead Palafox heir.

I vomit from anguish—but one of the med drones scans me and says it's radiation sickness, not a broken heart.

The skyline of Shreve out the window, fractured. But not obliterated, not poisoned for a thousand years. A city saved.

Col lying, torn, on the stone floor.

Instead of me.

CITY OF PAZ

I wake up in a softly lit hospital room in Paz.

There are flowers everywhere—on the windowsills, the bedside tables, climbing trellises made of silver wire. For a moment, I wonder if I'm a captive in a fairy den.

It's five days later, a doctors tell me. But it feels like a century.

They replaced my blood, my skin, some bones in my feet. They had to go all the way down to my poisoned marrow, deeper even than the pretty surge in olden days.

The doctors must have missed something, though, some spark of radiation inside me—after a groggy day awake, they put me in the tank again.

I come back with more new bones in my left foot.

As an afterthought, almost, they've given me my old face back.

But the mirror is no longer my friend. I want to smash that nose, split those lips, gouge those eyes.

Vengeance by proxy.

My sister doesn't come to visit.

She's too busy taking control of Shreve. Like everyone else, I've seen the speech she gave after the battle ended. So brilliant, so moving, somehow *humble*. Our father's blood still on her face, Rafi spoke of a new city, free and peaceful.

She didn't mention whose blood she bought it with.

The citizens love her—Boss Frey, the once-invisible sister now on every screen, her voice in everyone's ear.

She's decided it's still useful, being me.

She's better at it than I ever was.

A few hours later, I watch Teo's speech when he takes his honorary seat on the Victorian elected council.

He looks so somber in his black uniform. His citizens love him too, after all his family's sacrifices in the fight for freedom.

It's lonely in this bed, watching the word spin into its new shape without me. I lie here, too weak to intervene, aching with an emptiness as deep as the poison in my bones.

I could talk to the Paz AI. It's all around me, in the walls, the window glass, the wires of the trellis. Maybe even in the gene-spliced flowers, closing and opening as the sun moves across the room.

Paz might understand the way I feel, having once lost a hundred thousand pieces of itself, all those people who died in my father's war.

But the silence is already too bright and sharp; I worry that the sound of a friend's voice might cut my shiny new skin.

The day after my second awakening, a visitor finally arrives.

"No," I say. "Not you."

The avatar of the sovereign city of Diego smiles. "We're pleased that your recovery is complete."

"I wouldn't go that far. I can barely move."

"Radiation is a tricky thing."

"You don't say."

The avatar regards me impassively, letting the silence stretch. The host of machines might be processing a trillion thoughts a second, but still they have more patience than me.

"Why are you here?" I finally ask.

"To explain things." The avatar pulls a chair from the corner of the room and places it next to my bed but doesn't sit. "We've decided to leave your sister in charge of Shreve."

A laugh chokes out of me. "You didn't just forget who was who?"

The avatar shakes their head. "We know who you are, Frey. And none of the free cities will forget what you've done for the world. But removing Rafia from power that night, with five hundred rebels at her side, was not something we had the stomach for. And it only gets more complicated as the days pass."

"So you trust Rafi to run a city," I say. "You aren't worried that she's like him?"

"Are you?" they ask.

I close my eyes.

325

Rafi is the first daughter—the person I was born to protect. She's a brilliant leader, magnificent to behold, and to obey. The city of Shreve will be in better hands than it's been for twenty years.

But twenty years from now?

A week after our father's fall, dust has been detected in the air. No one knows why it's still there, but of course a whole city has never been cleared before.

Maybe it's just left over, leaking up from the topsoil. Or from old clothes, the tops of wallscreens, and toys shoved in the backs of closets—all the places normal dust comes from.

Or maybe some things never really change.

I love Rafi, because she was born and raised to make people love her. As her first victim, I love her better than anyone.

But I don't trust her anymore.

I've seen the trades she makes.

"You had a cam in my father's study." My voice is barely steady. "You saw what she did."

"We saw her save a million people, Frey. Her choice was logical and made under duress." They turn away from my expression. "And if your sister ever misbehaves, we can still show the world what happened that night. These days, Col Palafox is revered like no other."

At the sound of his name, a spire of anguish rises up from the center of the earth, through the floor, impaling me here in this bed. Everything spins on the axis of my heart, slow and lazy, grinding me away.

It takes a long minute before I can speak again.

"You trust Rafi because you can blackmail her."

The avatar nods.

"That threat won't work forever," I say. "Every day she's in power, how she got there matters less."

"True. We wish you could've stood with her that night, Frey, during those crucial hours of uncertainty."

"Yeah, I wasn't up to giving a speech."

"And Shreve needed a leader."

A beautiful leader. Not one who was wailing, puking, poisoned from slipping into a radioactive hole.

And wearing the wrong face.

The avatar finally sits beside me. "There's also hopeful news. We artificial intelligences have surmised the flaw in our thinking, the mistakes that allowed your father to become so powerful. We won't make them again. Not with your sister—not with anyone."

"The flaw in your thinking?" I ask. "That's what you're calling the biggest war in three hundred years?"

The avatar shrugs. "Call it what you will. We considered ourselves to be grown-ups—we forgot to believe in monsters."

"In other words, you failed when you were most needed."

Diego takes my hand, whispering now, like they're telling me a secret.

"It's how the powerful prove to ourselves that we're civilized. Victims are kept waiting, while monsters are offered every chance to mend their ways." The machine leans closer. "But we'll be watching Boss Frey."

"I'll be more than watching," I say.

"Careful." Diego pulls away from me. "The world has had enough of war."

"Something else, then. Not a war, but something."

The avatar waits, but I keep my mouth closed.

Eventually the room stops spinning, the steeple of pain fading into the floor. But it'll be waiting down there for me, always.

"We've brought you something that may change your mind," the avatar says into the silence.

"What's that?"

"A message from your sister."

DEAR LITTLE SISTER

We missed our birthday. That makes me sad.

First time ever, not together.

I understand you needed to sleep, all curled up in your surge tank. Getting the poison out. Getting healthy again.

But it feels wrong that we didn't turn seventeen in the same room, or even the same city.

Remember all those midnights, our own little parties?

Remember when it was just us two?

I'm so sorry how it all turned out.

I'm sorry, sorry, sorry—a thousand times, and more.

I know how important Col was. Hurting you like that was the hardest thing I've ever done.

But Daddy really was going to kill our city.

And I could never kill you.

It would have been the end of everything I am. You're my one and only, my always. My little shadow.

Maybe one day you'll forgive me. My heart is always open to you, Frey, even if it takes a thousand years.

—Rafia of Shreve

ALLIES

I read my sister's letter a hundred times.

The first dozen reads is for the pain—reliving those moments in the tower. Another dozen for the anger. Then for the tears, to know that my sister loves me, whatever happens next.

Only then can I start to pick it apart.

The childish writing, nothing like her elegant, perfect speeches on the global feeds. The flashbacks to our childhood, like we're littlies again, and she's apologizing for not bringing me cake from a party.

The fact that Rafi never mentions that she's stolen my name again, this time forever.

And her new nickname for me—*my little shadow.*

Finally, I count the words.

You appears six times in this letter.

The word *I*, seven.

I still have the photo of us I found on our bedroom floor. We're wearing costumes from some feed drama, Rusty-era dresses and ridiculous hats.

Hers looks handmade.

Mine is clearly printed by a hole in the wall.

Another patient comes to visit me.

It's Riggs, in a wheelchair, miraculously alive.

Her right leg is stretched out straight, the cast covered with data fiber and nutrient drips. An IV port is in her left arm, an airscreen over her head, full of wavy lines.

"What saved you?" I ask.

She cracks a smile. "You don't remember Zura's training sessions? Cats survive falls at terminal velocity."

I look at her straightened leg. The other's in a cast too, below the knee. But her arms seem okay—the wheelchair has wheels instead of lifters.

"Since when do broken bones take a *week* to heal?"

"Not broken—splattered. I'm practically growing a new leg." She winces a little. "My spleen was ruptured too, and some other stuff. Turns out you only need one lung."

My eyes widen. "Makes my radiation poisoning seem pretty tame. At least I can walk."

"Sure, but can you do this?" Riggs grunts, her powerful arms spinning her chair in a tight circle. Her skidding halt makes a rubber-wheeled *squeak* on the hospital floor.

A hoverboard in two dimensions.

I smile. "How long till you can walk?"

"Maybe never." She shrugs. "Lost three of my rebels in the battle too, but at least the rest are mine again. It's *Boss* Riggs, if you don't mind." She runs her fingers through her hair—the neat Shreve cut is already growing ragged. "Like we figured, your sister doesn't want too many rebels around, now that she's got her own city. Just a couple of crews, for old times' sake."

"Have you told them her real name?"

"Not yet." Riggs hesitates. "Do you think I should?"

"Depends on the timing, Boss. It might fit into some other . . . plans of mine."

Riggs glances at the open doorway, then rolls herself a little closer. "Do you remember our conversation about *Shame-Cam*? How I was just following orders, setting you up like that?"

"Hard to forget," I say. "You know, even the Rusties knew that *following orders* was a bad excuse."

"Fair," she says. "But back then, there was only one person I took orders from."

Of course. "How did Rafi send you an order in Shreve?"

"She didn't." Boss Riggs checks the doorway again. "It wasn't strictly her idea. But right before we all left for the mission, she pulled me aside. Pointed out that after your father fell, you two'd be making a speech to the citizens of Shreve. And she mentioned how you might . . ." Riggs's face screws up, like she's trying to recall Rafi's exact words. "You might complicate the narrative."

"What narrative?" I ask.

"About the twins coming home to make things right. Because you didn't have your normal face—the one that everyone in Shreve recognizes. You had Islyn's face." Riggs smiles. "It might strike a strange note."

I shake my head. "Everyone knows about camo-surge."

"But first impressions are important, Boss Frey said, especially during a change in power. She told me to look for ways to keep you from showing your face that night . . ."

I swallow. "Like making me the most hated person of the week."

Riggs nods, smiling at her own cleverness.

This hits hard, despite everything else my sister has done.

Even if I hadn't been puking from radiation sickness, Rafi never planned for me to appear on the feeds that night.

She never wanted me beside her.

I can still feel those fifteen minutes of shame, knowing the whole city hated me. A childhood nightmare bubbling up into reality.

But my sister was quietly pleased.

"Wait," I say. "You did this for Rafi *after* you knew she'd lied to you—about everything."

Riggs makes a half shrug. "Did myself a favor. Got her out of my life."

"Except now she's in everyone's life."

Riggs nods. "That's why I brought you some company. They share your concerns about Shreve staying in the family. You should meet them."

I follow her gaze at the open doorway. There are two shadows shifting out there in the hall.

My heart lifts a little.

The free cities are finished with war. Most rebel crews are still in love with Boss Frey. Victoria is too busy rebuilding, and Zura must hate me more than ever.

But maybe I still have allies.

"They won't come in till you declare privacy," Riggs says.

"This is Paz. Everything's private."

"Yeah, but this needs to be *extra* private."

"Fine," I say with a sigh, reaching over the small orange dome next to my bed with the Paz seal on the base. For the first time, I twist the fat dial clockwise until there's a *click*.

The city's familiar voice is instantly in my head: "Good morning, Frey. Are you well?"

"Lots better. Sorry I haven't said hello."

"Trauma has its own timeline."

I have to swallow before I speak again. "You're very kind."

"You are always welcome in this city," Paz says. "Each of these flowers is sent by one citizen. In thanks."

I close my eyes for a second, dizzy for a moment. I went to the Iron Mountain to hurt my father as much as to save Paz, but it is my favorite free city.

It takes a moment for this simple gesture to sink in.

"Tell them thanks." My voice stays steady. "I need a favor from you."

"Of course, Frey."

"I need to talk with the two people outside. In privacy—as much as you can give us."

There's a short, offended pause. "Privacy is always guaranteed in Paz."

"Sure. But my friends outside are very . . . secretive."

"I realize that, Frey," the city of Paz says. "Because I've already seen through their disguises. Boss X in particular makes for a poor clandestine operative."

Riggs groans in her chair.

I reach out and take her hand. "It's okay. Paz can keep a secret."

"Indeed I can," the city says. "And I hope you'll permit me to attend this meeting. I believe I understand the nature of your alliance, and wish to assure you that the sovereign city of Paz is on your side."

Riggs frowns. "I don't think—"

"You can trust this city," I say. "And if you decide otherwise, the AI will erase everything it knows. That's how it works here."

Riggs hesitates, an innate rebel suspicion of cities showing on her face. But finally she nods her assent.

"Okay. I'll tell them to come in."

"Excellent," Paz says. "I've always wanted to meet Tally Youngblood in the flesh."

AUTHOR'S NOTE

The characters Sara and Chulhee are named after Sara Leon of Little Village, Chicago, and US musician Chul Hee James Park, in honor of their contributions to Victorian firefighting efforts during the 2019–20 Australian bushfire season.

ABOUT THE AUTHOR

Scott Westerfeld is the author of the Uglies series, the Leviathan trilogy, the Midnighters trilogy, the New York trilogy, the Zeroes series, as well as the Spill Zone graphic novels, the novel *Afterworlds*, and the first book in the Horizon series. He has also written books for adults. Born in Texas, he and his wife now split their time between Sydney, Australia, and New York City. You can find him online at scottwesterfeld.com.

What – and who – are you willing
to sacrifice for your family?

IMPOSTORS

New York Times bestselling author

SCOTT WESTERFELD

Frey and Rafi are inseparable . . . two edges of the same knife. But Frey's very existence is a secret. Frey is Rafi's twin sister – and her body double. Their powerful father has many enemies, and the world has grown dangerous as the old order falls apart. So while Rafi was raised to be the perfect daughter, Frey has been taught to kill. Her only purpose is to protect her sister, to sacrifice herself for Rafi if she must. When her father sends Frey in Rafi's place as collateral in a precarious deal, she becomes the perfect impostor – as poised and charming as her sister. But Col, the son of a rival leader, is getting close enough to spot the killer inside her. As the deal starts to crumble, Frey must decide if she can trust him with the truth . . . and if she can risk becoming her own person.

SHATTER CITY

Her lies aren't the only things to crack

SCOTT WESTERFELD

When the world sees Frey, they think they see her twin sister Rafi. Frey was raised to be Rafi's double, and now she's taken on the role . . . without anyone else knowing. Her goal? To destroy the forces that created her. But with the world watching and a rebellion rising, Frey is forced into a detour. Suddenly she is stranded on her own in Paz, a city where many of the citizens attempt to regulate their emotions through an interface on their arms. Paz is an easy place to get lost . . . and also an easy place to lose yourself. As the city comes under a catastrophic attack, Frey must leave the shadows and enter the chaos of warfare — because there is no other way for her to find her missing sister and have her revenge against her murderous father.